Freedom to Love

FREEDOM SERIES

Freedom to Love

Seek Him & live.
Amos 5:6

Rhonda
Kulczyk

Rhonda Kulczyk

TATE PUBLISHING & *Enterprises*

Scripture quotations taken from New King James Version, New International Version, and New Living Translation

The opinions expressed by the author are not necessarily those of Tate Publishing, LLC.

Published by Tate Publishing & Enterprises, LLC
127 E. Trade Center Terrace | Mustang, Oklahoma 73064 USA
1.888.361.9473 | www.tatepublishing.com

Tate Publishing is committed to excellence in the publishing industry. The company reflects the philosophy established by the founders, based on Psalm 68:11,
"The Lord gave the word and great was the company of those who published it."

Published in the United States of America

ISBN: 978-1-60696-067-7
1. Fiction, Romance, Historical
09.07.22

Dedication

GOD   And He shall give you the desires of your heart!

WILL   Thank you for believing in me! 'I'm everything I am because you loved me.'

GRANDMA P.   Some will never know the influence they had in the life of another. I remember racing to your house after school, taking off my shoes at the door, of course, and diving onto your couch in order to read the latest short story in the most recent issue of *Good Housekeeping*. And then we would discuss the plot, characters, and setting. At times, I actually believed those characters lived among us!

But even before that, began our trips to the library in search of that rare book; a book that welcomed us into the wonderful world unknown. I truly believe those incidences paved the way for this new and exciting journey. And you, Grandma, were there at the beginning. I miss you.

Maxine Porter
October 15, 1916–January 30, 2005

Acknowledgements

ADELE LEACH You read this story not only once, but twice, and were so helpful with putting it all together. Thank you. You are a true friend.

WRITER'S BLOC To all of you at Writer's Bloc—thank you for letting me read my stories to you. You have been such an inspiration to me. Thank you, Cindy and Andrell, for your encouragement and prayers.

Foreword

Sometimes a great story is born out of the refining fires of an author's own experiences. Of course, the story will have different characters, a different setting and time, and a different plot than those of the author's life. Yet within the journey of the story's characters, a reader will in some way discover poignant echoes of the insights gained and lessons learned by the one who put pen to paper to make those characters come alive.

Freedom to Love is one of those great stories. It tells the tale of a young woman named Alana and her search for love and acceptance in an often-hostile world. Author Rhonda Kulczyk is most definitely a skillful storyteller who will keep you turning the pages to find out what happens next. But Rhonda is more than that. She is an intricate weaver of words, interlacing eternal truths and descriptive detail throughout the intrigue of the storyline all the way to the final, satisfying outcome. The discerning reader will find glimpses of glory in the life of young Alana—even in her moments of pain or peril. And in the end, the reader will be better for the experience.

Cynthia D. Hansen
Editorial Director
Rick Renner Ministries

June 3, 1841

"Jesse!" The young girl screamed his name over and over. She brought her horse to a sudden halt. Sobbing, she ran back to where he had fallen from his horse. She rolled him to his side. "Jesse!" she pleaded. "Please don't leave me. Please, Jesse. Please!"

Jesse opened his eyes and looked into the face of the woman bending over him, his wife of only three days. "Char ... Charise," he finally managed to say. "Go!" he rasped. "You ... you can st ... ill make ... it. Go!"

Charise pulled her gaze from his and looked behind her. The riders were quickly approaching. Freedom would soon be only an illusion. "I won't leave you. I won't."

Jesse knew that she wouldn't. It was one of the many things he loved about her—her strong will, her defiance to go with tradition. He pressed her hand tightly against his chest. He could see the fear in her eyes.

Was it her imagination or was the rhythm of his heart becoming slower and slower? "Jesse—"

"Charise," he interrupted. "I love you. Never forget that." He gasped as the shock of the gunshot wound to his left side suddenly turned into unbearable pain.

Charise screamed with the realization that his life was coming to an end. The scream echoed through the valley, and then all was quiet. The lively spirit that had once been so alive within her was snuffed out in that very moment.

CHAPTER ONE

April 5, 1858

She watched as the casket was lowered into the ground. Slowly dirt was shoveled on top, covering up everything she had, everything she knew ... her mother.

Her father had left years before. She had been eight years old at the time. He had gone into town. Going into town was not all that unusual for him. But on that evening eight years ago, he had not returned. Day after day her mother had watched for any sign that he might come home, but he had not. And as days turned into weeks and weeks into months, her mother's restlessness had subsided, and a sense of peace had come over her. The yelling had ceased. The tension had come to an end.

Her mother had never mentioned her father, why he had left, or where he may have gone. It was almost as if he ceased to exist altogether.

"Alana?" a voice questioned. Alana turned toward Mr. Raymond, the town banker. "Do you have a place to stay ... somewhere to go?"

Alana had refused to think about leaving the only home she had ever known. Taking care of her mother had taken every ounce of energy she could muster, both physically and emotionally. But of course now that her mother was gone ... the banker would want her to move. She knew they had stayed way past the date on the eviction notice. She looked up into the eyes of Mr. Raymond and was surprised by the compassion she saw there.

"My wife and I would like to offer you a place to stay, at least until you can find work … or family to go to. Will you stay with us?"

Alana pushed back the tears of gratitude. She would not cry in front of this business man. "I appreciate the offer, and I accept. Thank you."

Mr. Raymond touched her hand for a brief moment. "I'll be by to get you and your belongings this evening," he stated before walking away.

The preacher stood quietly a few minutes longer before finally offering his condolences and leaving the cemetery. Besides her, only the preacher and the banker had attended her mother's funeral. Alana and her mother had lived a sheltered life. Though often a topic of their small community, they rarely had associated among the residents.

Alana walked toward the trees, bending to pick up some yellow daisies. She slowly made her way back to her mother's grave. "Goodbye, Mother," she whispered as she laid the flowers on the new mound of dirt.

As she turned to leave she noticed two gentlemen standing off in the distance. The older man was the town doctor. She was surprised he had taken time out of his busy day to be there. The young man next to him lifted his hat as she drew nearer. She knew her eyes betrayed her surprise as she instantly recognized him. Shay. Shay O'Connell. The doctor's son.

"Miss Peterson, may I offer you a ride home?" he asked.

Alana felt the tremor that passed through her body.

Her thoughts went back to a specific day after school. He and two other boys had followed her home from school yelling insults at her all the way. She did have darker skin than most, enough for people to question her origin. She raised her dark brown eyes to meet his.

"Alana?" Shay questioned.

Alana felt her face redden as she realized he was waiting for her answer while she was dwelling on bad memories.

"No, thank you." As if she would go anywhere with him.

"I'm sorry about your mother. You'll be in my prayers."

Alana nodded as she turned toward home.

º º º

The afternoon slipped by unnoticed as Alana went from room to room, wanting to remember every memory, every good memory with her mother. Charise had tried so hard to be everything Alana needed. And Alana was grateful, and yet deep within she wondered how she would survive in such a cold world as the one she resided in. Her mother had sheltered her. Living life without her mother was unnatural ... and terrifying.

Alana closed the door to the bedroom she had shared with her mother the last three weeks. Knowing her mother's time here on earth was drawing to a close, she had tried to be with Charise every moment possible. Most of their discussions had taken place in the dark hours of the night, when death had seemed so frightening and real. Alana had not wanted her mother to die alone, so she had stayed with her, held her mother's frail hand, and pretended to be stronger than she really was.

Alana moved toward the kitchen, carrying the only belongings she had. She walked to the window but saw no sign of Mr. Raymond. She sat her belongings on the table and retraced her steps back to the bedroom. She couldn't leave the quilt.

Walking back into the bedroom, she retrieved the blanket from the floor. It had a rather large tear in one corner, but it had been the first quilt she had ever received from her mother. She had been six years old at the time. As Alana turned to leave, a book fell out of the folded blanket. She picked it up and fingered through the first few pages, recognizing at once her mother's handwriting. It was a journal. Could it be her mother's? An envelope protruded from the top of the journal, and Alana slowly withdrew it.

The single word *Alana* was written on the front. She unsealed the flap before slowly retrieving the letter.

Alana,

I began writing in this journal years ago when I was a child. As you grew up, I always hoped we would one day look at it together. But I could never cultivate enough courage to share with you the words on these pages. And now my day is drawing near, and I will not be here to share these things with you. I only hope that you have the courage to bear the words that fill these pages. Sadly, this is the only thing I leave you.

I hope that in reading these pages, it will decrease your fears and release your hope. I do love you. You are the only thing I have created that truly makes me proud. I leave you with this advice: "Live life to the fullest. Make wise choices. Follow your heart. And may you find true love."

I have one wish and one wish only. Go west. You have

an uncle who lives in Dalles, Oregon. His name is James Bratten. I've never spoken of him to you. There is much you do not know. That is why I leave you this journal. But, please, do as I say. Go west as soon as you are able.

Your loving mother,
Charise Peterson

Alana's eyes continued to read the two words, *go west … go west.* How could she ever endure a journey as the one her mother prescribed alone?

A knock sounded at the door. Alana quickly wiped her tear-streaked face and gathered her belongings once again. It was Mr. Raymond waiting with his wagon. "May I go in and get your belongings, Alana?"

"These are my belongings," Alana replied. She saw the sad look in his eyes as he surveyed what she had in her arms.

"Well then, let's be on our way." He helped her into the wagon. She studied the house one last time as they pulled out of the yard. Tears welled up in her eyes, but she refused to let them fall. The house meant nothing to her now. It was her mother who had made the house a home.

Mrs. Raymond met them at the door. "Welcome, Alana. We are so glad you have come. Please let me show you to your room. I hope it will suit you. It is quite bare, but at least it will keep you warm and dry." Alana followed her up the staircase while Mrs. Raymond continued to discuss various topics on the way.

The bedroom was beautiful. A vase of flowers stood on the dresser. Alana turned to admire the canopy bed. She had never seen a bed such as the one that now stood in front of her. But then she had never been in any other bedroom besides the two in the small dilapidated home she had grown up in.

"Is it all right, Alana? Oh, I do hope so. We could bring in some more furniture from the parlor—"

"No … no … it is perfect. Thank you very much for allowing me to stay with you."

Mrs. Raymond scurried around the room making sure everything was in order. "I do hope you are comfortable. Be sure and tell me if you need anything, and I mean anything at all. I would hate—" Mr. Raymond appeared in the doorway and motioned for his wife to leave the room. Mrs. Raymond did not return that evening.

○ ○ ○

On Saturday evening as they ate supper, Alana listened quietly as Mr. Raymond conversed with his wife about the events of the day, though Mrs. Raymond did do most of the conversing. Alana's mind was elsewhere when she heard her name being spoken.

"Alana? We would be grateful if you would attend church with us in the morning. And afterward there is to be a potluck outside. Will you join us?" Mr. Raymond inquired.

Alana found herself agreeing to the request even though it was the last thing she wanted to do. She did not want to go to his church to be inspected by all the townspeople. But how could she refuse when she was sitting at his table, eating his food?

When she finally retired to her room, anxiety was already eating at her. She tossed and turned all night, trying to come up with a valid excuse to tell the Raymonds come morning. As dawn began to break forth, she could stay in bed no longer and found herself pacing the room, listening for any sound that indicated the Raymonds were awake and moving about.

The knock at the door startled her. "You sure are up bright and early this morning," Mrs. Raymond exclaimed as she moved into the room. "I heard you moving around and thought I'd bring these in." Alana studied the dresses draped over Mrs. Raymond's arm.

"Our daughter, Rebecca, refused to take these dresses with her when she married and left us for the exciting life in Boston. She said they were old and out of fashion. The dresses I mean. They certainly look fashionable to me, don't you think? Why don't you try them on and see if any of them fit. You must be near my Rebecca's size. Here you are now." She pushed the dresses into Alana's hesitant arms.

"We'll be eating breakfast within the hour," Mrs. Raymond stated as she left the room as quickly as she had come in.

Alana fingered the hem on the lavender dress. She had never owned such fine dresses. Her mother's words echoed in her head. *We don't take handouts. Everyone expects something in the end.* But she couldn't bring herself to give them back, for she had nothing to wear to church. After all the Raymonds' generosity, the last thing she wanted to do was embarrass them in front of their acquaintances at church.

An hour later, Mr. Raymond generously helped Alana down from the wagon, exclaiming for the third time that morning how lovely she looked in the lavender dress she had chosen to wear. Alana blushed. She wasn't used to compliments from men, and she didn't know how to respond. The only attention she had ever

received from any man was from her father, and it had never been kind.

Alana felt all eyes upon her as she entered the church. She kept her eyes downcast, refusing to acknowledge their stares, though she could not keep from overhearing their hurtful comments. "*Why would the* Raymonds *take in such a thing? This could certainly hurt his business.*"

When they reached the pew where the Raymonds routinely sat, a family already seated had spread themselves out providing no more empty spaces. It was obvious what they were doing. Several other previously empty spaces were now full as the people began to spread themselves out, making less room.

Mr. Raymond questioned the man he usually sat next to. "Mr. Hansen, could you kindly move in closer together so we can take our seats?"

Mr. Hansen could not bring his eyes to meet Mr. Raymond's. "I'm sorry, but these seats are taken this Sunday."

Mr. Raymond was stunned at their behavior. Had he known the people would have responded this rudely, he never would have subjected Alana to this kind of cruelty. These people went to church. They had listened to hundreds of sermons, many of which told them to love others unconditionally, forgive the unforgivable.

The townspeople had hated Alana's father. Clyde Peterson had been a conniving, ruthless man who had little concern about the people he came in contact with. But if anyone had cause to denounce Alana because of her father, it was Mr. Raymond. Her father had borrowed and swindled money from his bank on several occasions. But didn't the Bible say in order to be forgiven, you must first be willing to forgive?

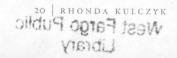

Mr. Raymond saw a hand wave at him from the back, signaling some empty seats. Mr. Raymond motioned for his wife and Alana to follow him to the back. He offered Shay a smile of gratitude before taking his seat. There was no time to talk, but Mr. Raymond found himself wondering why Shay O'Connell was at home.

The last time he had talked to the boy's father, he had been as proud as any father could be over his son going away to school to become a doctor. Shay was the younger of Luke's two sons. Cal, the oldest, headed west shortly after he had finished school, and the mantel had fallen to the younger son. Mr. Raymond knew Cal had been pressured from a young age to follow in his father's footsteps, but Cal had managed to escape his father's expectation. Had Shay finished school already?

○ ○ ○

Shay couldn't help sneaking a glance at Alana. He couldn't believe how she had grown and matured. She was a beautiful girl ... woman. His eyes took in her black hair that went to her waist, but it was her eyes that were so captivating.

He felt a sudden pain of regret over the way he had treated her during their childhood. He had been a spoiled child with little respect for people. Perhaps if he had been raised with more discipline during his child-hood years, he would have been a more caring person, but there had been no one willing to nurture that side of him.

His father had worked all hours, day and night. The few hours he was home, he was studying, trying to find better alternatives to medicine and surgery.

And his mother had never been content. She was

constantly in search for something or someone to make her happy. And sometimes she would find some temporary relief, but it was never lasting. She was tolerated, as she was the doctor's wife, but she wasn't pleasant to be around.

Shay had left for doctor training two years ago, to fulfill his father's dream of at least one of his sons taking over his practice someday. His brother, Cal, had kindly left the trade to him, and since Shay had nothing else planned for his life, why not?

It would be the first of several good decisions he had made. During his first year of training, he had met Thomas, another aspiring doctor. Shay had admired Thomas from the very beginning. He was confident, respectful, and when he had invited Shay over for supper at his parents, Shay knew his life would never be the same.

Shay had no idea that relationships could be trustworthy. Instead of taking from each other, they were giving. Shay had only been exposed to relationships in which love was based on what the other person could give you, not what you could give the other person.

All through Shay's life, he had done what others told him to do because he wanted to be accepted … admired. Here he was, going to school, practicing to be a doctor, when he had no desire to do so.

The topic arose one day as Thomas and Shay were eating lunch. Thomas began to question Shay about his life, his dreams. The more Shay spoke, the more he realized that he didn't even know who he was. He didn't have a dream. One thing he did know was that he wasn't intended to be a doctor.

Shay began attending church with Thomas. Thomas's father, the minister of the church, began to mentor Shay, and it wasn't long before Shay knew beyond any doubt that God was real. He quit school, but couldn't bring himself to face his father quite yet. Eldon, Thomas's father, invited Shay to assist him in remodeling the church. Shay moved in with Eldon and his wife and began working with his hands, something he had never done before. It wasn't long before people realized that Shay was gifted, and he hired out for several other jobs.

Everyone believed Shay had found his purpose. It would have been so easy to settle there, and yet Shay knew that there was still something more elsewhere. His mind began to dwell on going west, and he sent his brother Cal a long letter.

Cal had written back, more excited than ever about Shay's interest in coming west. Shay was surprised to learn that his brother had married and was expecting a second child.

Shay was now home to pack his belongings and prepare a wagon to head west. He looked forward to spending time with Cal. Although they had grown up in the same household, they had never formed a close relationship, something Shay hoped to rectify.

Shay had hated the disappointed look in his father's eyes when he had told him of his plans to leave. His father had tried to change his mind but finally realized his son was intent on leaving and no amount of bribery would change Shay's mind.

Shay glanced over at Alana again. This time their eyes connected and held for several seconds. Shay had never seen such beautiful eyes. He offered her a smile, but she quickly blushed and turned away. Yes, she was incredibly beautiful.

°°°

As soon as church ended, Mr. Raymond ushered them out the door. He had no intentions of staying for the potluck, not after the humiliation Alana had just endured. Instead he found himself asking Shay to join them for lunch at the local hotel. Shay accepted, and they walked the short distance across town.

"Enough of the suspense—what are you doing back in town, Shay? I know you aren't done with school quite yet. There is no father more proud than your old man."

"I didn't finish school, Mr. Raymond."

"Orville," Mr. Raymond stated.

"And I'm not in town to stay, Orville. I will be heading west as soon as the wagon train departs. My father is slightly disappointed, but I feel pressed to go. Even if I don't stay there permanently, I would like to see the country, and of course see my brother and his new family. I have a nephew I've never seen, and they're expecting another baby soon."

Mrs. Raymond's eyes widened at this bit of news. "I had no idea that your parents were grandparents. I wish I had known. I could have sent a baby quilt or a bonnet along with you. Your mother must be thrilled."

"I wish that were the case, Mrs. Raymond, but my parents only just found out themselves. You see, they haven't spoken to Cal since he left for the west. I guess they're a bit stubborn in their own way."

"But that was five years ago. That is entirely too long to have no contact with your child," Mrs. Raymond gasped.

"I agree. I most certainly agree." Shay looked away, embarrassed by the admission.

Mr. Raymond quickly changed the topic lest his wife cause a scene. "I must admit, Shay, I find myself somewhat jealous. I would love to go with you to explore the wild countryside. You young fellows just leave your old men here to slave away while you run off to the untamed west." Everyone laughed. Even Alana could not suppress a smile.

"What are your plans for the future, Miss Peterson?" Shay questioned, trying to include Alana in their conversation.

"I'm not sure yet," she responded with little enthusiasm. She refused to meet his gaze.

"Do you have family nearby?" Shay inquired.

"No, I have no family nearby." Alana again refused to look at Shay's face, gazing instead at her hands folded on her lap.

Shay turned toward Mr. Raymond. It was obvious Alana didn't want to share any more than needed. He wondered who she really was ... what kind of personality was she hiding underneath the wall she had constructed around herself. If the rumors of her father were true, then he could understand her fear of men.

Finally, near the end of their meal, Alana's eyes met his, but she quickly glanced away as if afraid she might reveal too much. Shay realized at that moment he would likely never see her again unless he happened back to Independence someday. The thought saddened him.

CHAPTER TWO

March 16, 1836

Mr. Martin gave me this journal for my birthday last month. He said that writing down one's feelings was a good way to diminish emotional outbursts. He meant my emotional disturbances, I'm sure. I reminded him he is merely my instructor, not my priest. He only smiled that smile I have come to detest.

And yet I must remember that he is the one who allows me to play with Jesse once a week. For three years he has kept this from my parents, so I do owe him this small measure of sacrifice.

I write now in hopes that perhaps Mr. Martin is correct, and it will help to express myself on paper, for some days I truly wonder how much longer I can survive trapped in this world of no independence.

Sometimes I wonder if my parents are punishing me for Jack's death. It was six years ago today when Jack drowned in the pond behind our house. Johnny, James, Jack, and I had gone ice-skating on the pond that day. The winter had been a cold one, much colder than usual, and we wanted to enjoy the frozen pond behind our estate one last time before spring came.

After a couple hours, Johnny and James had tired of the event and had returned to the house. Jack, shivering and wet, had wanted to return as well, but at six years old, I wasn't quite ready to leave. I begged and pleaded until he agreed to stay with me for a while longer.

Why didn't we leave with Johnny and James? Why had I been so persistent to stay? He chased me around the pond, and I can still hear my giggles as he caught me in his arms each time. I remember taking off my mitten so I could eat the ice I had picked off the tree branch above me. The wind caught my mitten and blew it out toward the thin ice. I began to cry, knowing mother would be angry with me for losing my brand-new mitten.

"Sshh, Charise, I'll get your mitten. Don't worry." And Jack had gone to do just that. I remember reaching for another piece of ice from the tree above me and then hearing the deafening sound of the ice breaking behind me. I turned around, but Jack was not there ... he was nowhere to be found. The hole in the ice was the only evidence that proved he had been standing there only moments before. I was too frightened to go back out onto the ice, so I ran toward the house as fast as my feet could carry me, screaming all the way. James met me half-way, having heard my screams, and I fell into his arms sobbing.

I remember nothing else after that. When I awoke several hours later, my governess was beside me. She said I had fainted and should remain in bed for the night. The memory of the cracking ice prevented me from sleeping. I wanted to ask her about Jack, but instead I said nothing, asked nothing, because inside I already knew he was gone.

My mother took to her bed for three weeks. I remember one afternoon my mother asked to see me. I made the long trip from the third floor to my mother's room on the second floor, clutching my governess' hand the entire way. But as we stood outside mother's closed door, I realized I could not face her yet. I was afraid she'd look into my eyes and see the truth. She would see that it was I who had killed Jack. I ran down the stairs to the first floor and out the door to the gardens.

Judas, who was digging in the gardens, stood to his feet when he heard my sobs of despair. I fell into his arms, not caring that he was beneath me, not caring that he was merely our gardener. And I cried for the first time since Jack's death. "Sshh, don't ya' worry, missy. Don't ya' worry." Judas held me like I longed to be held. He comforted me as I longed to be comforted.

Alana closed her mother's journal, no longer able to read due to the tears that blurred her eyes. What a terrible tragedy for a six year old to face. Alana placed the journal on the table beside her and then snuggled down under the covers. She tried to collect her thoughts as she contemplated what she had just read. Her mother was the youngest of four children—four children! Growing up, Alana had always thought her mother was an only child.

The letter Alana had read three days ago had told of one brother out west. But three brothers! Of course, Jack was no longer living. James had gone west. But where was Johnny? And what of her grandparents; were they still alive?

Alana turned out the light and lay quietly in the dark. Numerous thoughts were running through her head. Why had her mother left home? Why had her mother never told her any of this?

Suddenly, she thought of Clyde, her father, and she wondered why her mother had married such a man. Clyde had hated her very existence. Even as a small child she had sensed his revulsion. She was never allowed at the table while he ate. She was not allowed in the parlor while he read the *Independence Post*.

Why doesn't he like me? How many times had she lain in bed, trying to understand the reason her father could not stand the sight of her? *If I don't talk too much, maybe he'll love me. If I do better in school, maybe he'll love me.* But no matter what she did, it never made her father love her.

In school one year the teacher had them make sculptures using clay. She had worked on her piece for weeks, wanting it to be perfect. *For if it is perfect, maybe he'll love me.* She had made a sculpture of his horse. The one thing he showed affection to. And then she had given it to him as a gift for his birthday. He had laughed. The ears were too short. The eyes were too far apart. He had discarded it in the wastebasket as a worthless piece of trash. Just like her...worthless.

Her mother had tried to make up where her father had fallen short. When Clyde was gone, they had played together, read together, and talked together. But deep inside, she had always questioned her significance. Why was she here?

Alana's eyes grew heavy, but before she fell asleep, she began to plan her destiny. She would go west. She would find her uncle, if only for her mother. It was the very least she could do.

o o o

Alana spotted the wagons up ahead and slowed her pace, questioning what she was about to do. She did not converse well with strangers. She had never been given the opportunity. Now she had no choice.

"Where can I find Mr. Leaver?" Alana asked the first

man she saw. She did not care for his lingering gaze, and she shifted her eyes toward the trees pretending she did not notice. He signaled to the wagon at the end of the camp, and she made her way toward it.

She could hear snoring coming from within and wondered what to do. Should she knock, or wait? Finally, gathering her courage she knocked on the side of the wagon.

Silence…and then…a loud voice. "What do you want?"

Alana jumped and then steadied herself. "I'm inquiring about the wagon train."

She heard movement from within. A few seconds later he appeared. He was shirtless with a pair of very dirty trousers on. His hair was disheveled. He looked to be in his fifties. Mr. Leaver studied her intently from head to toe. "What would you like to know?"

Alana blushed, quickly looking away from his piercing stare. "I need to go west. I need to find my uncle."

"We leave in four days," he said as he began to close the canvas.

"But, sir … is there someone who could take an extra passenger? I—"

"Ma'am, the wagons are full. You are a stranger. The only ones interested in having you share their quarters are the bachelor men, and I will not tolerate that on my train. Now … go on home where you belong."

The canvas swung closed. Alana stood in shock. She hadn't expected to be turned away so suddenly … or rudely. She had no money to purchase a wagon, and even if she did, she could not take on a team of oxen by herself.

Tears coursed down her cheeks as she turned to walk

away. She lost her balance as she bumped into someone. "I'm sorry," she mumbled before running toward the road. She heard her name being called, but she didn't stop. After several minutes, she was out of breath, and Alana slowed to a walk.

Was she to live with the Raymonds forever? Eventually, they would tell her to leave. Perhaps some man would marry her, but wouldn't that be doing what her mother had done years before?

She heard a horse approaching from behind. She quickly brushed away the evidence of any tears, hoping desperately the rider would not stop.

Her hope was disregarded as the rider did stop. He quickly dismounted his horse and hurried his step to catch up with her. "Miss Peterson, are you all right? I tried to stop you back there, but you took off before I had the chance."

She finally glanced up, and her wobbly smile went straight to Shay's heart. "Listen, I overheard your conversation with Mr. Leaver. I think I may have a solution. Are you interested?" Alana quickly nodded. "I plan on leaving with the wagon train at the end of the week. I already have a wagon. You could ride with me. Of course, we'll have to put up a good front, like husband and wife, or sister and brother. The latter would probably be better under the circumstances."

Alana studied Shay with a shocked expression, but he could tell she wasn't completely opposed to the idea. "And you think we could pull this off?" she questioned. "Would they believe us? Mr. Leaver knows who I am now … I'm not sure … "

"Mr. Leaver couldn't care less about who is traveling as long as we all get along. We'll be the least of his problems I can assure you."

"I don't have any money," Alana stated.

Shay smiled. "Oh, I do think I'll be getting the better end of the deal. Good cookin', a clean wagon, and I'm sure there'll be plenty more for you to do to earn your keep."

"Your thoughts may change, Mr. O'Connell, after you've tasted my cookin'."

Shay stopped and stared at her. Had she just mocked him? Her full fledged grin was proof enough that she had. And never had he seen such a beautiful smile. He laughed. The girl did have a little spunk after all.

"Well, Mr. O'Connell, I will accept your offer."

Shay smiled. "And now that we are sister and brother, shouldn't we be on first name basis?" Alana nodded her consent.

Shay remounted his horse. "I'd offer you a ride back to town, but since you refused a ride in my wagon just a few days back, I doubt you'll agree to ride double on my horse! I'll be by in a couple days to let you know when the wagon train pulls out." With that said, he turned his horse back toward the wagon train.

Alana stared after him. Before turning the corner out of sight, Shay turned, lifting his hat in farewell. Alana's face reddened at being caught staring. A smile formed on her face as she turned back toward town.

º º º

"Who's your father, Alana? Or is it your mother who is black?"

Alana hurried her steps toward home. Why did

they hate her? She glanced at her hand, studying it carefully. Her skin was darker than her mother's. It was darker than the other children she attended school with. But her father was not black, nor her mother. She just had darker skin, just as Gina had brown eyes when both her parents had blue eyes, or Molly who had a narrow nose when both her parents had short stubby ones. Everyone was created different. Weren't they?

Jake jumped out from behind the tree, his eyes full of hatred… hatred of her. Alana went to walk around him, but another boy jumped out, and another… until finally she was surrounded with no way of escape.

"Please, I need to go home. My mother is expecting me." Alana's eyes focused on her feet, no longer able to look at the spiteful faces that surrounded her.

"Are you sure she's your mother?" a voice sneered. "I heard your mother was a slave, and she died while giving birth… "

"It's not true," Alana screamed. "It's not true." Tears coursed down her cheeks, and she hated herself for not being able to stop them. She knew her tears only encouraged them to taunt her more.

Jake withdrew his hand from behind his back… lifted it into the air…

Alana awoke drenched in sweat. She tried to recall what it was that had awakened her and was reminded of the reoccurring dream she had been having for six years. It was always the same. She was standing in the middle of a group of boys. The boys were holding stones, screaming at her, and then suddenly stones were flying from every direction. She always awoke before the stones hit her, unaware of her surroundings and frightened.

She had been teased all her life. Being called names by the children she attended school with was not an unusual occurrence. She did her best to ignore them. But on one particular day a rock had struck her in the back of the head. She remembered the tears ... the pain. She had no idea who had thrown it. But she remembered the three faces: Jake, Jared, and Shay. Shay O'Connell. He had hated her. Why was he helping her now?

The incident had brought about some good. It had been the last time they had followed her home. She was sure it had been her mother's doing, for when Alana had come home from school in tears, her mother had left. She had not returned until later that evening. Every once in awhile a discriminating remark would be said, but they had never again tried to hurt her.

∘ ∘ ∘

Mr. Raymond knocked on the door to Luke and Lydia O'Connell's home. He knew Shay was staying with his parents. "Mr. Raymond?" Luke looked surprised to find the banker outside his door. "What can I do for you?" Luke questioned.

"I'm looking for Shay."

"He's out back putting together some crates to haul his belongings in. Still can't believe he's heading west. I couldn't keep either one of my sons here." Mr. Raymond could hear the sadness behind his words.

"I do know the feeling. Our daughter left us for Boston. It hasn't been quite the same without her."

Luke guided Mr. Raymond out back. Shay glanced

up and welcomed Mr. Raymond. Luke soon left their presence saying he had some medical cases to study.

"Alana said you offered to take her west?" Mr. Raymond questioned. "And I'm not so sure I like the idea. There hasn't been any correspondence from her uncle in seventeen years. What if he is no longer there? Or worse still, what if he is dead? What will happen to Alana then?" Mr. Raymond waited patiently for an explanation.

"I understand your concern, Mr. Raymond," Shay admitted. "But what will happen to Alana if she stays here? You know her past, the way people treat her. Who is going to marry her? Who will hire her for work, besides Stilt's Saloon? The odds are against her if she stays here. You know it. I know it. Hopefully, her uncle is still where she last heard from him, but if he's not, at the very least she can have a fresh start somewhere where nobody knows anything about her ... or her past."

Mr. Raymond pondered Shay's words. Shay had obviously given the situation quite a bit of thought, and he was right. Alana had nothing to keep her here.

"I'll see that she is settled wherever she stays," Shay added.

Mr. Raymond nodded. "I suppose you are right. She is determined to go. At least if she leaves now, she'll have you to look out for her." He reached out and grasped Shay's outstretched hand. "I appreciate what you're doing for her, Shay. I pray God blesses you for it." He turned and walked away.

°°°

This new chapter in her life brought forth some excitement for Alana, especially after the mundane life she had previously been living. She would never forget the Raymonds or their generosity. Mrs. Raymond had been running to and fro since the news of Alana's soon departure. She had food already packed and ready to go. Mrs. Raymond had also finished two quilts for the cool nights on the trail. When Shay arrived later in the week, Alana was surprised at the sudden sadness over having to say goodbye.

Mr. Raymond handed her an envelope. "Don't read it until later," he stated. She nodded, giving him one last hug before he helped her up behind Shay.

"It seemed foolish to bring the wagon to town," Shay acknowledged.

"I understand," she offered, though she did feel a bit uncomfortable with the close proximity. As they neared the edge of town, Alana noticed the cemetery.

"May we stop … for a moment … " she asked in a soft voice.

"Whoa," he called to the horse. He jumped down before reaching for her and setting her on her feet. She walked to her mother's gravesite. Grass was already beginning to take root. The flowers she had placed there previously had blown away. "Goodbye, Mother. I'm leaving … just like you asked. I'll find James. I know I will. I love you."

Shay watched from a distance as she ran her hand along the ground. She was doing well under the circumstances, having just lost her mother only days ago. Alana stood to her feet. Shay swallowed past the lump in his throat at the sight of the fresh tears that now traced down her cheeks.

CHAPTER THREE

February 4, 1837

It was my birthday today. I'm now thirteen. Thirteen is certainly old enough to take a walk by oneself. Thirteen is definitely old enough to ice skate on the frozen pond without parental supervision. But I fear if I leave my independence up to my parents, I will never be old enough to do anything ... at least not anything alone.

I see my future planned out for me already. I will marry at age eighteen, like all the eligible women of my stature. I will marry some man twice my age, for any man younger would not be prepared to take care of such a "vivacious creature," or so my father always says. I often wonder if I am the only woman on earth who craves freedom. And by freedom I simply mean, no one making my decisions for me. Is there such a life in which one is in charge of her own destiny?

Jesse understands my desire to be free. He understands my yearning for privacy. I once thought I wanted to be alone, but I've come to realize being alone is not what I want; rather, I need someone to recognize I have desires and wants of my own, regardless if they are shared by any other person.

Why was I made this way? Mother says God expects children to obey their parents and those in authority. I'm afraid God has not been very happy with me as of late.

For the last three weeks I've sneaked out of the house. I've gone against my parents rules. I've met Jesse at the frozen pond behind the trees, and together we've skated until my toes were frozen, and I could not feel my nose. It is in these moments that I truly feel alive. But must one work so hard to simply feel alive?

I realized something today, and it took me by surprise. As Jesse and I were skating around the pond together, he grabbed my hand when I lost my balance, and for the first time ever I realized I no longer thought of him as different than myself. And I wondered when this transformation had taken place.

I was nine years old the day my instructor introduced me to Jesse. Of course, I already knew who he was. I had seen him from afar. I knew that he was Judas' son. But that day, standing face to face with him, I was shocked at how much darker his skin was than mine. I was shocked at how brown his eyes were. And every time we played together, it was so very hard to ignore. But somewhere along the way, I have come to accept that we really are not that different from one another. In fact, I am certain there is no other person more akin to myself than my best friend Jesse Blackwell.

Alana closed the journal and placed it underneath the bed with her other belongings. She pulled back the canvas, slowly climbing down from the wagon. The wagon was awkward to get out and in, but she was sure she'd get used to it in time. She glanced around at the wagons that surrounded her.

Mr. Leaver was busy inspecting the wagons. They would be pulling out within the next couple hours. Alana was worried that he would recognize her and question her relationship with Shay, but if he did remember her, he certainly didn't let it show. The voices of the people were full of excitement. They spoke of the west, a new start, and some spoke of seeing family once again.

Alana kept to herself by the wagon. She studied all the wagons making the long trip west. The trip was expected to take approximately six months. She wondered what she would find when she arrived in Dalles, Oregon. What if her uncle was no longer there? It had been so long since her mother had heard from him. But it was useless to worry about something she could not help at the moment.

She glanced over to where Shay was talking to some of the men. He was very sociable. He had a very likeable personality, not at all like she had thought him to be. And he was so unlike herself. She was shy and cautious. He was talkative and outgoing. Shay noticed her lingering gaze and waved for her join him. She cautiously made her way toward him, wishing she had never glanced in his direction.

Shay introduced her to each of the gentlemen present. A couple of the men tipped their hats to her, and Shay noticed the interest displayed in more than a couple of the men's faces. He realized that with his posing as Alana's brother, she was fair game to the single men in camp. His last thought was that he would then have to play an overprotective older brother.

∘ ∘ ∘

They had been traveling for several hours already, and Alana had been walking the entire time. She had promised Shay she would let him know when she was tired and needed to ride. Alana felt someone's presence behind her and she turned. It was a young woman who looked to be near her own age.

"Hello, my name is Maggie." Alana slowed to let the woman catch up. "What is your name?"

"Alana."

"Where will you and your husband settle?"

Alana hesitated before answering. It was unnatural to lie, and yet she couldn't tell her the truth. "I am traveling with my brother."

"Your brother? You don't look much alike. Not that it matters. I don't look anything like my older brother either. I have blond hair. His is red. That's my husband over there." Maggie pointed to a young man driving a wagon a few spots back. "My husband wants to go west to farm. The land is supposed to be good farm land and inexpensive. Why are you going west?"

"I am going to stay with my uncle."

"Where are your parents?" Maggie questioned.

"They are … dead."

Maggie's eyes widened in shock. "I'm so sorry. Here I was feeling sorry for myself because I had to leave mine behind." Alana found herself warming to the young woman. They talked until their legs were numb. Finally Maggie excused herself and Alana quickened her step to catch up with Shay.

° ° °

Shay was relieved that Alana was finally riding beside him. She had walked a great distance. "I noticed you speaking to Tom's wife. I haven't met her yet, but I met her husband the other day, and he is a real nice man."

"She seems real nice too," Alana offered.

Shay smiled. Alana was one of few words. "If you

are tired, you are welcome to use my shoulder as a pillow," Shay offered.

"I'm fine … but thank you." Her face reddened at the thought.

Stubborn too, Shay thought to himself. Several minutes passed in silence with only the oxen's feet plodding on the ground. He felt Alana's head rest against him. He glanced down at her and smiled. She was sound asleep. He shifted a little hoping to make her more comfortable.

It was difficult to keep his eyes on the road rather than on her. She was so still and at peace. He took the opportunity to really study her features. Her big almond colored eyes were closed in a peaceful sleep. Her nose was … perfect. His eyes moved to her mouth … soft and moist; her skin … beautiful. Alana Peterson. Who would have ever known, these many years later, he would be escorting her west.

He fixed his eyes back on the road ahead. It was a wonder she had even agreed to come with him, after all the mean things he had said to her as a child. He wished he hadn't been so cruel. At the time he had wanted the other children to notice him. He had wanted them to look up to him. They had laughed at his comments … encouraged his mean words. And now he realized how immature he had been, seeking recognition at the expense of another person. It was too humiliating to even think about it.

o o o

Alana opened her eyes. She could feel movement. Finally her senses came back to her and she remembered being in the wagon … next to Shay, yawning … she must have fallen asleep. She realized with great embarrassment that she had fallen asleep with her head on Shay's lap.

She lay motionless for several minutes before finally accepting the fact that she would eventually have to face him. She certainly couldn't stay in this position forever. *One ... two. ... three ...* She gathered her courage and sat up.

Shay suddenly started laughing, and she knew her face was red as a beet. "I wish you could see your face right now. I believe I've just witnessed one of your most embarrassing moments." He laughed again. Alana's face reddened even more. "My leg has been asleep for the last hour," Shay added with humor in his voice.

Alana finally turned to face him. "How long have I been asleep?" she inquired.

"It has been over an hour. I know that much. And my leg knows it even more." Shay began to massage his leg just to emphasize his last words. Alana finally smiled. His smile was contagious.

"I heard you tell Mr. Leaver that you were trying to find your uncle?" Shay voiced, now more serious.

Alana nodded. "My mother's brother lives in Dalles, Oregon. She asked me to go west to find him."

"Have you sent him a letter telling him you are coming?"

"No. I figured he would have no time to reply," Alana stated nervously.

"If he has moved on, then more than likely someone from Dalles will know where he moved. I'm sure you'll find him."

"I hope so," she voiced.

"We can send him a telegram from the next town

we stop at. Then if he is still in Dalles, he'll be expecting you."

"Thank you," Alana voiced.

"Tell me about you?" he questioned, hoping to find out more about her.

"There's not much to tell." She knew she sounded evasive, but she had so much she still needed to learn about herself, and she didn't even know where to begin.

"We may have grown up in the same town, but you know as well as I that we know very little about each other's families."

She turned toward him. "Then, you start. Tell me about your family." He smiled. *She may be shy, but she was clever as well.*

"All right. My father is a doctor. My mother... she... is my mother." Shay pondered his next words, realizing that sharing information about his family was awkward, especially when it was information he didn't wish to share. Perhaps that was why Alana was so cautious when she spoke.

"Why did you decide not to be a doctor?" Alana inquired, changing the subject.

"Being a doctor requires sacrifice, not to mention a caring disposition. I realized I didn't have it in me."

"But that's not true. You have sacrificed in order to bring me along, and I have watched you around other people. You are caring as well."

Shay smiled. "Well, I thank you for your vote of confidence. Let's just say I found something else I enjoy more."

○ ○ ○

When the wagon train stopped for the night, Alana moved toward the edge of the camp. Shay had already shown her where to find the food to start supper. She walked between the big oak trees, trying to find large pieces of wood with which she could start a fire. Her arms were loaded down with wood when she finally headed back to their wagon.

Shay had taken the harness off the oxen. They were hobbled and grazing nearby. He quickly took notice of her arms full of wood and took the pile from her.

"I'm fine," she insisted. "I'm sure you have more important things to do."

He ignored her and carried the wood to the spot he had already arranged to start a fire. "Have you ever started a fire before?" he asked.

"We had a fireplace," she stated.

"Starting one outside is more difficult because there are no walls to break the wind. We need to find some tiny pieces of wood about the size of your finger."

"My finger?"

"To get the fire going. Then once a fire is going, we'll add a few more pieces of wood … about the size of your arm. And finally, once it is really going good, we'll add these nice, big pieces of wood." He signaled to the wood he had just deposited on the ground.

Shay watched Alana make her way back out into the trees. He hoped he hadn't hurt her feelings, but it would take all night to start a fire with the green wood she had just gathered up. Alana soon reappeared with some much smaller pieces of wood.

"Now … the drier the wood the hotter the fire, so if you break this twig in half and it snaps easily, then that means you have a dry piece of wood." Shay bent one of the twigs. It slowly bent but did not break.

"You could have told me that useful piece of information before I began searching for the wood." Alana turned in a huff and made her way back into the forest. Shay laughed as she disappeared from sight. It was nice to see she did have some emotion inside that very calm exterior.

It wasn't too much longer before Shay had a fire going. Alana did know how to cook. It was one thing she had done a lot of. She could hear Shay talking with another man. He was on his way back with some water from a spring nearby. Alana smiled, pleased that she already recognized his voice.

She handed Shay a plate of food, and he wolfed it down in a hurry. Had he even tasted the food? He held his plate out for seconds. "Now you said you couldn't cook. That there was the best meal I have ever tasted." Alana blushed at his compliment. She began to gather up the dishes to wash and was surprised when Shay began to help.

"I can do this. I am trying to earn my keep." She reached for the plate he was holding.

"I didn't say I couldn't help," Shay insisted. He held the plate just out of reach. Hearing laughter, they both turned to find Maggie and Tom watching their silly discussion. Shay finally relinquished the plate and turned toward their company.

"The men are meeting over at Mr. Leaver's campfire to discuss our first day on the trail," Tom stated, still trying to hide his smile. Shay winked at Alana and moved toward Tom. They soon were out of sight. Maggie moved toward Alana to help with the dishes.

"I feel bad you are helping me clean my dishes when you have probably just finished your own."

"Oh please, Alana. I really don't mind. Besides, staying here with you over listening to all those men talk about who knows what ... I do think our discussion will be more enjoyable." Alana smiled. "I enjoy your company," Maggie added.

As Maggie shared about her childhood and her family, Alana couldn't help but feel a twinge of envy. Maggie had grown up with a loving mother and father. She had brothers and sisters, and now she was married to a good man. Her life had been quite painless.

"Where is your brother going to sleep?" Maggie inquired. "There is only one bed in your wagon."

Alana tried to think of a reasonable answer. The wagon was very small and now that she thought of it ... there was only one bed. "I ... Shay ... " The men returned, saving Alana from answering Maggie just yet.

Alana made some coffee and they sat around the fire. "We found out some valuable information tonight," Tom said with a smile.

"And just what was that?" Maggie inquired.

"Shay here is a doctor. So if there are any injuries, which there are sure to be a few on a journey like this, we have ourselves covered."

"I said I had some medical experience," Shay corrected. "I'm no doctor."

"But your father is a doctor," Alana voiced. "Surely you learned a lot growing up in a household like that." Alana realized her mistake as soon as the words were spoken, but she could not take them back.

Maggie glanced at Alana surprised. "But I thought your parents were ... dead."

Shay stared at Alana wondering what to say next. He didn't want to lie, but he didn't want Alana to suffer, either. He turned to Maggie. "Alana and I have different fathers."

"That explains why you both have such different features," Maggie answered.

When Tom and Maggie left, Shay and Alana both shared a quizzical smile. "That was somewhat awkward," Shay announced. "I'm confused. Did our father die, or is he a doctor?" Alana smiled at Shay's teasing. "Perhaps we should have come as husband and wife; at least it would be true." Alana turned away, hoping the darkness covered the blush she knew was creeping onto her face.

"Where am I going to sleep?" Alana voiced, changing the subject.

"You'll sleep in the wagon ... on the bed."

"Where are you going to sleep?" Alana questioned.

Shay smiled as he listened to the concern in her voice. "Well, I don't suppose I can sleep in the same bed, now can I?" Even in the darkness, he could see the blush forming on her cheeks. "Actually, I plan on sleeping out here by the fire. I have a mat, and I'll be plenty warm."

Shay noticed her worried stare. "Now don't go worrying over me sleeping outside. I've slept outside plenty of times. In fact, I'll be more comfortable outside than in that cramped wagon."

Alana wasn't convinced. "But this is your wagon. You hadn't planned on having me along."

"Alana, I asked you to come. And I knew the implications of asking you to share the wagon. I don't mind. End of discussion. Now get up in that wagon and go to sleep."

Alana climbed up into the wagon. She found the bed

in the darkness and began to undress. She was exhausted even though she had barely done anything all day. Traveling seemed to take its toll on a person. She closed her eyes in anticipation for sleep to come, but it evaded her. Perhaps she was overtired.

She suddenly remembered the envelope from Mr. Raymond and reached down, retrieving her parcel from under the bed. *Alana Peterson.* She opened it, and her mouth fell open as the money fell out into her lap. Why? Why had he given her this? She pushed the canvas back in order to let the moon shed light to the paper in her hand.

Alana,

The bank sold your property last week. I could not let you leave with no provision for your future. Of course, most of the money went to pay the debt of the property, but there was this small amount left over. Take it and start a new life. My prayers are with you as you travel.

Sincerely,

Mr. Raymond

Tears pooled in Alana's eyes. Mr. Raymond had no reason to give her this. She knew her father had outstanding debts he had never paid back at the bank. Any money left over should have gone to pay those debts. "Thank you, Mr. Raymond," she whispered into the night.

CHAPTER FOUR

July 17, 1839

I attended Lilly Dunlap's wedding today. She is only two years older than I. Only seventeen and already married to a man who is losing his hair and looks as old as my own father. She smiled during the ceremony. And even during the dinner reception, she smiled as if instructed to do so. Perhaps some were fooled by her joyful expression, but not I. I glanced across the table during dessert and realized her eyes did not mirror the smile plastered on her face. And when Mr. Grant, her husband, reached over and caressed her shoulder, I saw her brief hesitation. And yet, she did as her parents wished. She married a man she does not love. How can she pretend to be pleased about it?

And that is where I differ from all the young women around me. I cannot pretend to like something, or someone I do not. I cannot pretend any longer. I am suffocating, and no one around me cares. When we returned from the ceremony, I retired to bed early, saying I was tired from the dancing, which was not entirely untrue. I had danced well into the evening with several men my parents approved of, yet none I could ever love. Jared Dobbs asked if he could begin calling on me. I told him I was not ready to receive callers. He must have then spoken to my father, who invited him to supper next Sunday. My parents care nothing for what I want.

I do not care that Mr. Dobbs comes from a very influential family. I do not care that Mr. Dobbs can offer me everything I ever wanted. He cannot offer me love, for I have already found it. Yes, I, Charise, have found love, unexpected love. And I mourn, for it can never be. He cannot have me, and I cannot have him. He loves me too. I know he does. I see it in his eyes...the way he looks at me... the way he touches me.

Alana traced her mother's writing with her finger and smiled. Her mother had fallen in love! At the tender age of fifteen, she had loved another, and he had returned her love. It comforted Alana to think her mother had enjoyed a loving relationship with some man before she had married her mean, cruel, overbearing father. Who had her mother loved? And why could her mother not be with him? Were her mother's parents so cruel that they would come between her wish to marry another?

Alana sat the journal down and turned her focus to the task at hand. She plunged her hands into the now lukewarm water as she rinsed the plate. Her eyes were closed. She was more tired this evening than most and looked forward to a good night's rest.

Each day was spent doing the very same thing they had done the day before. It felt as if they relived each day over and over again. They awoke as the sun came up. They ate breakfast. They traveled for as many miles as possible before dark. And then they made camp again. After six weeks, Alana and Maggie had already formed a deep bond. Alana also was opening up more to Shay. He was a generous man who noticed when someone else was in need. And he was often at someone else's campsite each evening fixing a broken harness or a broken axle.

Alana jumped as a hand touched hers from beneath the sudsy water. A tingle ran through her body as she looked up into Shay's blue eyes. He took the plate and dried it. An awkward silence passed before she returned to her senses and reached for the next plate. His hand brushed hers each time, and she tried to focus. Why would his touch bring forth such emotion? It was a feeling she had never experienced before. She focused her eyes on the trees in front of them, afraid she might give herself away.

"The Hensons should be fine to travel tomorrow. I sure am glad that they had that extra axle along. If it had been up to Mrs. Henson, she would have packed that china set instead."

Alana smiled. He would have to throw in a comment like that. "It would be hard to part with a china set." Shay laughed, and she enjoyed the sound of it.

Shay dried the last plate. "You look beat. You head to bed. I'll dispose of the water."

She opened her mouth to disagree, but he placed his hand over it. "Go to bed," he insisted. She moved past him, still tingling from his touch. "Goodnight, Alana."

"Goodnight," she whispered.

After dressing in her night gown, she peaked out the canvas one last time. Shay lay by the campfire, propped up by one arm. He was reading the Bible. He read it every night. She yawned. Dropping the canvas, she crawled into bed.

o o o

The following evening, after the dishes were clean and put away, Alana turned toward Shay. "Maggie asked me to come by her wagon this evening."

"Do you mind if I walk with you? I have something I wish to discuss with Tom."

Alana nodded, and they headed toward Maggie and Tom's wagon. "I notice you read the Bible. Do you find it interesting?"

"Yes. I do. It teaches me how to live. I want to be a good example to others. Though I fail at times, the Bible encourages me to try again." Their conversation ended as they came upon the Stewarts' wagon.

"Hi, Maggie."

"Are you ready?" Maggie inquired. "I'm so excited, I can barely contain myself," Maggie stated with excitement.

"Be careful," Tom exclaimed. "And if you see anything that could be dangerous, scream with all your might. Do you have the gun?"

"Where are you going?" Shay asked with a concerned look.

"Mary said there was a hot spring down the trail," Maggie answered. "Alana and I are going to bathe. We haven't had a true bath since we left Independence," Maggie acknowledged.

"My skin is layered with dust. I'm afraid I'll never be clean again," Alana voiced to Maggie as they made their way toward the trees.

"Are you sure they'll be safe," Shay asked Tom, his eyes still on Alana as she walked out of sight.

"I've taught Maggie how to shoot a gun. They'll be fine." Tom motioned for Shay to take a seat.

◦ ◦ ◦

Alana felt somewhat uneasy about undressing in front of Maggie, but any discomfort soon fled as she watched

Maggie throw her clothes in every direction and plunge into the warm water. "Oh, Alana, it is simply heavenly. I will never forget this moment for as long as I live." She closed her eyes as if memorizing the entire experience.

Alana undressed and waded into the water as well. It was an amazing feeling. To have your entire body engulfed by hot water was delightful. Maggie shared her small bar of soap. The lavender smell soon filled both their senses.

"One has to believe in God after experiences like these."

"You believe in God?" Alana voiced.

Maggie turned toward her. "Yes, of course. Don't you?"

"I've never given it any thought before."

Maggie eyes widened with Alana's brief acknowledgement. "When we get back to the wagon, I want to give you something."

Several minutes of silence passed as they each enjoyed the peaceful moment.

Alana heard the sound first, as the leaves in the bushes began to rustle. "Maggie … what is that?"

"I'm not sure, but keep still." Maggie moved slowly toward the bank where she had left the gun.

"Maggie," Alana hissed as more movement came from the bush. She could now hear a rattling sound.

"Ssshhh," Maggie hissed back.

A snake soon peered over the top of the bush. Alana's eyes widened in fear, and she let out a piercing scream.

○ ○ ○

Shay jumped to his feet. "Did you hear that?" he questioned Tom.

"What?"

"I swear I heard someone scream. Do you think they're in trouble? Perhaps I should follow the trail … "

"I'm sure they are fine, Shay. Like I said before, Maggie is a good shot … " A loud gunshot echoed through the camp. Both Shay and Tom were on their feet. Neither voiced their concern as they ran toward the path the women had taken.

∘ ∘ ∘

"Alana, you can open your eyes now. The snake is dead."

"Dead? Are you certain?" Alana cried.

"Yes, I'm certain. Everything is fine now."

Alana moved toward the bank where Maggie now stood wrapped in a blanket.

"That certainly put a damper on that wonderful feeling. At least the snake waited until we were fully washed; though, I wish we could have enjoyed the spring a little bit longer, don't you, Alana?"

Alana heard voices echoing through the trees. "Someone's coming, Maggie!" She dashed back into the water.

"It's probably Tom. He could have heard the gunshot. Or perhaps it's Shay … "

"Shay! Maggie, I don't have any clothes on … "

Both Shay and Tom rounded the corner at the same time.

"Maggie … "

"Alana … " both men said in unison.

"You're both all right?" Tom questioned.

Maggie nodded. "We're fine. We saw a rattle snake is all. I shot him."

Alana wished she were anywhere but where she was at the moment. Her body was fully under water, but it was a spring, and the water wouldn't be as murky as a pond or river. Could they see anything? At the moment she was sure they were too worried to notice. She could no longer avoid Shay's gaze, and when she finally allowed her eyes to meet his, she was sure he could see into the depths of her soul.

His shirt sleeves were rolled up, displaying muscled arms not afraid of hard work. His blue eyes revealed deep concern for her well being. But beyond the concern she could sense a devotion that went beyond that of caring for a friend. He couldn't possibly be falling in love with her, could he?

"Since we are not yet fully clothed, I do believe it would be wise for you to wait beyond the trees. It is going to be dark soon," Maggie added for emphasis. Both Tom and Shay turned at the same time, finally realizing the women were indeed not fully clothed.

"We'll wait for you then. Don't be long, we didn't bring the lantern," Tom stated.

When the men were out of sight, Alana moved out of the water. The night air was definitely cooler than when she had gone in. Maggie held the blanket out to her and Alana quickly dried off. In spite of the snake, it did feel good to be clean once again. When they were both fully dressed, they made their way toward the waiting men.

Shay could not take his eyes off of her. Her wet, black hair hung loosely around her shoulders. And she smelled amazing. Darkness had quickly descended, but the full moon lent quite a bit of light to the darkened trail. Shay reached for Alana's hand, rubbing his thumb against the back of her smooth skin. He told himself that he was only looking out for her. He didn't want her to trip and fall, but who was he fooling? Shay could no longer resist the urge to touch her.

As they neared the camp, Shay relinquished her hand. Others saw them as brother and sister. He didn't want it to become any more complicated.

"Wait, Alana," Maggie insisted as she climbed into her wagon. She soon appeared with a Bible. "This was my mother's. She gave it to me the night before we left. I want you to have it."

Alana pushed the book back toward her. "You should keep it as a keepsake. Shay has a Bible. I can read his."

"Keeping this as a keepsake will do neither one of us any good. Please, I want you to have it."

Alana reached for the Bible. It looked like it had never been touched. "Thank you, Maggie."

° ° °

Shay lay trying to sleep, and instead relived the night he had just experienced. The gunshot and overwhelming fear that something had happened to Alana had surprised him. The relief that had filled his entire being, seeing her alive and well in the spring... and then the feel of her hand in his... he could not get that thought to leave his mind. In only a few short weeks, he had fallen in love with her. He was shocked at the feeling... the feeling of wanting to take care of her for the rest of his life.

A scream pierced his ears, and he instantly scrambled to his feet. He heard it again. It was coming from the wagon. Alana? He hurried to the wagon, and pushing back the canvas he peered inside, trying to find Alana in the darkness. He could hear her crying. He moved into the wagon.

"Alana," he whispered as he came near the bed. He sat down gently on the edge of it. "Alana?" he said again. She didn't answer and he realized she was not yet fully awake. Shay gently began to shake her, softly whispering her name.

He was not prepared for the terror displayed in her eyes. He reached for her, but she inched backwards. "It's me, Alana. You're fine." She fell against him and he held her for a long time, waiting for the tenseness of her body to subside. When he heard her shallow breathing, he knew she had finally fallen back asleep. Carefully he eased her back into the bed and covered her with the heavy quilt. He quietly left the wagon, wondering if she had ever fully awakened.

Sleep continued to evade him well into the night. Alana had memories from her past that continued to plague her mind. He knew her father had been a hard man. Had he hurt Alana like he hurt his wife?

Shay remembered the night Alana's mother had come to their home. He had answered the door and remembered the pained face of Charise as she had waited patiently for Shay's father to return from delivering a baby so he could reset her arm. Shay had known it had not been an accident. He could read the sadness in his father's eyes. Shay's father had not believed the made-up story any more than Shay had. As Charise left the O'Connell house that day, father and son had both stared at her retreating figure as Charise walked into the night, fearing that someday it would not be a simple broken bone, but rather a lost life.

Alana was distant in the morning, causing Shay to wonder if she had any remembrance of the evening before. He decided it would be best to wait for her to bring the incident up. He didn't want to embarrass her, even though he was concerned. Was it a nightmare she routinely had?

As they ate supper that evening, each silent in their own thoughts, Alana finally blurted out, "I'm sorry about last night."

Shay cocked his head to the side. "That's quite all right. Would you like to talk about what was bothering you?"

"I've had the nightmare frequently...since...a long time ago. The nightmare is always the same. I'm surrounded by people who hate me. They are screaming...yelling...and then suddenly they begin throwing stones from every direction. It sounds silly, I know. But at night, in the dark, it feels so real."

Alana noticed as Shay's eyes suddenly clouded. He remembered the incident, and she couldn't keep herself from asking. "That day after school, when I was hit with the rock, who threw it?"

Shay dropped his gaze, no longer able to look into her hopeful eyes. He had known she would ask someday. In the beginning he had hoped she wouldn't remember he had been one of the boys, but who could forget hurtful moments like that. It was a wonder she didn't hate him for those awful days from the past. At least now he finally had a chance to tell her the truth. A feeling of relief pushed away the sorrow.

"I challenged Jake to throw it. I dared him to do it.

I'm sorry, Alana. If I could go back in time and change that part of our lives, I would."

"Why did you hate me? What did I do?" Shay reached for her hand, intertwining his fingers with hers. His strain eased when she didn't pull away.

"Everyone in town spoke of you. It was alluded to often that your mother had been a slave. When you began school, everyone was curious about who you really were. I suppose it had already been bred into us that colored people were not one of us."

Alana searched his eyes. "The color of my skin isn't so different from yours," she insisted. He studied their hands, intertwined together. They really weren't so different.

"All kinds of stories went around, but the one that seemed to have the most clout was the one about Caty's Cavern."

"Caty's Cavern?" Alana questioned with interest.

"It was said that your mother found you in Caty's Cavern and raised you as her own."

Alana gasped. "But Caty was a slave. She escaped from a plantation in Georgia and was found in a cavern near Independence." Precariously close to the time Alana had been born, but Alana left that part out.

Shay nodded. "She hid in the cavern for several days before hunger forced her out. The slave owner's dogs followed her smell, and they found her a few hours later. The cavern was called Caty's Cavern from that day on."

"So, did you believe the story? I mean the part where I was her child."

"I suppose it was exciting to think it might be true. But we all knew it was a preposterous story. I would be foolish to believe it now." He reached out with his free hand and brushed her cheekbone with his hand.

"In this manner, therefore, pray: Our Father in heaven, Hallowed be Your name. Your kingdom come. Your will be done on earth as it is in heaven. Give us this day our daily bread ... "

Alana listened as Shay read from the book of Matthew. For an entire week now they had been reading the Bible together each night. Sometimes it felt as if he were reading in another language. Some of the words were foreign to her. It was peaceful though, listening to him read.

"For if you forgive men their trespasses, your heavenly Father will also forgive you. But if you do not forgive men their trespasses, neither will your Father forgive your trespasses" (Matthew 6:14–15 NKJV).

Shay stopped reading and glanced at Alana. He marked their place in the Bible and closed the book. He could tell she had questions.

"So, in order to be loved by Jesus, I need to forgive everyone, even those people who have purposefully hurt me."

"God loves everyone, and nothing we do or don't do will make Him love us more or less. His love is unconditional. Hard to fathom, I know." Shay nodded toward the Hubbards' wagon. "He even loves Joe Hubbard over there."

Joe reminded her of her father Clyde. He was angry most of the time. He had no patience. And Alana and others heard him yelling at his wife on different occasions. His wife Ellen was quiet and kept to herself. They had a small son. It was almost identical to the home Alana had grown up in, only it was a little boy with a horrible father, instead of a little girl.

"When we choose not to forgive, we harbor bitterness in our hearts, and the only person we hurt is ourselves."

Alana looked down at her hands. "Forgiveness is a hard thing to do," she responded.

"It is. Especially in our own strength. But with God it becomes a whole lot easier."

"Have you ever had to forgive anyone, Shay?"

Shay studied Alana, aware she was waiting for an honest answer. "I didn't realize it until later, but I held a lot of bitterness toward my parents. They didn't spend much time with Cal or me when we were growing up. My father was too busy, and my mother was too selfish with her time. Forgiving requires letting go. So I had to let go of the bitterness. It's a matter of choice. Some people don't like to hear that, but it's the truth."

"Your family seemed … perfect." Alana's eyes beheld amazement at his confession.

"You can't always know what goes on behind closed doors." He leaned back and gazed up at the stars. "There is always a lesson to be learned. See, I could have chosen to stay bitter, becoming a person no one wants to be around. Instead, I chose to forgive and learn from the experience."

"What have you learned?" Alana asked curiously.

"I know now that I want to be a husband who enjoys his wife and children. I want to be a husband who spends time with his family."

o o o

Mr. Leaver, the wagon train guide, had called a meeting asking for only the men to attend. Shay walked Alana over to Maggie's wagon, and then he and Tom continued on to the meeting.

Mr. Leaver counted the men in attendance, and then with a satisfied sigh, he began to speak. "I asked you here tonight because I want you to be aware of the dangers that lie ahead. I am sure many of you have heard of the massacre that took place two years ago. Twenty individuals lost their lives to the Blackfoot Indians in their attempt to go west. And this massacre took place not too far from where we are standing tonight.

"During the next couple weeks, we will need to be very cautious and constantly on the lookout for any evidence that Indians may be nearby. We will have someone on watch constantly. I will need the aid of each one of you. Each man will take two hour watches until we reach the last man, and then it will start over again. I am not relaying this information to frighten you, but I do want you to take extra precautions.

"Keep an eye out and your gun handy. If we do spot Indians, we will make camp quickly in an attempt to provide protection for not only ourselves but also our women and children. You may wonder why I chose to keep this information from the women. I did not want to cause them any unneeded worry or stress. Women are easily frightened, and when frightened, they carry on something awful." All the men nervously chuckled at the comment.

"I will let you know when the danger has passed. On duty tonight will be Andy, followed by Thomas, then Travis, Orville, and finally John. Are there any questions or concerns?"

○ ○ ○

Alana walked down the dusty road, tired of feeling sticky, dirty, and grimy...

"I have some wonderful news!" Maggie called from behind.

Alana smiled, turning around to wait for Maggie to catch up. "Please tell me ... don't keep me in suspense a moment longer."

"Tom and I are going to have a baby! Can you believe it? A baby!" Suddenly Maggie turned serious. "Am I ready to be a mother, Alana?"

"Of course you're ready. You have nothing to worry about, Maggie. You will be an amazing mother. Do you know how far along you are?" Alana inquired.

"Tom and I were trying to decide that very issue last night. I'm not entirely sure, but I may already be two months along. So that would make me due about the end of December ... or the beginning of January. Tom was very relieved to know we would be off the trail by time the baby comes."

Maggie squealed unashamedly, and Alana looked around to see if anyone was watching. "I have so many thoughts going through my head. Will it be a boy or a girl? Will he have my blue eyes or Tom's brown eyes?"

Alana laughed. "It will be a boy, and he'll have blue eyes just like his mother."

"Are you mocking me?" Maggie voiced with good humor.

"No, I would never do that." They both laughed. "I'm happy for you, Maggie. You really will be a wonderful mother. Just look at how the children follow you around. They love you. You're good with children."

"I hope so. It's an entirely different feeling when you realize the baby you carry is your full responsibility."

"Yes," Alana agreed. "I'm sure it would be. I, myself, have never been around children. At least you have had experience with them. Imagine what kind of mother I'd be!" Alana laughed.

"First, Alana, we need to find you a husband. I've noticed Allan Hadley watching you from a distance."

Alana blushed. She had noticed as well. The man could not keep his eyes off her. He seemed nice enough. And he was handsome: tall, brown hair, brown eyes. But it didn't matter if he were the most handsome man on earth; Alana knew her heart was already taken.

"Alana, you look at me right now … you have someone you like already … I can see it in your eyes. Now, I demand you tell me who it is this instant," Maggie cried.

"Maggie, ssshhh, someone will hear you … ."

"Hear what?" Shay said as he came into view. Alana's face went crimson red.

"Hear that Alana … "

"Maggie, you shush right now, you're embarrassing me."

"Surely telling your brother the news will not hurt anything," Maggie retorted.

"Yes," Shay teased. "As your brother, I believe I do have a right to know.

"Alana is infatuated with someone in our camp," Maggie quickly stated. Alana threw her a look of contempt.

"And who might you be infatuated with, Alana?" Shay persisted. His eyebrows were now raised in curiosity.

"I have no intentions of telling anybody that private bit of information." Alana quickly turned and walked away. She could hear the laughter of Maggie echoing behind her.

CHAPTER FIVE

January 5, 1841

The strain in my family is unbearable. I hate James for leaving me here. I envy him for escaping this prison. When James told me of his decision to go west, I was heartbroken. Besides Jesse, James was the only other person who seemed to care about me—to really love me, but then he abandoned me. Even Johnny has escaped my parent's control. He moved into town four years ago. He has worked beside father at the bank for eleven years, in hopes of taking over the business in the future. And now I am the only child they have left. What little independence I did have is now only a distant memory.

My father declared over supper his intentions of announcing the engagement of his only daughter to Mr. Jared Dobbs at Atlanta's banquet next month. I begged him to give me one more year. I am still just sixteen, yet my father reminded me my seventeenth birthday is only weeks away. I wish I were six again. I wish I had never gone ice-skating with my brothers. I wish Jack had not died. I wish ... I wish ... I wish. Yet all my wishing has changed nothing.

I ran from the supper table in tears. No one came after me. I suppose they expected my outburst. I escaped to the barn, where I searched in earnest for Jesse, but could not find him anywhere. Finally hearing my sobs, he found me in one of the stalls weeping in the hay. He knelt down beside me, concern evident in his eyes. I told him what my parents had planned, but he said nothing in my defense. And in shock, I watched as he backed out of the stall and walked away.

"Jesse," I screamed. "Jesse, I love you." But he acted as if he hadn't heard me. I cried awhile longer, but the cool air forced me to return indoors. I have never felt more alone.

◦ ◦ ◦

The wagon train had slowed to a stop. Alana hurried toward their wagon somewhat confused. Why were they stopping when there were several hours of daylight left? She watched as a cloud of dust signaled riders coming. "Indians!" one man shouted. Mr. Leaver ordered camp to be made. A few women began to panic. Some husbands tried to comfort them, while others chose to ignore them.

As camp was quickly set up, Mr. Leaver continued to give orders. "We will not fire the first shot. We will wait and see what they want first. Some are just interested in bartering. Others want medicine ... or whiskey ... which is why I don't allow whiskey on my train. If they fire upon us, you have my permission to fire back."

Alana counted twelve Indians as they road into camp. One Indian rode up to the front. "Son hurt. Need medicine. Need doctor."

Several women and children were crying. Alana looked over at Shay. Could he help them? Was it safe to go with them?

The Indian reached for his gun. "I know you have medicine. You not take long journey without medicine."

Shay stepped forward. The Indian turned his gun toward Shay. "I have experience with medicine. What is wrong with your son?"

"His leg twisted and hot with fever."

"How was he hurt?"

"He fell from horse."

Shay turned toward Mr. Leaver. "Give me the medicine used to treat infection. I will also need the antibiotic cream to treat the wound. It sounds like his son has broken his leg and infection has set in. I will go with him to see if I can set the leg."

"I don't think that is wise, Shay," Mr. Leaver admonished. "Give him the medicine, but leaving the wagon train could cost you your life. What if his son dies before you get there? We cannot wait around for you to return. The wagon train cannot afford to lose valuable time." Mr. Leaver walked away to get the medicine.

"You come," the Indian insisted.

Shay knew he would go in order to protect the rest of the wagon train. He turned to Alana. "Go on as usual. You've driven the wagon on several occasions. Listen to the instructions I've given you. You'll be fine."

"But how will you catch up?"

"I'll take my horse … Star. Traveling by horse is faster than by wagon. It won't take me long to catch up."

He reached out and brushed the tear from her face. "I'll be back," he promised. *Please let me come back.* He took the medicine from Mr. Leaver, mounted his horse, and followed the Indians back in the direction they had just come.

∘ ∘ ∘

Shay entered the Indian tepee. It already smelled of

death. *Please, Lord, give me strength to do what I need to do.* The father pointed to his son. Shay bent and felt his head. He was burning up with fever. He pulled back the blanket and gagged.

The boy's leg was indeed broken. Shay turned from the ghastly sight. The bone was protruding out of the leg. *Oh God.* He pulled the medicine from his bag, taking deep breaths to calm himself. Shay focused his eyes on the boy's face as he poured a small amount of medicine into the boy's mouth. Shay then pushed his finger back into the boy's mouth until the boy swallowed.

He turned to the father. "I need hot water. I also need a knife, needle, and thread." He made motion like he was sewing. Did the man understand him? He must have because he turned and left the tepee.

Shay turned back to the leg. How long had the leg been like this? Would the bone heal when he snapped it back in place or was it too late? He knew he had to at least try.

The father returned with the supplies he asked for. Shay showed him how to hold his son's arms lest he begin thrashing around. It took several moments of stretching and pulling but he soon had the bone back in the leg. After a few more minutes Shay felt confident that the bone was back where it was suppose to be. He cleaned the area thoroughly before applying a disinfectant cream. He then wrapped the boy's leg tightly.

Shay followed the Indian back outside the tepee. He breathed in deeply the cool mountain air, yet the smell still lingered.

"He cannot put any weight on his leg for at least four weeks." The Indian shook his head confused. Shay pointed to his leg and then bent and slowly drew thirty-one lines in the dirt. The Indian nodded his head acknowledging that he understood.

"Give him medicine when the sun comes up and when the sun goes down." The Indian nodded again.

Then the Indian pointed to the ground. "Sleep here. Check son tomorrow." Shay sighed and turned to the mat the Indian offered. He would not be leaving tonight.

o o o

Alana dipped her hands into the soapy water once again. She grimaced at the burning sensation. She should have worn the leather gloves. But she had not remembered until the train was already moving. As the afternoon turned to evening, and Shay had still not returned, Alana's anxiety only worsened. Surely a broken leg would not take this long to set.

Tom had graciously taken care of the oxen when the wagon train had come to a stop. And she had eaten supper with Maggie and Tom. *Please come back. Please.* She wished she knew how to pray like Maggie … or Shay. Perhaps praying would ease her frightened heart, but she did not know the Lord like Maggie or Shay. Maggie said all she had to do was ask Him to come live in her heart. And Shay had read the scripture only a few days ago that said if you believed in your heart and said with your mouth that Jesus was Lord, you would become His child. But did she believe?

Alana poured the water out on the ground and reached for the lantern. Tomorrow she would remember the gloves. *Oh please Shay, be here tomorrow when I awake.* She crawled into the wagon, but sleep was a long way off.

Shay awoke to find the Indian man staring at him. "Come," he insisted. Shay got to his feet and followed the Indian back into the tepee. The boy's eyes were open and he was alert. He was still hot to the touch. The boy was mumbling, but Shay did not understand his words. He turned to the father.

"Need water and leg hurt much," the father interpreted.

"He should heal if he stays off the leg. Do not let him up for several more days. And remember, don't let him stand on the leg for thirty-one days."

"I remember," the father stated.

"The medicine will heal the infection … take the hot fever away … "

The Indian nodded. "You go now. You go back to your people."

Shay left the tepee and walked toward his horse. He was free to leave.

○ ○ ○

Alana tried to focus on the tasks at hand. When she had awoke that morning to find Shay still gone, fear had overtaken her. *Where was he? Had they killed him?*

"May I help you with anything?" She turned to face Allan, a young man also heading west to farm. "It looks as if you could use some water." He picked up the two buckets next to the wagon and made his way down to the river. At least she wasn't entirely alone. The people were willing to help, and for that she was thankful.

When Allan returned, he began to tend to the oxen, and he soon had them harnessed to the wagon. She knew he had no wife to return to, so she offered him breakfast.

"I hope that your brother returns soon," Allan offered.

A tear ran down her cheek, and she turned away from his compassionate gaze. *Not her brother, but rather the man that she loved.*

When the wagon train pulled out that morning, she did not forget the gloves.

○ ○ ○

Dusk was falling. Shay pushed the horse hard. He did not want to spend another night away from the wagon train. He was sure Alana was worried enough as it was. As he came over the next hill, he could see the wagons way off in the distance. He urged the horse on. He would be with her again soon.

Shay was cloaked with darkness when he came upon the camp. "Who goes there?" a loud voice loomed ahead.

"It's me … Shay O'Connell."

Blake stepped out into the moonlight with a smile on his face. "Shay! You made it back. We all thought … when you didn't return yesterday … we just weren't sure."

"How's Alana faring?" Shay knew he'd see for himself in a few moments, but he couldn't stop himself from asking."

"You can certainly be proud of your sister, Shay. She's done a right good job guiding the oxen. And plenty of people have pitched into help, especially Allan Hadley." Blake said the last part with a lopsided smile. "I think he's taken quite a likin' to that sister of yours."

"Good-night, Blake." Shay turned his horse and moved down the line of wagons until he finally came to his own. Alana sat eating supper ... with another man. Had she even noticed he was gone? He watched as Allan made a comment, and Alana smiled back at him. Shay scowled. He had forced himself to complete exhaustion to come back to this! Had he misread the signals she had given him? Or was she just too bashful to tell him she had no feelings for him?

Shay moved the horse forward, and Alana was the first to see him. She jumped to her feet, splattering food everywhere. "Shay!" she squealed with excitement. Her eyes danced with animation. But was it because of him or because of ... Allan?

Allan also stood to his feet. He walked toward Shay and held out his hand. Shay shook it, hating himself for the anger he felt toward the man. None of this was Allan's fault.

"Glad you made it back safely," Allan voiced. "We've been worried about you," Allan stated with a glance in Alana's direction.

We ... as in they were a couple? Shay turned away before he said or did something he shouldn't. "I've got to tend to Star. I've ran her hard today." *Because I didn't want to miss one more second of time spent with you.* He didn't say the last part, though he wanted to. He glanced briefly at Alana before leading Star to the river. A perplexing look had now crossed her features.

Shay stood at the river, lost in thought. Had he overreacted? No. Overreacting would have been throttling Allan and telling Alana he never wanted to see her again. He had contained himself pretty well under the circumstances. But inside he felt like a fool. She had invited another man to eat with her. How many ways was he supposed to take that? Either she liked Allan ... or she really liked him. Evidently she liked him. He knew her enough by now to know she wasn't one to throw out invitations. Asking Allan to supper was a big deal ... for her.

Shay yawned. He was tired. He hadn't slept well the night before. And now ... thanks to Alana ... he probably wouldn't sleep well tonight, either. The horse had stopped drinking and was staring at him. He patted Star's head and led her back to the wagon. Allan was gone when he returned, and Alana had left a full plate of food by the fire. He could see the outline of her figure as she moved inside the wagon.

He sat down by the fire and took a bite of the hot food. He closed his eyes in satisfaction. The meal was very tasty, just like every other meal she made. When he opened his eyes again, Alana was climbing down from the wagon. She made her way toward the fire and sat down across from him.

"I'm glad you're back," she whispered.

"Are you?" he retorted.

Her eyes retreated from his and went to her hands. "Of course. Why would you say such a thing?" She continued to study her hands.

Shay wasn't one to hide his feelings. When he was happy, everyone knew it, and when he was mad, everyone knew it too. He wasn't going to pretend everything was all right when it wasn't.

"It seems like you found someone to take my place rather quickly."

"Allan? Allan has been helping out around here. I couldn't do everything alone."

"And you didn't want to eat alone either, I take it."

"I offered to pay him, but he wouldn't hear of it. The only other way I could think of repaying him was by feeding him."

"And he readily accepted, I'm sure." Shay continued to shovel food into his mouth, waiting for her to look up. She would look up at him any moment now. Though shy, she was spirited. He wouldn't have the last word, not if she could help it.

"Are you jealous?" she finally voiced. Her eyes met his in an even stare.

"Should I be?" he questioned.

"No! No, and it is absurd that you would even think so. I thought you knew…" He watched her rub her hands together, enjoying her discomfort.

"Knew what?" he persisted.

"Knew that I … that I … ," she groaned and stood to her feet. "You are so aggravating, so very, very aggravating." She stormed back into the wagon.

CHAPTER SIX

February 18, 1841

I turned seventeen two weeks ago, and tonight my father announced my engagement to Jared Dobbs. My hands tremble at the thought. I hate my father. I hate Jared Dobbs. I hate my mother. And I even hate Jesse Blackwell. How could he desert me when I so desperately needed him? Had I only imagined his feelings toward me?

I wish I had never been born. I wish . . .

I've changed my mind about one thing, and one thing only. I do not hate Jesse Blackwell. While writing earlier I heard a noise outside my window, but still so distraught, I ignored the sound at first. But when it persisted, I had to go to the window to check and see what or who was making the sound.

Imagine my fright when I found Jesse perched in the tree outside my window. I screamed and then covered my mouth to muffle the sound. Jesse told me he could not keep his feelings at bay any longer. He does love me! He truly does.

Father has sold him to a plantation on the other side of Atlanta. Does he know of our relationship? He must; why else would he part with one of his hardest workers. Jesse and I have agreed to escape. We will marry and head west to be near James! I love Jesse Blackwell.

Alana stood at the river deep in thought. After reading more from her mother's journal the evening before, Alana now had so many unanswered questions. Her mother had loved Jesse Blackwell, a slave. It was all so difficult to fathom. The woman in the journal and the mother Alana had grown up with were two entirely different people. What had happened to the vibrant woman in the journal?

Alana turned as she noticed Ellen struggling to fill her buckets in the stream next to her. Her son continued to venture away from his mother, preventing Ellen from fulfilling the task at hand.

Slowly, Alana advanced upon them. "May I help you?" she asked. "I could follow behind with your son while you carry your water back to your wagon." Ellen nodded.

Alana reached for the little boy's hand. "What is his name?"

"Jesse," Ellen replied. *Jesse, like the man Alana's mother had loved.* Alana watched as Ellen bent to fill up her buckets with water and couldn't help but notice Ellen's protruding belly. *She's pregnant!* Alana thought to herself. Alana said nothing as she turned to follow Ellen back to her wagon.

"Hi, Jesse. My name is Alana. Can you say Alana?"

"Lana," Jesse said.

Alana laughed. Jesse pointed to the flowers … the trees … the birds. Everything was intriguing to him. He was a beautiful child with sandy blond hair and piercing blue eyes like his mother. Alana looked at his small hand in her own, so tiny … so light. Her hand looked especially dark next to his.

By the time Alana and Jesse had come to the wagon,

Ellen was ready to take her son. "Thank you," she offered before walking away.

"Will you come for supper this evening?" Alana invited. "We read the Bible together in the evening. You are welcome to join us." Alana surprised even herself at the offer. The words had come out of nowhere. Ellen did not respond.

A few hours later, Alana was dishing up Shay's plate of food when Ellen showed up with her small son behind her. Shay's eyes met Alana's several times during supper. He too was surprised by Ellen's presence.

When it came time to read the Bible, Maggie and Tom also came by. They all took a seat around the fire, even Ellen silently sat down with Jesse seated on her lap.

Silence fell over the group as Shay began to read from Second Corinthians, chapter five. "Now then, we are ambassadors for Christ, as though God were pleading through us: We implore you on Christ's behalf, be reconciled to God."

"What does ambassador mean?" Alana asked.

"I believe that it is a person that represents Christ," Maggie offered.

Shay agreed. "Every day we are faced with decisions. And we are held accountable before God for our decisions. The world sees God through us." Shay paused as he glanced at Alana. He wasn't doing too great a job lately in that department. She raised her eyebrows at him. He smiled sheepishly before turning back to the scripture.

° ° °

The night was dark, but Alana couldn't help but read further in her mother's journal. She had to know if Charise married Jesse. What had happened between them? One thing was certain; her mother had not remained at home. Alana reached below the bed and retrieved the journal, opening up to where she had left off.

September 3, 1841

My life is meaningless. I can hardly believe Jesse is gone ... dead ... and has been for three months. My father hired men to find us ... and he killed my husband; for that alone I shall never forgive him.

My instructor was gone when I returned. My engagement to Mr. Dobbs, of course, annulled. I contemplated taking my own life on several occasions. I was so overcome with grief, and then a ray of hope broke through the darkness. I am with child...Jesse's child. And I know I have to leave. Raising this child conceived from our love is my utmost concern.

My parents are leaving for the weekend to attend a distant cousin's wedding. And since I am no longer accepted among their prestigious society, I will be left at home, watched by the butler, maids, and other servants, of course, but my chance has finally arrived.

I will leave tonight. The hired help is having a celebration, and my absence will not be noticed until it is too late.

Her mother was with child? Did Alana have a sibling? Surely her mother had not abandoned the baby. Alana hurriedly skipped ahead to the next entry.

November 9, 1841

I have made it as far as Independence, Missouri, but I have no money, no food, and no roof over my head. Mr. Scott Peterson offered me temporary work in his shop, but come December I will once again be out on the streets.

Scott's son, Clyde, has made his intentions known. He wishes for us to marry. He frightens me, and yet I must keep my baby's well-being my first priority. I am alone and beginning to show. I do not want to marry Clyde, but what other choice do I have?

Alana once again flipped the page, her curiosity heightening by each moment.

March 4, 1842

My daughter was born this morning. She is beautiful, more beautiful than I ever imagined she'd be. The doctor glanced at me in shock upon her birth, instantly realizing the child was not fully white. She was indeed dark in complexion, but as soon as I gazed into her almond-colored eyes, so much like her father's, I fell in love with her. Does every mother feel as protective as I do at this moment?

I have named her Alana ...

Alana dropped the journal. March 4 ... Alana ... it was she! She was the daughter of Jesse Blackwell! She was black. Alana quickly closed the journal and shoved it beneath the bed.

○ ○ ○

Alana was filling two buckets with water at the creek, and her thoughts were on the passage of scripture Shay had read the evening before. Peter had asked Jesus how many times he should forgive his brother when his brother sinned against him. Jesus' response bothered her. *I tell you, not seven times, but seventy times seven.*

The topic of forgiveness had been discussed on many occasions. Deep down she knew she needed to forgive Clyde. She could forgive her mother for the life she provided for her. She could forgive the townspeople for treating her as an outcast. She could forgive Shay for hating her when she was a child. But the thought of forgiving her father was almost unbearable. He had been so cruel, so terrible. How could God ask her to forgive him? Surely He knew the terrible things her father had done to her; and not just her, but her mother.

If God knew not only every sparrow that fell from the sky, but also every hair on her head, then of course he knew about the beatings she didn't deserve. But He was asking too much when it came to forgiveness. She couldn't forgive her father. She wouldn't.

She was on her way back to the wagon when she heard the shouts. It was coming from the Hubbards' wagon. Alana listened as he screamed insult after insult at Ellen. She sat the buckets of water down and made her way closer.

"I can't believe you! I've told you over and over again, and yet still you forgot to tie the bin shut. We've lost a whole week's oats because of your stupidity." Alana rounded the corner just as Joe reached out his hand and struck Ellen in the face.

Alana flew at Joe in a rage. Joe, who had no idea he had a spectator, was completely caught off guard. He stumbled to the ground. Alana continued to hit him with all of her might. Finally, Joe's strength returned, and he shoved Alana back as hard as he could.

It was at that moment when Shay arrived on the scene. He watched as Alana was thrown backwards. Joe came to his feet only to be knocked unconscious with the solid blow of Shay's fist. Joe lay in silence on the ground.

Shay rushed to Alana's side. She had a deep cut on the side of her head. Any lower and it could have damaged her right eye. Already it was beginning to swell. Shay pulled Alana to her feet. "What is going on here?" he demanded.

Alana tried to free herself from his grasp. Shay held tightly and used one hand to pry her hands free from her face. Her eyes displayed deep anguish.

"He's not my real father," Alana shrieked. "He's not my real father."

"What are you talking about?" Shay inquired.

"Let me go!" she screamed.

Shay freed her and watched as she quickly ran into the trees. It was then that he noticed Ellen. She was holding her son in her arms, rocking him back and forth. Her eyes were on her husband lying on the ground, still unconscious.

"Can I help you with anything?" Shay asked.

"She was only trying to help. Don't be angry with her."

"I'm not angry … just worried. Are you all right?"

"I'm fine."

Shay took a step toward Joe. "Just leave him be." Ellen's voice was sharp. "He's been drinking. Hopefully he won't remember what has taken place." Shay nodded and then walked away.

His first instinct was to follow the path that Alana had taken, but she had made it clear she did not want him near her. *He's not my real father.* What was she talking about?

∘ ∘ ∘

Maggie followed the path that Shay had pointed out to her. The concern etched in Shay's eyes when he came to their wagon made Maggie hurry her step. She saw Alana in the distance, lying underneath an oak tree. Maggie stooped down beside her.

"Alana, are you all right? We're worried about you."

Alana turned her face toward her. "Oh Maggie, I don't know what came over me. When I saw him hit her it brought back such terrible memories. My father used to beat my mother. I remember watching him hit her over and over. I hate him. I do, Maggie. I hate him."

Maggie patted her shoulder. She kept silent, hoping that Alana would continue to bear her soul if needed.

"And my mother—why did she let him do it? Why? Why didn't she defend herself? Why didn't she strike him back? Why didn't she leave? When I saw Joe, I wanted to kill him, Maggie. I wanted to hurt him like he was hurting her."

The tears came then, and Alana cried for quite a while. *Poor Alana, no wonder she struggled opening up to people.* A tear coursed down Maggie's face. "What you did wasn't wrong. You were trying to defend another woman in trouble."

Maggie continued to rub Alana's shoulder. "I'm sorry about your father. At least he is no longer a part of your life."

"And I won't forgive him. I won't." Alana spat out.

"God doesn't ask us to forgive others for their benefit. He asks us to forgive others for our benefit."

"But he doesn't deserve it," Alana protested.

"You are right, he doesn't. But you do. You are not forgiving him because he deserves it, but because you deserve it. You deserve to live your life free from him, free from thoughts of what he did to you and to your mother." Alana stood to her feet and Maggie followed suit.

Alana began to walk away, but Maggie reached out

and grabbed her hand. "Shay loves you. He loves you so much."

Alana's head shot around and she searched Maggie's face. "Shay loves you with a love between a man and a woman ... not the love of a brother and sister."

Alana stared at Maggie with disbelief. "How long have you known?"

Maggie smiled. "I cannot pinpoint the exact day, but I have seen the glances he sends your way. And I wondered about your shyness around him. Then I began to notice the way he looks at you ... the way he touches you." Alana's look changed from shock to panic. "Don't worry, Alana. I'm not going to say anything. No one else has noticed. I guess I am the only one with extra time on my hands."

Maggie joined hands with Alana as they made their way back to camp. "Why are you so afraid of allowing him to love you?"

Alana sighed. "I've never loved anyone before, besides my mother. What if he decides he doesn't love me anymore? What if I'm not who he thinks I am? I'm afraid to trust him."

Maggie sighed. "I don't know what kind of life you've lived that makes you so wary of people, Alana, but Shay is different than the father you grew up with. You need to open your heart and learn to trust him."

"But how do I do that?" Alana asked.

"You begin opening up in small ways. Look into his eyes when he is speaking to you. Talk to him about your fear of being rejected. Talk to him about your past. Each day will bring you one step closer. And you'll have my prayers every step of the way."

They turned back toward camp. Maggie's words

continued to haunt her. *Talk to him about your past.* She wasn't ready to tell him about her past. How could she share her past with another when she wasn't willing to face it herself?

o o o

Alana was still shocked by the news of her ethnicity. Now that she knew, everything else began to make sense: the teasing she had endured as a child, the reason Clyde had hated her. Being black opened up another fear as well. How would Shay feel about the news? As children, Shay had disliked her when he thought she was of black descent. What would he think if he knew it was no longer an imaginary tale, but, rather, the truth?

Alana could no longer bring herself to look into his eyes, afraid that Shay would read the truth behind her own eyes. She knew deep down she could never be with Shay. She could never marry him. What man wanted Negro blood running through the veins of his children?

"Alana..." She heard Shay's voice from outside the wagon.

"Yes," she whispered. Alana couldn't even bring herself to walk to the front of the wagon.

"The camp is meeting to celebrate the June birthdays. It's about time to head that way."

"I'm not going," Alana stated. She closed her eyes. "I'm not feeling well... I'd like to rest."

The canvas parted, and Shay poked his head in, concern written on his face. "You're sick?" he questioned. "What symptoms are you having?"

Alana looked down, fingering the edge of the quilt her mother had made for her. "Nothing serious," Alana voiced. "I guess I'm just tired and in need of some sleep."

"Or are you hiding from me?" Shay persisted. "You can't even look me in the eyes. Why? Did I do something to make you angry ... frightened?"

"No ... no ... nothing like that, I just need some time." Alana closed her eyes. *I just need some time.* What kind of answer was that.

"Fine," he voiced with no emotion. The canvas swung shut, and she was alone ... as she would most likely be for the rest of her life: alone.

It wasn't long later that Alana heard a soft knock outside the wagon. "It's me, Alana," Maggie's voice acknowledged.

The canvas once again parted, and Maggie moved into the cramped space. "Small quarters are good for newly married couples," Maggie voiced with a smile. "Any arguments are quickly quenched when you have no choice but to deal with the anger the moment it surfaces."

Alana smiled. "Do you and Thomas argue?" she asked.

"Of course, every couple has their moments. Thomas is soft-spoken. I'm ... not!" Alana laughed. Maggie sat down on the bed next to Alana. "What's wrong, Alana? Are you going to make Shay worry for the remainder of the trip?"

"No ... is that what he said?" Alana voiced with surprise.

"Of course not. Shay was quiet tonight, which is very unlike his character. When I asked him where you were, he said you were feeling under the weather. But I spent all day with you, and you said nothing about not feeling well."

Alana blushed. "I cannot bring myself to face him, Maggie. I'm scared—"

"Scared of what? Shay is the last man on earth you should be afraid of."

"I know," Alana cried. "But I've learned something…from my mother…about my past. I am not who Shay thinks I am. And if he knows for certain, he'll push me away. I know he will."

Maggie sighed. "Shay would not push you away because of your past. That is part of love—accepting people the way they are and then helping them grow. You love Shay. I know you do. You need to give him a chance. Let him prove his love to you."

Alana looked up into her friend's eyes, hoping Maggie would give her the strength she herself did not have.

"How can you possibly allow the love between you and Shay to die? Wouldn't you rather face him, tell him your circumstances, and take the chance that he could push you away?" Maggie paused and then pushed forward. "There is always the chance Shay will tell you he loves you in spite of your past and that he would allow nothing to come between you."

Alana hopefully grabbed her friend's hand. "Could he?"

"Yes, he most certainly could."

o o o

Alana sat up in bed. Slowly her mind began to focus. She hadn't been dreaming, but something had awakened her. Then she heard it again. Thunder. Thunder so loud it sounded as if rocks were falling from the sky. The wind was howling, and then it began to rain. Small drops at first and then sheets of rain began coming down.

Alana's thoughts turned to Shay. He couldn't stay out there. He would already be soaked, she was sure. She crawled out of the warm bed and reached for the canvas. Cold rain splattered in her face as she called Shay's name. She couldn't even hear her own voice. "SHAY!" she screamed. Suddenly he was there, wet from head to toe. He entered the wagon shivering.

"Are you all right?" she asked.

He nodded. "I'm a little cold, but all right." He searched for the lantern and matches. Soon light invaded the small wagon. Water dripped from his clothing onto the floor. "I do need to change," he said with realization.

Alana crawled back into bed. "I'll cover my head. Go ahead and change."

She heard him fumbling around for clean clothes. After several minutes had passed, she peeked out from beneath the covers. Shay was standing there, dressed in dry clothes, but deep in thought.

"What if I had still been dressing?" he teased.

"Not even an eighty year old man would take that long to dress himself. I knew you were done."

Shay laughed. It felt good to laugh with her again. The last few days they had barely said a word to each other. Shay grabbed a dry blanket with the intentions of laying it down on the soaked floor.

"Don't do that!" Alana voiced with alarm. It was the blanket her mother had made. "The floor is wet and muddy. Besides, you can't sleep down there."

"Where else do expect me to sleep, ma'am, if not outside or here on the floor."

"Here," she pointed to the bed where she was seated. The smile fled Shay's face, and he shook his head. "We'll have our own blankets," she continued, "and we are brother and sister, are we not?"

Shay inched toward the bed with the quilt in his arms. There was really no other alternative, unless of course he wanted to get wet again. Alana scooted far over to the corner. Shay laid his blanket down next to her and blew out the lantern.

He hesitated briefly before laying down. He wouldn't be able to sleep. The woman he loved was sleeping next to him. He could feel her warmth … smell her skin.

"Shay?" Alana whispered in the night.

"Hmm?" he answered.

"Are you sleeping?" Alana asked.

"Yes," he replied.

Alana smiled. "If you were sleeping, you wouldn't be answering me right now." Even in the dark she could sense his smile.

"Remember that day when Joe hit Ellen and I was upset … "

Shay felt the mood begin to change. How could he forget that day? "Yes … I remember."

"Clyde … he wasn't my real father. And I'm glad he wasn't. He was not very nice … to me or my mother."

He's not my real father. He's not my real father. He had wondered about the meaning of those words. Now it made sense.

"My father … he … he passed away before I was born." Why couldn't she just say it? *My father was black. My father was a slave.*

"I'm sorry you never knew him. He would be proud of you."

"Proud of the fact I asked Allan to supper?" Alana giggled.

Shay turned toward her. "Why, you little tease…" He clasped her hands in his own and tickled her side with his free hand. She buried her face in her blanket.

"Stop, Shay. Please stop." Shay let her go, but not before tickling her one last time. He fell back on his side of the bed.

"Shay?" Alana said.

"Yes." He replied.

"I … I love you."

Shay pulled her against him. With three words, she had changed his world. He knew he would never be the same again.

Alana waited for him to say something, but he didn't. And then she felt tear drops on her skin. He was crying.

◦ ◦ ◦

When Alana awoke the next morning, she was alone. The memory of the night before came flooding back to her. Had she really told Shay that she loved him? Alana smiled as she quickly dressed. It had stopped raining shortly after her declaration of love, and Shay had reluctantly returned to his bed by the fire.

The sun was shining when she crawled through the opening of the canvas, and the sky showed no sign that it had been raining only a few hours before.

Alana began to prepare breakfast. She was so involved in building a fire that she didn't hear Shay approach. He walked up from behind and encircled her waist with his arms. Her neck began to redden.

"Do you need some help, ma'am? Not even an eighty year old woman would take this long to build a fire."

Alana laughed. Shay took the matches from her hand and soon had the fire burning hot.

He stood to his feet and pulled her back against him. "Did you tell me you loved me last night?" he questioned. She could not see his eyes and wondered if he was serious or teasing.

"I did," she answered.

"I thought you did. And would you like to know if I return the sentiment?"

"It may be beneficial—yes."

He turned her around and brought her chin up with his finger. "I do . . . " He paused as Star whinnied from behind him.

"You do . . . what?" she pressured.

"When a horse raises her ears like that it means someone is coming," he stated.

"Or it means that some man isn't ready to make his sentiments known," she retorted.

Shay dropped his arms, just as Allan rounded the corner. "I'm headin' to the river. Can I fill these up for you, Alana?" he asked as he retrieved the buckets by the wagon.

Alana looked at Shay who now had a scowl on his face. "Thank you, Allan. I'd be appreciative." Alana smiled as she turned back to the fire.

○ ○ ○

As Maggie and Alana were walking one day, Alana noticed Ellen up ahead. "Let's go catch up with Ellen, Maggie. I think she is lonely." Maggie agreed. They hurried their pace. Ellen came frequently when Shay and Alana read the Bible. She didn't stay long, but at least she was reaching out.

Alana noticed the black and blue mark near her neck, but made no mention of it. Why had she married Joe? It may have been a situation like her mother's: pregnant, homeless, and no place else to go.

"When is your baby due?" Maggie inquired.

"Sometime in August," she answered. Alana knew that they would most definitely still be traveling at that time. Was she afraid? Nervous?

"I'm going to have a baby, too, and I know I have a lot to learn. Perhaps you'd be willing to show me how to take care of a newborn. The whole idea is both exciting and frightening all at the same time."

Ellen smiled. "I'd be glad to help, Maggie. And when this little one is born, you can come observe if you think it would help."

"Oh, could I?" Maggie exclaimed. "Thank you, Ellen. I've never missed my mother more than when I found out I was having a child. I'm glad I have someone to talk to who knows all about it."

Ellen's eyes had a far away look in them, as if she, too, were remembering better days. "Jesse had an older brother ... Daniel was his name."

Alana searched her new friend's sorrowful eyes. "What happened to him?" Alana asked.

"Daniel ... we called him Danny...he died when he was two. He was sick ... just a cold at first that got worse with time. We couldn't afford a doctor ... and by the time Joe ... we realized Danny was in need of one, it was too late." A tear slipped down her cheek. Ellen turned her eyes toward the wagon. "I'd better go. Jesse's sleeping in the wagon. I'll see you this evening." She left with a small wave.

"She left something unsaid," Maggie voiced. "I

think it was Joe who wouldn't spend the money on a doctor for his own son ... he makes me sick." Maggie let out a loud sigh. "Why does she stay with someone like him, Alana? Why?"

"Because she's afraid of the unknown, the unexpected. She'd rather live the life she's living instead of face a life of other cruelties like hunger, no roof over her head, the necessities most take for granted."

° ° °

"Mr. O'Connell," the woman nervously stated as she came upon their campfire. Shay immediately stood to his feet.

"This morning Chad had a fever and threw up. I kept him inside the wagon to rest the entire day. Now Kent also has a fever." She continued to wring her hands as if in discomfort. "I'm afraid, Mr. O'Connell. Could it be ... ?" She couldn't speak the awful word. She knew how devastating that one small word could be.

Shay knew what she meant. Cholera. *Please Lord, don't let it be that,* he prayed silently. Alana moved to follow him. Shay quickly pulled her aside. "Alana ... I want you to remain here. If it is some sickness or disease, you will only increase your chance of contracting it."

Her eyes narrowed, a frown pulling at the edges of her mouth. "But you're going. And we are in contact with one another."

He shook his head. "No ... stay here." He walked away before she could answer.

Hannah led him to their wagon, and he went inside. He suddenly wished his stomach were not full at the moment. There was a lingering smell of waste. He moved to the bedside, taking the youngest boy's hand in his. "Kent, how are you feeling?"

"Not too well," the nine-year-old boy answered. Shay's eyes moved to Chad, who was sleeping, his face was also colorless.

"Tell me where it hurts," Shay questioned while he looked the boy over.

"My stomach aches, especially when I'm about to throw up. And I'm so cold. Mama keeps bringing us blankets, but I'm still shivering."

Chad suddenly sat up in bed, incoherent of his surroundings. His eyes frantically searched the wagon. Shay reached out to steady him. "Chad, it's me, Mr. O'Connell. Your mother is worried. I came to check on you." Chad slowly eased back into the bed, his eyes still open.

"Chad, can you tell me if you ate or drank anything in the last few days that might have made you sick?" Shay desperately hoped the sickness wasn't a result of the water they had all been drinking.

"Nothing unusual … just water … and what mama's cooked for supper." Chad rubbed his eyes.

"Have you only drunk the water from the spring?" Shay insisted.

Chad nodded, and then instantly hesitated as if remembering a detail long forgotten. "Three days ago, we were following the wagon like usual. Kent was thirsty … and the thought of chasing down our wagon for a drink of water was too tiring. We stopped at a water hole along the road."

"And you both drank from it?" Shay asked, concern etching his face. Both Kent and Chad nodded. "I think we found the culprit. Those water holes are not clean.

Look at all the garbage and dead animals that litter the sides of the road. When it rains, the water streams to these holes ... " He didn't have to say more; understanding was already transparent on their young faces.

"You'll be fine," he reassured. But do what your mama says, even if you don't feel like it. You should feel better in a couple days." Shay stood up and left the wagon.

"Hannah," Shay stated. She turned from the fire, tears coursing down her cheeks. "I think everything's fine. The next two days should tell for sure. They drank some water off the road the other day ... and their bodies are trying to rid themselves of the bacteria. Make sure they drink lots of fluids ... I don't want them to get dehydrated. No food ... but lots of water, all right? If they won't drink the water, mix up some chicken broth. Something salty will be easier to stomach."

She nodded. "Thank you, Mr. O'Connell."

"I'll be by to check on them in the morning," Shay said as he walked away.

○ ○ ○

The Bible reading was increasing in size. Maggie and Tom continued to come, as well as Ellen. Jake, a bachelor, also started coming, and he brought along his guitar so they could sing some songs, which in turn brought more people, like Martha, Ben, and their four sons. Allan also saw an opportunity for more time with Alana and started attending as well. And when Kent and Chad finally returned to health, Hannah also began coming, her two sons forced to attend with her.

Alana enjoyed Jesse. He was used to her now and not quite as reserved in her presence. She often cared for him during the day so that Ellen could rest or do chores. And sometimes he would venture over onto her lap during the Bible study.

As May turned to June and June to July, Ellen could no longer hide her pregnancy. Mr. Leaver was upset by the situation because he had strict rules, one of which stated no women knowingly pregnant before departure were aloud on the journey. "A wagon train is no place for a baby to be born," Mr. Leaver had disgustedly remarked.

Shay and Alana continued to form a deeper bond. They enjoyed any time they had alone together, which wasn't much. Alana loved the way he took extra moments during the day just to be near her. At night, while washing dishes, he would let his hand purposely linger near hers before finally taking the dish and drying it. They were careful about physical contact, so as not to disturb the wagon train of the belief that they were brother and sister. But Shay's eyes said a lot when he'd draw her gaze to meet his.

○ ○ ○

One evening as Mr. Leaver was making his nightly rounds, he came upon the Hubbards' wagon. He never should have allowed them to come. Joe Hubbard was an irresponsible man who had only one thing on his mind ... himself. And with a wife who was about ready to burst...well it was not a comfortable situation for Mr. Leaver. Not comfortable in the least.

Mr. Leaver knew of Joe's violent behavior. Shay had spoken with him about it as had several other spectators. But if he ordered them to leave the train now, what would become of the woman and child? Mr. Leaver was said to be a cold man, but he wasn't heartless.

There was a lantern glowing from within the wagon, and Mr. Leaver debated passing the wagon by. He had on other nights, but tonight he thought better of it. "Hello … anyone there? It's Mr. Leaver. I'm just making sure everyone is accounted for."

He heard the whimper of a small child coming from within. "Hello?" Mr. Leaver said again. Still nothing. Mr. Leaver slightly moved the canvas to peek inside. He noticed the boy at the foot of the bed. But where were his parents?

"Where is your mama?" Mr. Leaver questioned the boy. The little boy avoided him, offering no information. It was then that he heard the moan. Then he saw the heap bundled up under the covers. "Mrs. Hubbard? Are you all right, Mrs. Hubbard?"

He moved into the wagon and over to the bed. Slowly he removed the blanket. Bruises and swelling had already formed on her body. He knew what had happened. "Where's Joe? I'm going to kill that worthless scoundrel."

Mr. Leaver left the wagon and began his search for Joe. Joe was nowhere to be found. Word spread that Mr. Leaver was on some sort of man hunt, and he soon had spectators following him.

Mr. Leaver made his way down to the river. Joe was sitting under a tree, drinking the last of the whiskey he had managed to smuggle into his wagon.

"Get out!" Mr. Leaver blared. "I am hereby ordering you to get your filthy, no good carcass away from my wagon train."

Joe stared at him in disbelief. "You can't abandon me and my family here in the wilderness."

"The only one I intend to abandon is you. Your wife and child are free to stay." Joe stood to his feet intending to fight, but there were now seven gentlemen standing directly behind Mr. Leaver. Joe knew he didn't stand a chance. He had no choice but to leave.

Mr. Leaver, along with the other men, escorted Joe to his wagon. Joe made several threats along the way. It didn't take Joe long to pack his belongings. He saddled his horse and tied his pack to the saddle horn. "You can have them," meaning his wife and child in the wagon. "They've only always been a burden." Joe quickly rode out of sight.

o o o

Alana was undressing for bed when she heard a loud voice outside the wagon. "Shay, is Alana around? I just came from the Hubbards' wagon, and Ellen is asking for her."

Alana redressed and swiftly left the wagon. Mr. Leaver turned to her and motioned for her to follow him. Alana passed him and ran all the way to the Hubbards' wagon. From a distance, she could hear moans coming from within the wagon.

Ellen was in great pain. It was etched all over her face. Jesse was at the end of the bed huddled in the corner. Alana reached for him and carried him to the entrance of the wagon. She handed him down to Mr. Leaver. "Take him to Maggie Stewart's wagon," Alana stated.

Jesse tensed and reached his arms out for Alana. She cringed at the fear she saw in his eyes. "Jesse, I'll come for you soon. I promise." She turned away, no longer able to bear the fearsome look in his eyes.

Alana hurried back to Ellen's side. Ellen's hair was damp from the sweat off her forehead. It was then that Alana noticed the bruises on Ellen's face. Alana's heart ached. She knew where the bruises had come from. Why? Why would a man treat someone with such cruelty?

"Ellen, what can I do?" Alana reached for her hand and held it, stroking it gently with her own. A sharp pain seared through Ellen's body. Ellen bit down on her lip to bear the pain, and her lip began to bleed. The pain soon subsided. Alana used her dress to wipe the blood from Ellen's mouth.

"Please ... I have one request." Ellen's voice was labored. "Take Jesse. He ... he loves you. He's never taken—" Another pain gripped her body, and they both waited for it to pass.

"He's never taken to anyone else before you." Ellen lay back against the pillow, exhaustion overtaking her small frame.

"Don't talk like that. Ellen, don't give up. You have so much to live for. Jesse needs you. He needs his mama!"

"Alana ... I ... need to know ... "

"I'll take him ... you know I will." A relieved smile formed on Ellen's face. They waited as the next pain subsided. Ellen reached for Alana's hand again. "I want ... Jesus in my heart. Pray with ... me."

Pray? Alana looked toward the entrance of the wagon. She needed Shay. Who was she to pray with this woman in pain? But the pleading in Ellen's eyes stole any misgivings Alana had.

"Lord ... Ellen wants to know you. She ... we believe

you died for us. And we want you to be the Lord of our lives … amen."

"Amen," Ellen whispered.

Shay entered the wagon as another pain ripped through Ellen's body. He rushed to the bed. Alana moved away to make room for Shay. Shay moved to the end of the bed, quickly lifting the covers.

"Ellen … the baby's head has crowned. On the next contraction, I need you to push. Can you do that for me?" Shay's eyes met Alana's in silent concern.

"Push! Push, Ellen!" Shay wiped the sweat from his own brow. "Push … one more time."

Alana did not like the look in Shay's eyes. She watched as he tried to resuscitate the small infant, but he could not find a heart beat. Shay rushed to Ellen's side, but both could see she was no longer breathing. Shay picked up the baby girl and laid her next to her mother. Then he reached for Alana. He pulled her against him and caressed her shoulders. Sobs shook her entire body. He had never seen her look so mournful, not even after the death of her own mother.

° ° °

Mr. Leaver was standing outside the wagon when Shay and Alana emerged. He knew without asking that Ellen was dead. "The baby?" he inquired. Shay shook his head. "I was doing my nightly rounds when I found Mrs. Hubbard in the wagon … "

Shay again shook his head. Mr. Leaver stopped short. Shay didn't know if Alana could handle anymore devastating news.

"I'm going to check on Jesse," Alana said as she walked away.

Shay turned back to Mr. Leaver. "One of Joe's blows must have severed the umbilical cord. The baby has been dead for several hours."

Mr. Leaver's face blanched. He wished at that moment he had shot Joe Hubbard. "I ordered Joe to leave the wagon train. He's gone now…but I guess the damage is already done."

"I need to make sure Alana is all right." Shay began to walk away.

"I'll take care of the bodies, Shay. We'll have a burial tomorrow morning, before the wagon train leaves."

"Thank you, Mr. Leaver. That will mean a lot to Alana." Shay moved to follow Alana. These things were not suppose to happen. Not to innocent women like Ellen. How would Alana deal with this tragedy?

Shay watched from a distance as Alana spoke with Maggie. There were fresh tears on Maggie's face as well. Jesse was sitting by the fire, playing in the dirt. He looked up and saw Alana. Scrambling to his feet, he ran to her with his arms open wide. Alana knelt and folded him into her arms.

Without words being spoken, Jesse seemed to understand that his mother was gone. Tears coursed down his small cheeks. Alana brushed them away with the hem of her dress. The same dress that had just moments before wiped away the blood of his mother.

Shay could see the determination in Alana's eyes. He had heard Ellen's request that evening, and he knew that Alana would honor it. She would raise Jesse as her own.

CHAPTER SEVEN

April 23, 1846

Alana is four years old, and the most beautiful four-year-old girl that has ever lived in Independence, Missouri, I am certain. I fear I am making the same mistake my parents made with me, suffocating her very existence. I'm afraid that someone will question her ethnicity, so I try to keep her indoors as much as possible during the day. In the evenings, we take walks along the river, and I share with her the names of all the birds or flowers we meet along the way. Today she asked me how I know so much about everything. My knowledge is due to Mr. Martin, my instructor who diligently taught me. For the first time, I am glad I know these things, for Alana's sake.

Clyde becomes worse by the day, and I am worried about his treatment of Alana. I try to keep Alana preoccupied in her room as much as possible when Clyde is home. Thankfully his work keeps him away for several days at a time. It is during these moments Alana and I are able to finally relax and enjoy our days together.

Alana looks like her father, though a lighter version. The shape of her eyes reminds me of my mother, but the color is identical to Jesse's. She also shares Jesse's high cheek bones. And her hair, almost black, is a beautiful sight to behold. Thankfully, Clyde also has dark hair, and his hazel eyes allow the townspeople to believe this child is his. Though I will always be grateful she is not.

○ ○ ○

"Is mama coming back today?" the small voice asked. It was the same question Jesse asked her every morning since his mother had died nearly two weeks ago.

Alana pulled him onto her lap. "No Jesse, your mama is in heaven … with Jesus."

"I miss her," he voiced.

"I miss her too."

Alana was slowly becoming accustomed to having a child underfoot. Jesse clung to her and refused to let her leave his sight. Her tasks now took much longer to complete. Her time was no longer her own, but she was willing to share it. Jesse needed her.

At three years old, he was no longer a baby and was awkward to hold for long periods of time, yet Alana could not bring herself to put him down. She shifted Jesse to the other hip.

"Here, let me take him," Shay offered. Alana was trying to cook breakfast and hold Jesse at the same time. She began to relinquish the boy, but Jesse screamed out. Alana quickly pulled him back against her.

"He won't get used to other people if you pamper him like you do," Shay stated, somewhat annoyed.

Alana turned back to the task at hand. "He just lost his mother. Surely a bit of pampering is in order."

Shay walked away, turning his focus to something less irritating. His efforts toward the boy were futile. If Shay tried to talk to Jesse, Jesse turned away from him. And any time he held the boy, which wasn't often, Jesse cried at the top of his lungs.

Shay hated to admit it, but he was somewhat resentful. Alana had her hands full, and they now had very little time together. Even a smile across the burning fire over supper was an incredible effort. How could a small child change their lives that drastically?

Shay led the oxen down to the river. "Good morning, Paul."

They had debated leaving the Hubbards' wagon alongside the trail, but in the end, Martha and Ben Henson's sixteen-year-old son, Paul, had offered to drive the wagon and he was doing a fine job of it.

"Good morning, Shay. Are you ready to pull out this morning?" the young lad questioned.

"As ready as can be, I suppose."

○ ○ ○

"Lana, I'm hungry," Jesse announced.

"We'll be stopping real soon, Jesse. Look, there's Maggie. Maybe Maggie will tell you another one of those stories from the Bible."

Jesse smiled, but gripped her hand even harder as Maggie came upon them.

"Hi, Alana … Jesse." Maggie reached down and caressed his soft cheek.

"Jesse was just saying how he would love to hear another one of your exciting stories," Alana voiced for Jesse.

"Did you like that story of David and Goliath?" Maggie stooped down to his level.

Jesse nodded his head.

"Have you ever heard the story of Daniel in the Lions' Den?"

Jesse buried his head into Alana's skirt, but Maggie could still see him as he shook his head back and forth. Maggie and Alana laughed.

Alana sighed with relief. Jesse was finally sleeping. She bent and kissed his forehead before walking to the entrance of the wagon. If she had any sense at all, she would go to bed herself. Taking care of a child was very tiring—pleasurable, but definitely exhausting. She glanced outside the wagon and could see Shay sitting by the fire. She climbed down and made her way toward him.

"Jesse's sleeping?" he asked as he watched her come near.

"He is … for the moment, anyway."

He motioned for her to sit next to him. "Are you enjoying being a mother?" He reached for her hand.

"Yes … he is not a difficult child and so easy to love." Shay looked away. She knew it was not as easy for him.

"I can see there is a barrier between you and him," she acknowledged.

"I can't seem to reach him. He wants nothing to do with me." Shay met her eyes then. "What if he never likes me?"

"He's afraid of men. But he will eventually see what a kind-hearted person you are. He will learn to love you."

Shay tipped her chin. "Like you learned to love me?" he voiced huskily.

"Well, perhaps a somewhat different kind of love … but, yes, as I learned to love you."

"Different as in how?" he teased. He moved his mouth toward hers.

Alana dropped her eyes. Was he going to kiss her? Here? What if someone … His mouth pressed against hers and all questions subsided. The kiss deepened, and her hand moved to the back of his head. His hair felt good between her fingers. He pulled her nearer.

"Mama!" the voice cut into the still night air. Alana pulled back. Shay groaned.

"I'm sorry," she apologized as she moved toward the wagon.

○ ○ ○

Another week passed, and if anything, the barrier between Shay and Jesse only deepened. Alana found herself defending Jesse's actions toward Shay. But in doing so, Shay became more distant. The time Shay spent with her and with Jesse was slowly lessening.

Mr. Leaver stopped by that evening. "Shay ... Alana." He tipped his hat to them both before he took an offered seat. "Some folks have brought up some issues with the young Hubbard boy, and I must admit they do seem like valid ones. I've called a meeting. Will the next hour be all right?"

"What do you mean?" Alana questioned. "What kind of issues?" she demanded.

Mr. Leaver stood to his feet. "Why don't we just wait until the meeting to bring all this out into the open?" Shay nodded and said they would be there. Alana watched as Mr. Leaver walked away.

"What do they want? Jesse has done nothing wrong." Alana studied Shay, knowing he must know something. He knew everybody in the wagon train.

"Alana ... you're jumping to conclusions. They don't have anything against the child." Shay reached for her hand, but she turned away.

He doesn't understand. Jesse was hers now. What con-
cerned Jesse concerned her.

An hour later, Alana, Shay, and Jesse made their way toward the inner circle in silence. All eyes focused on them as they took their seats.

"Martha and Ben have brought up several issues concerning the boy," Mr. Leaver began. "Martha, why don't you share with the O'Connells what you shared with me earlier?"

Martha stood to her feet. "Well, my husband Ben and I have raised four boys. And we know the importance of raising a child right. A child needs a mother and a father to look after him, to provide a good home with love and discipline."

Martha turned to Alana. "You're a young girl. And you're not even married. Taking on the responsibility of a little boy is simply too much for an unmarried girl your age."

Ben, Martha's husband, stood up next. "Alana, what my wife is trying to say is that we would be more than happy to take over the responsibility of young Jesse. We have plenty to offer him, and he would have older brothers. He needs a family." Both Martha and Ben sat down. There were many assents that went around the circle. Alana waited for Shay to say something ... anything in her defense, but he didn't. He sat there as if he agreed with every word that had just been spoken.

"Shay?" Mr. Leaver questioned. "As Alana's brother, don't you think it would be a wise decision for Alana to allow the Hensons this opportunity?"

Shay couldn't bring himself to look at Alana. "Well ... I ... " Shay had never been one to stutter with words, but he was caught between a rock and a hard place. He had no special bonding with the child. It would be easy to let the boy go with the Hensons. After all, Jesse was the reason that Shay and Alana were now struggling in their own relationship.

Yet if Shay sided with the Hensons, Alana might give up on him altogether. And this led to an entirely different predicament. The entire wagon train believed Alana to be his sister. He couldn't just shout out that he intended to marry her, thus giving Jesse a father … a family. What a mess.

He didn't have to think any further, because Alana stood to her feet. Never had he seen her so angry, so defensive. "I know I am young, but I promised his mother on her death bed that I would raise Jesse and always be there for him. I fully intend to keep that promise."

Alana turned toward Martha and Ben. "You have a wonderful family. You are a good mother, Martha. And you are a good father, Ben. But I know in my heart that Jesse is to stay with me. I may not be able to offer him all that you have offered your sons, but I will offer him my best."

Finally Alana turned to Shay. She was angry with him; there was no doubt about that. "I am keeping this boy, and I defy anyone who would try to take him away from me. If it means marrying the first man who will have me, why, I'll do it."

Allan appeared out of no where. "Why, I'd be obliged to marry ya', Miss O'Connell."

Shay jumped to his feet. "This is absurd," he cried out. "Alana is keeping the child. But she'll marry no one … at least not right now." Alana could hear Maggie's laughter coming from the back.

"We appreciate everyone's concern, but the boy is staying with us. Alana does a right good job with him, and he'll never lack as far as love goes."

Mr. Leaver nodded. "Besides all that, I don't believe he would let go of her skirt long enough to let anyone else claim him, anyway." Everyone glanced at the boy and laughter echoed through the camp as they noticed Jesse's head buried in Alana's skirt.

"What were you thinking?" Shay hissed as soon as they were out of earshot. "You can't just up and marry the first man who proposes to you."

"If it means keeping Jesse, I'd do it. At least Allan had the unction to propose," she finished.

Shay grabbed Alana's hand and pulled her around to face him. Is that what she was waiting for—for him to propose? "You're not marrying Allan," Shay told her. "I have someone else in mind."

"And just who might that be?" Alana voiced mischievously. Shay didn't answer. He turned Alana around once again, walking her back to their wagon. He then dropped her hand and stooped to grab the water buckets from beneath the wagon. He winked at Alana as he passed by, glad that he had gotten to it before Allan had the chance. He could hear Alana's laughter following him all the way down to the river.

ooo

Nothing more was said of the situation with Jesse. It seemed that everyone realized how useless any effort toward taking the boy away would be. Jesse was now less clingy and more inclined to play with the other children.

They had long since passed through the Indian

Territory, so when one of the children ran to his father screaming, "Indians are coming … Indians are coming!" Mr. Leaver was caught off guard. They quickly made camp waiting for the arrival of the five Indians on horseback. They carried their weapons above their heads, signaling they came in peace.

One of the Indians was leading a beautiful palomino horse. Shay recognized him as one of the men traveling with the father of the hurt child. The group of Indians stopped, and the Indian searched the crowd, finally resting his eyes on Shay. He moved toward him, still leading the horse. He dismounted and led the palomino over to Shay, offering him the lead rope.

"Gift for healer. Son live."

Whispering spread through the camp. These Indians had ridden days to deliver this gift to Shay. Shay hesitantly reached out his hand for the lead rope. The Indian again mounted his horse, and they rode back in the direction they had just come.

The horse was beautiful and well trained. Shay had many visitors come by the wagon to look at the horse, even Allan, who seemed to admire the horse almost as much as he admired Alana.

"She's almost sixteen hands tall," Allan voiced after measuring the horse. "She's a beauty. Will ya' consider trading me straight across for Jasper?" Allan joked.

"No … I don't think I could do that," Shay stated with a smile.

Allan turned away from the horse and met Shay's gaze, a more serious look displayed on his face. "I'm worried about Alana. Taking care of a child alone is too much for her, don't ya' think?"

"It is hard work for sure," Shay responded. "But she'll adjust in time."

"But she has no time for anything else," Allan responded. Shay only nodded, not sure what to say.

"I have a question, Shay. You're her brother, and ya' know her better than any of us. Could she ever be interested in a fella like me?"

Shay turned back toward the horse. He had known this conversation would arise someday. Allan had been interested in Alana for weeks now, and he wouldn't wait around forever. "Alana's shy..." *and not interested...* why couldn't he just tell the man? Shay stroked his chin in thought. "She... needs time... to... admit her feelings."

Allan smiled. "Well, if it's only time that lies between us, I've got all the time in the world." Allan walked away whistling some happy tune.

○ ○ ○

Jesse was fascinated with the palomino horse. One evening as Alana was busy making supper, Jesse began inching his way closer to the horse that was hobbled nearby. Shay walked toward Jesse. Jesse startled and ran back behind the wagon.

Shay picked up the horse brush and made his way toward the horse. He slowly began to brush her. Eventually Jesse moved toward the horse again.

"Do you like horses?" Shay spoke. Jesse nodded. "This horse needs a name, but I'm just not sure what to name her. What do you think, Jesse? What should we name this horse?"

He felt Jesse's head beneath his elbow. Timidly, Jesse reached out his hand and touched the horse. Light filled his eyes. "Heaven," he whispered. "Name the horse Heaven."

Tears stung Shay's eyes. They had talked about heaven last night during their Bible study. Alana had told Jesse that his mama was in heaven. Jesse seemed to understand a lot more than they gave him credit for.

"Heaven it is. How would you like to sit on Heaven, Jesse?" Jesse reached his arms out toward Shay. Shay picked the small boy up and sat him atop the horse. Jesse giggled with glee. Shay stood next to horse watching for any signs that the horse might spook, but Heaven didn't seem to mind a bit that Jesse was sitting on her back.

"I love Heaven," Jesse stated, still smiling.

"Well, I'll tell you what. If you'll help me take care of her ... give her water ... feed her hay, then I'll let you ride Heaven. What do you think of that?"

"I like that," Jesse replied. "I like it a lot."

○ ○ ○

Alana smiled as she studied the lights visible from the town nearby. They had been in the wilderness for too long, and she was grateful to see small civilizations popping up along the trail. Several men had gone into town to buy supplies they had previously run out of. The women were grateful they would once again have sugar and other necessary ingredients for cooking.

"It's hard to believe we are almost to the end of our destination," Maggie declared. "I'm going to miss you."

Alana hugged Maggie briefly before turning and taking Jesse's hand. They began walking back toward the wagons. "I did not expect the men to be gone this long," Alana stated.

"Me either. Though, if the women had been allowed to go to town, I am sure we would not have come back at all." They both laughed.

"Look, there's Shay," Jesse voiced with excitement. Shay had promised him some licorice, and Jesse had been searching for Shay's return since the moment he had left.

Behind Shay were six other men. Alana was curious to why there were only seven returning when eight men had gone to town, but she brushed the thought aside. Shay quickly dismounted and handed Jesse a small sack. Jesse peered inside, his smile widening by the second.

"Thank you," Alana mouthed. Shay smiled. The other men's wives made there way toward their husbands. Everyone was relieved they were near the end of their journey.

Conversation was abundant, as the women were interested in Redding, the nearby town. Alana noticed Jane making her way toward the group, looking for her husband. A look of desperation penetrated through her soft eyes. "Where is Jay?" Alana quietly asked Shay.

Shay's smile suddenly turned into a frown. "He ... stayed in town."

"Why?" Alana persisted. Shay did not answer. "His wife is looking for him," Alana acknowledged. She watched as Shay finally noticed Jane. He let out a deep sigh and made his way toward her.

Jane closed her eyes as Shay spoke quietly to her. A tear slipped down her cheek unchecked, and she quickly turned and made her way back toward the wagons.

"Jane," Maggie called, but Jane ignored her and hurried from sight. "What is wrong with Jane?"

Shay refused to answer, but the other men were

more than willing to share Jane's dilemma. "Jay went to the saloon. He wanted to play a few rounds of cards before calling it a night."

The other women present instantly jumped at the topic at hand and began talking about the couple.

Maggie turned toward them, her anger easily recognized. "Instead of gossiping about those less fortunate than ourselves, why don't we instead be thankful our husbands chose not to stay in town." She walked away. Alana followed close behind her.

"May Alana and I come in?" Maggie questioned outside Jane's wagon. The canvas parted and Alana and Maggie climbed inside. Jane's tears had subsided, but the evidence that she had been crying remained. "What can we do to help?" Maggie asked.

"Nothing can be done. He took the money we had saved to put down on our parcel of land. He is now in town gambling it away." Jane swiped at a strand of hair in her face.

"Perhaps he won't play too long. Maybe he'll return soon," Maggie stated hopefully.

"No ... once he starts to play, he can't stop."

"Shay could go back to town and force him to come back," Alana offered.

Jane shook her head. "No ... he won't listen. He won't." She moved to the other side of the wagon and reaching far back into a small storage area she pulled out a small canister. "I hid this from him. It is money I saved last year." She held it out toward Alana. "Please ... take it and put it in your wagon."

Alana's eyes widened. "Are you sure?" She hesitantly reached out her hand for the canister.

"Yes, I am sure. He'll be back when he runs out of

money, and he'll search the wagon for more. If it is here, he'll find it. At the end of our journey you can give it back, and, hopefully, I can put it down on our land that same day." Another tear appeared on Jane's cheek. "It will only pay for half of the payment, but perhaps they will be lenient with us."

Maggie and Alana hugged Jane and left the wagon. Maggie walked with Alana back to her own wagon where they then said their goodbyes. Alana moved inside the wagon and sat on her small bed. She stared at the small canister in her hands.

A thought occurred to her, and she opened the canister, pouring the money out on the bed. She quickly began to count it: forty-four dollars and twenty cents. She reached under her bed and pulled out the envelope. She smiled. Mr. Raymond had given her forty-five dollars. She quickly stuffed the money in Jane's canister before scooping up Jane's saved money and returning it to the canister as well. Alana put the money under the bed, just as she heard Shay and Jesse's voices coming near the wagon.

o o o

"We'll be in Dalles, Oregon, in three to four days. We'll stay for one day in order to restock our supplies." Alana could hardly believe they were nearly to their destination. Shay had sent a telegram to her uncle notifying him of her arrival that fall. But had he received it? Did he want to see her?

And what about Shay? She knew he had a brother in Sheridan. How much farther would he be traveling? She shuddered as she thought of how far it could be from Dalles.

"How far is Sheridan from Dalles?" Alana voiced aloud.

"Another two weeks by wagon. A little faster if you're traveling by horse." Shay suddenly understood her worry. "I won't leave you in Dalles by yourself, Alana. I'll wait until you can come with me. We have an entire day to find your uncle. If we can't find him, then we'll continue on to Sheridan."

Alana had mixed feelings. She desperately wanted to find her uncle. Yet at the same time she didn't want anything to come between the plans Shay had already made for himself.

Later, as Maggie and Alana were walking together behind the wagons, Alana realized this could be their last walk together, for if Alana found her uncle, she would no longer be traveling with the wagon train. Alana looked ahead to where Jesse was riding in the wagon with Shay. Their relationship had indeed blossomed since the incident with the horses.

"God has done amazing things in your life, hasn't he?" Maggie voiced as if reading her thoughts. Alana nodded. She had no words to adequately express her feelings.

"I feel so selfish, Alana. I really hope that you won't find your uncle. I don't want you to stay behind. I'll be so lonely if you stay." A tear glistened on Maggie's cheek.

Alana grabbed her hand. "I'll see you again, Maggie, you can be sure of that."

"How will Shay manage without you, if you decide to stay?" Maggie inquired.

"He plans to stay in Dalles with me if I find my uncle."

"But … I thought … he—" Maggie stopped suddenly.

"Maggie, tell me what you know," Alana insisted.

"I overheard Shay tell Tom some time back that he needed to claim the land his brother was holding for him by the end of the month or he would lose it. If he's not there to sign the deed, he'll lose it for sure. Tom and I are in the same predicament."

"So if Shay stays, he'll lose his land?" Alana said with surprise. Maggie nodded her head. Why had Shay told her he would stay if he knew … and then it hit her: He didn't want her to base her decision on him. He wouldn't come between her longing to find her uncle.

∘ ∘ ∘

Alana awoke early to fix breakfast, thankful that Jesse still slept. She turned when she heard the loud voices.

"Mr. Bratten, I am sorry, but we do not have a Miss Peterson on board. I would know. After six months of travel, I know each and every one of these passengers, and not a one of them is a Miss Peterson."

The other man's voice was just as persistent. "The telegram said she was traveling with this wagon train. I'll just take a quick look around."

"I will not have you upsetting the passengers by looking through their wagons. Perhaps your niece decided to come on the next wagon train."

Alana made her way toward the men. She studied the man next to Mr. Leaver. He had light brown hair. There was no mistaking the resemblance to her mother. She knew at once that he was her mother's brother.

"Uncle James?" Alana whispered.

He turned when he heard his name. "Alana? Is that you?" The man studied her for a moment before he ran toward her and picked her up off her feet. Alana gasped at his fierce embrace. He swung her around in a circle.

"Well, somebody had better start explainin' what in holy tarnation is goin' on here," Mr. Leaver blared. Silence followed Mr. Leaver's outburst. Alana looked at her uncle, her face crimson red.

"Her name is Alana Peterson, though I certainly wouldn't mind if it were Alana O'Connell, under totally different circumstances." Alana shot a quick look in Shay's direction. He actually had a smile on his face. How could he even think about laughing at a time like this? They were under the scrutiny of the entire wagon train. He turned his smile her direction, but she quickly looked away.

Mr. Leaver moved toward Shay. "I'm disappointed in you, Shay. I was going to talk to you about joining the wagon train business as you have a good head on your shoulders and have been invaluable to me on this adventure west. But now ... now I'm not so sure."

"Lying is not something I have a habit of doing, but if you had known the truth of our relationship, she would have been left back in Independence, and she desperately needed to leave. If it is any consolation, I do plan on marrying her in the very near future."

Mr. Leaver's stern face soon turned to a smile and then he began to chuckle. "I suppose you had your reasons," he stated as he strode off.

"You look like your mama," James pronounced as he studied his niece. "I still miss that woman. But we'll talk more of her later. Mary is expecting you. We have a room made up for you, and I do not plan to let you out of my sight until I've had the opportunity to find out all about you." He patted her hand.

Alana was cautious about bringing up Jesse. He soon awoke, and she had no choice but to share his story. As James listened about his mother's death ... his father abandoning him ... tears of sadness filled his eyes. "Mary will be thrilled. She loves children."

∘∘∘

Later, while James was in town buying last minute supplies and allowing her a chance to gather her belongings, Alana set out to find Shay. She saw him down by the river watering his horses. They stood for a moment in awkward silence.

"Shay, I need to stay. I cannot pass up this opportunity. He is a part of my mother I never knew. I didn't even know he existed until after my mother died. I read about him in her journal. James knows all about my father. I can learn a lot about myself from him."

"You don't need to talk me into it. We'll stay. You deserve this opportunity. I won't take it away from you."

"I'll stay." She covered his mouth with her hand when he began to disagree. "I know about the land—that if you don't go, you'll lose it. I won't be the reason you lose your land. I won't. You can't give up an opportunity like the one that is in your grasp right now. Please go. Go without me."

Shay pulled her near him and waited for her to look up. "What are you saying? I love you, Alana. Land does not mean more to me than you. I would rather stay here with you than be there without you."

Alana rose up on her tip-toes and kissed him square on the mouth. "I'll be waiting right here. When you are settled in Sheridan and have a place for Jesse and me, then we'll be ready."

Shay sighed with relief. She still loved him. She still wanted him. She was only allowing him the freedom to fulfill his own dream. "I'll be back," he whispered against her hair.

"Then I'll be waiting." Alana moved into his arms, realizing this would be the last time he would hold her for a long time.

"Oh, I have one small favor to ask." Alana voiced against his chest.

Shay smiled. "All right … "

"I have some money hidden under the bed in our wagon. It is Jane's. Please give it to her when they depart the wagon train in Oregon City." Shay raised his eyebrows, but did not ask any questions.

James soon returned and began loading the belongings of Alana and Jesse. "Mr. Bratten, may I ask a favor of you?" Shay voiced from behind.

"Of course, and please, call me James. It sounds like we may be family one day soon." He patted the young man on the back.

"Jesse is taking it a bit hard being that we are to be separated for awhile. I was wondering if I might leave my horse Heaven with him, as a pledge to him that I'll be returning."

"We'll take good care of your horse, Shay." Shay left to prepare Heaven for Jesse.

Saying goodbye to everyone was difficult. Maggie sobbed on Alana's shoulder. It helped to know their separation was only temporary. "I'll pray for a healthy baby and a safe delivery," Alana stated between Maggie's hiccups. Maggie sobbed all the harder. Tom led her away to console her.

Alana turned to Shay. She already missed him. He reached for her and pulled her against him one last time. Gently he brushed his lips against her cheek and then withdrew. He then knelt down to say goodbye to Jesse. Jesse, still overcome with the news of their separation, took a step back. Shay stood up. He wouldn't pressure him.

Alana grabbed Jesse's hand, and they began to make their way toward Uncle James' awaiting wagon. It was then that Jesse noticed Heaven tied to the back of the wagon. Abruptly, Jesse turned and ran back to Shay. Shay scooped him up and held him tight. "You'll be back?" Jesse voiced with uncertainty.

"I'll be back. I promise," Shay assured. Jesse smiled and then struggled to be put down. He ran back to Alana with a smile on his face.

CHAPTER EIGHT

Atlanta, Georgia: October 23, 1858

The man continued to glare at the death certificate. Charise. Charise Catherine Bratten Peterson. His sister. A knock sounded at the door. It creaked open slowly, and one of his attendants slipped his head inside.

"Mr. Bratten, do you have a moment?"

Johnny waved his hand in frustration. The door quickly slammed shut. The young attendant knew better than to provoke Mr. Johnny Bratten, the president of the Bratten Bank, especially when he was in one of his moods.

Johnny turned his attention back to the death certificate. It did not arouse good feelings within him. How he hated her. Even in her death, he hated her with a vengeance. She had destroyed their family. First by marrying that good-for-nothing slave, and then as if that hadn't been sufficient enough, she had run off again in order to have his child.

When Charise had left the second time, Catherine, their mother, had lost her mind. For two years she lived in oblivion, not knowing who she was, no longer recognizing the identity of her own husband...her own son. Eventually, she had died of starvation, not only from lack of food, but from mental and emotional loss as well.

John Sr., his father, had slowly lost interest in everything, even his bank which had been in the Bratten family for years. If it hadn't been for Johnny, the bank would have gone to pieces altogether. Fortunately the loss of a daughter and the death of their mother had actually increased the patronage of the people. They had felt sorry for the Bratten family and had sympathized with them during their despair.

For years Johnny had envisioned getting rid of his sister. He wanted to make her pay. Regrettably, his father still had love in his heart for his only daughter, even after all the pain she had caused him. He had secretly sent men to seek her whereabouts. He only wanted to know she was alive and taken care of. All of this had been done without Charise ever becoming aware. John Sr. had known that if his daughter knew she'd been found, she would only run again. For some odd reason it had brought comfort to Johnny's old man, knowing that his daughter was alive and well.

The only consolation Johnny had received was the knowledge that Charise had married a no-good-drunk, who couldn't even take care of himself, let alone a wife and her child. But his father had seen to his daughter's welfare. He had privately found a woman in Independence whom he had paid handsomely to provide employment for his daughter. For several years, Charise had worked for this woman, cleaning her house, mending her clothes, ignorant of the fact that her income came through her employer via her own father.

Johnny had waited. He had waited patiently. His father had not been expected to live long. How he had lasted fourteen more years after the death of his wife was a puzzle to the doctors and to his son. How ironic only three weeks after his father's death Johnny would receive word that his sister had also succumbed to an illness. It looked as if he would not get his vengeance after all.

It had been such a splendid plan. There had been a reward posted for that slave husband of his sister. Of course, he had died during his sister's first flight from home. But it was clearly stated that the same reward stood for any children that had been produced of the slave. It would have torn his dear sister apart, watching her beloved daughter be taken into slavery. But before he could act, Charise had died. Johnny slammed his fist down on the desk in frustration.

And then suddenly he realized, maybe he had missed his chance with Charise, but he could still get revenge. It was the only way to put an end to his wrath. He couldn't remember the girl's name. It started with an *A. Alice?* No … that wasn't it. His father would have known, of course, but he was useless to him now. Johnny quickly stood up and strode to the door.

"Mr. Cohn," he yelled. The young attendant quickly appeared. "Mr. Cohn, I am going to send you on an errand. You will be gone for several days."

"Where to, sir?"

"You'll be going to Independence—Independence, Missouri. I will have Marie get everything ready for you. You leave tomorrow. When you have obtained the information I desire, then and only then may to return. Do you understand, Mr. Cohn?'

"Yes, sir."

"Send Marie in here." Mr. Cohn hurried to do his bidding.

Johnny smiled to himself. Those who knew him

were well aware that he never stopped until he got what he wanted.

° ° °

Dalles, Oregon: January 23, 1859

Alana watched as Jesse rode Heaven in the round pen. He was proud of the fact that Uncle James had taught him to ride. In three months, he had already grown out of any babyish behavior. He even looked like a little boy instead of a toddler. Alana figured he had to be four by now, but not knowing when he had been born, she didn't have a specific date to go by.

"Mama," Jesse yelled. "Look at how fast I am going!" He had begun calling her mama over a month ago. How it had touched her heart the first time he had said it.

"Good job, Jesse. Be sure to hold on with both hands," she admonished.

"When will he be back?" Jesse questioned. Alana knew Jesse was speaking of Shay. Jesse missed him almost as much as she did. Shay had written twice, telling her about their land and then in the second letter, about their house. It gave her hope, the way he stated *our* in his letters. It meant that he still intended on coming to claim her and Jesse, though he made no mention of when he might return. She hoped it would be soon.

"When will he be back?" Jesse asked again, this time in a louder voice, thinking she hadn't heard him the first time.

"I don't know, Jesse. Probably when it begins to warm up. It would be difficult to travel in the snow."

"Well, when will it be warm again?" Alana smiled. He was such an inquisitive child. And not very patient, either.

"In a couple months."

"A couple months? How long is a couple months?"

Alana laughed. "Not that long," she finally said.

○ ○ ○

James Bratten watched his niece as she swung Jesse around in the yard. She was a good mother. And to a boy that wasn't even her own. It amazed him. He was so glad she had come. She was the only thing left of his dearly beloved sister. Alana had some of his sister's features, though she was darker in complexion. Charise had been so fair.

Charise. Poor Charise. James could not forgive himself for leaving her in Atlanta. Had he known her life would turn out the way it had, he never would have left her. He had every intention of sending for her after her eighteenth birthday, but that day had never come. His parents had written shortly after she turned seventeen, asking if she had come to him. James waited for months, hoping against all odds that she would find her way to him. The next letter from his parents came notifying him of his mother's death.

Sixteen years had passed. Sixteen years of not knowing where his sister was. Sixteen years of not knowing if she was dead or alive. And then, finally, the telegram had arrived announcing Alana's soon arrival. Alana had shared the news of his sister's recent death, and he had been saddened at the loss of his sister, but overjoyed that she had a daughter … a daughter that was coming west to meet him.

Alana soon joined him on the porch swing. Tired and out of breath, she offered him a smile before leaning her head back and breathing in the mountain air. After a few moments, she spoke. "Children have an amazing amount of energy, don't they?"

"That they do. That they do. Wish I had a portion of it."

"Did you get the mail?" she questioned, knowing he had gone to town that morning.

"I did. But there wasn't anything from Shay. I'm sure you'll hear from him soon, though." He hated to see her disappointment. Though he would be thrilled if she continued to stay with him, he hoped for her sake that Shay would come back soon. Alana was missing him quite a bit.

"I've enjoyed these last three months with you," James stated.

Alana smiled, instantly forgetting there had been no mail for her. "I have too. I wouldn't have missed it for anything."

They had learned a great deal from each other, making it easier to let go of the past and look to the future. But even amidst all the information, James still felt she was keeping something from him, though he couldn't pinpoint why he thought so.

He had told her of his family. How Johnny, his older brother had taken over the Bratten Bank. Everyone had thought James a fool for going west when he had everything in his grasp right there in Atlanta—wealth, recognition ... yet it had never been enough. He had impatiently waited for the day he could escape it all. The tension in his household had been nearly unbearable. All he had ever wanted was to be accepted ... loved ... not for being what his parents expected, but simply for being who he was.

How could Johnny and he turn out so differently

from one another? Johnny had seemed hardened to it, even at a very young age. His only ambition was to make it to the top, even if it required hurting the person who stood in his way. Then there was James. James with the big heart. He couldn't stand seeing anyone hurt. Jack had been quiet and reserved, keeping mainly to himself. Poor Jack had been taken from them all at too young an age.

And finally there had been Charise. She had broken the mold when she came into the Bratten family. Even as a baby, she had been so strong willed. Neither his father, John, nor his mother, Catherine, had known what to do with the child. They had been overly protective of their only daughter, which in return had only resulted in increased opposition from her, the exact reverse of what they desired.

James only remembered Charise as a child. She had been only eight when he had left for the west. They had exchanged letters often until she turned sixteen. He had never heard from her again. He had written his father several times inquiring from them if they had heard from Charise. His father had never replied.

From Alana he had learned that Charise had made it as far as Independence, Missouri. There she married a man named Clyde Peterson. Alana was born, and Clyde later abandoned them, leading James to believe that the marriage had not been a happy one.

Something other than Clyde had caused Charise to discontinue her trip west. She had never been one to give up easily. Alana was hiding something. James hoped she knew by now that he loved her dearly and would never cause her harm in any way.

Mary watched her husband James from the window as he conversed with his niece. He had become his old self again when Alana had arrived. God had answered her prayers. When she had met James over twenty-three years ago, he had been so full of life, full of dreams, and full of adventure.

They had been so young, he at age nineteen and she at age sixteen. She had fallen in love with him immediately, and they had married two years later. James had wanted to wait until he had enough income coming in from his farm to provide a good home for her and the family they talked about having. They had a happy marriage and three sons had been born.

Clay was twenty. He had married his childhood sweetheart at age eighteen, and they already had a son. Cole was nineteen. He was engaged to be married in June. And Cody was eighteen. He had moved into town to assist the town deputy.

Even as a small boy, Cody had dreamed of being a deputy someday. He had carried his little gun and holster everywhere he had went. Even to church. Everyone had thought he'd grow out of it, but he never did. Now he was training to be just that, for the current town deputy had high hopes of retiring by the end of the year.

○ ○ ○

One evening James was sitting by the fire, reading a book. Jesse had already been put to bed. Alana was sitting on the sofa, reading her Bible. She read the book often.

James put the book down. He could always read a

book. But Alana—she could be gone in a few weeks if Shay returned soon.

"Your mother, she was so full of life. Her energy exhausted our whole family. No one could keep up with her." He noticed the sadness in Alana's eyes. "That's not how you knew her, was it? Alana shook her head. "What made her stay in Independence, Alana?" James had to know.

Alana was hesitant. But if she couldn't tell her uncle who she really was, then who could she tell? He was family. He would love her no matter what she told him.

"She was with child. Clyde was not my real father. When she got to Independence, she was out of money and desperate. Clyde agreed to marry her. I guess by then, she had lost all hope."

"It wasn't a happy marriage, was it?"

Again, Alana shook her head. "Clyde was … he was … he drank a lot. He was not a nice man. We were relieved when he finally left."

"I'm sorry. Charise deserved so much more than that." He wouldn't press Alana for more. In fact, he didn't want to know. He'd rather remember his sister the way he knew her before.

Alana took a quick breath before venturing forth. "Uncle James … do you remember a man who worked for your father? His name was Jesse Blackwell."

Remembrance immediately mirrored James features. "Yes … of course I do. He was the son of our family gardener. I believe his father's name was Judas. Yes, Judas Blackwell. Father had a special liking for the man and even allowed his son Jesse to attend school during the winter when the work was slow. Why do you ask?" He found it odd that Charise would tell her daughter about Jesse Blackwell, yet hide her own family from her daughter.

Again Alana hesitated. "Jesse … Jesse was my father." She watched as James expression shifted from disbelief to shock and then to utter amazement.

"How? Why?" James stuttered.

"I'll be right back," Alana stated. She left the room and soon returned with her mother's journal. "Mother left this for me when she died. It told me everything. Here … take it. I want you to read it. She explains it better than I ever could."

Alana held out the journal and James reached out his hand to receive it.

"Alana … I … "

"It's all right. You don't have to say anything. We'll talk later." Alana quickly left the room.

∘ ∘ ∘

Shay grimaced as the hammer missed the nail and hit his thumb instead. A perfect indication that he needed to quit before something worse happened. He had only a small amount left to finish before the house would be complete. His house. And hopefully Alana's as well.

She had written him once since their separation. He had read the letter so often he now had the words memorized, but it didn't stop him from retrieving the letter from his shirt pocket and reading it again. He traced a word with his finger. Her hand had penned this letter. The same hand he longed to hold.

He was thankful for the one letter, but he wished there had been more. Part of him was afraid she had changed her mind. That she had found someone else.

Shay packed up his tools and carried them to the

finished barn. He then saddled his horse Star and made his way to his brother's house. He could see Cal's house off in the distance and was glad that he would live near his brother and his brother's wife Annie. Cal had done well for himself. He enjoyed farming. He also enjoyed being a father. And Annie was a nice girl. She was very exuberant and talkative, quite the opposite of his brother who was quiet and calm.

They had a small boy named Peter, named after Annie's father. Shay had arrived in Sheridan only days after their daughter, Candice, had been born. Shay looked forward to bringing Jesse here. He would enjoy playing with Peter. It would be good for him to be around other children. And he was glad that Alana would have Annie, though he was sure Annie would overwhelm her a bit at first. Alana had been handed a hard life and was still in the process of coming out of her shell.

"Uncle Shay!" Peter called out as he rode into the barn. "Mama said supper is almost ready," he stated as he put the last kitten into the box.

"Well, then I came just in time didn't I," Shay teased.

"Why do you have to leave? You just got here," Peter meandered over to help brush the horse down.

"I won't be gone long. And when I come back, you'll have a cousin your own age to play with. What do you think of that?" Shay laid the saddle over the barrel next to the horse stall and then led Star into the stall and swung the door shut.

"Is he nice?" Peter timidly asked.

"Jesse is a real nice boy. He's a mite shy, but if you give him time, you'll be the best of friends, I'm sure of that." Shay dumped the oats into the horse bin.

"Will you still play with me, Uncle Shay?"

Shay ruffled Peter's hair. "Of course. Why you'll be over at our house all the time. We'll play even more than we do now." That earned Shay a full-fledged smile. Peter grabbed Shay's hand as they made their way to the house.

o o o

Atlanta, Georgia:

Johnny sat at his desk, intently studying the information he had only just moments before received. His young assistant, Mr. Cohn, had returned two days ago. How it had taken Mr. Cohn so long to obtain this small amount of information was beyond Mr. Bratten. It irked him quite a bit. But he kept his cool, for he knew he would need Mr. Cohn again in the very near future, and he certainly did not want to train another assistant just when he had finally trained Mr. Cohn

Johnny glanced back down at the paper. *Alana Peterson left for the west over eight months ago. She left with a man named Shay O'Connell. Her destination was Dalles, Oregon. She was going to stay with her Uncle James...*

His brother James had always been too kind-hearted. And he had loved their dear sister. James had written many times requesting information about Charise's whereabouts. Johnny had disposed of the letters before his father ever saw them. The last thing Johnny needed was for James to get involved.

"Mr. Cohn," Johnny yelled. Mr. Cohn slowly pushed open the office door. "Come in, Mr. Cohn, and close the door." Mr. Cohn closed the door and walked over to the desk. Johnny studied the young lad. Alex Cohn was young. That's why Johnny had chosen him.

He was young and impressionable. Johnny knew he could groom the young man well. Alex would be his right-hand man in the years to come. "We will be leaving by the end of the week."

"But I just got back…"

"Mr. Cohn, do you value your job?" Mr. Cohn nervously nodded. "We are going west to find Alana Peterson. We will be gone for some time."

Mr. Cohn's face changed from surprise to excitement. He was a young man, only twenty-one, and every young man dreamed of seeing the west.

"Now get out," Johnny ordered. Mr. Cohn turned and walked back out the door.

Johnny walked over to his safe. He pulled out the warrant he had held there for over sixteen years. Johnny read the words at the bottom of the page: … *this also stands for any descendants of Jesse Blackwell.* Johnny smiled. Without this warrant, he wouldn't be able to lay a hand on the young Blackwell girl … but with it … he could do just about anything.

∘ ∘ ∘

Dalles, Oregon:

A soft knock sounded on Alana's bedroom door. She rose from the bed and answered it. Her uncle James walked into the room. It had been two days since she had told him the news about her father.

"Alana," he voiced as he took a seat by the window. "As I read the journal I remembered your mother's letters." He handed her a small box. "I kept most of them. I thought maybe you'd like to have them. And here is your mother's journal. I just now finished it. Thank you for letting me read it. I know it was very personal to you."

"Thank you for the letters, Uncle James." She took the lid off the box and gently took out one of the letters. Her mother had penned this letter many years ago. *James Bratten, Dalles, Oregon.* Are you sure you want me to take these? They were written to you."

"Yes, take them. I can no longer bear to read them. All of them beg me to return for her. Had I, she may have lived a much happier life."

"You are not to blame for her choices, Uncle James, surely you know that."

"Mary says the same thing, yet my mind tells me differently. But enough of that. I came to talk to you about your ... father." His face was pensive. He turned from her and looked out the window. "Alana ... it doesn't really matter to me who your father was. To say that I wasn't shaken by the news would be an outright lie, but it does not change how I feel about you in any way."

James turned back to her. "I am concerned. I'm concerned that if this information ever got into the wrong hands, it could be used against you significantly. As terrible as it sounds, the people who are prejudiced in our society greatly outweigh those who are not. What I have learned, I will take to my grave. I wish to never speak of it again. And I ask you ... beg you ... never to share this information with another person."

"But what about Shay? Surely I should tell him before we marry." She studied her uncle, fear evident in her eyes.

"You have not told him?" James sighed. "I wondered." He brushed a hand through his hair, obviously not optimistic by the news.

A tear slipped down Alana's cheek. "I've tried to tell him on several occasions but ... I'm afraid. I don't want to lose him."

James pulled her into a fatherly embrace. "It's not fair, is it? Life is simply not fair. None of this is your fault, yet you are left to deal with the consequences of it. I am offering you counsel as if you were my own daughter. Don't tell him. He hasn't questioned you. He loves you. And he is a good man. The less people know, the better."

Alana nodded her head against James' shoulder. Finally, James released her and walked to the door. He turned before walking out. "I love you, Alana. I love you very much."

CHAPTER NINE

May 1, 1850

Clyde has been gone for over three weeks. This is the longest he has ever been gone, and I am finally accepting the fact that he is never coming back. I have heard rumors that he headed west to California in order to mine the abundant gold promised to be found, and I desperately hope the rumor is true. The peace Alana and I have enjoyed these last few weeks have been a gift to us. To think we may enjoy this peace for the remainder of our lives is too good to be true.

The money is tight, but my employment with Mrs. Cleaver has picked up pace. Now that Alana attends school, I am able to work longer hours. Mrs. Cleaver pays me well to mend her clothes, iron her husband's suits, and do other odd jobs she creates for me during the week. I am thankful for the work.

I've tried to put aside money, wondering if I could ever save enough to go west to be with James. If something should ever happen to me, it would be a great relief to know Alana would still be taken care of. I will never share the secret of her ethnicity, not because I am embarrassed by it. I loved her father very much, and he was more of a man than the esteemed Jared Dobbs could ever hope to be. But I am concerned about what others would think. Her father was a slave, and the nimber of prejudiced people in our society completely outweigh those who are not.

There are too many secrets, and I wish I could tell her everything, but she is shy and tenderhearted. Would she have the strength to bear the truth? Someday I will share with her the details of my life, but not now—not yet.

◦ ◦ ◦

Alana walked with Mary into the post office. *Please let there be a letter. Please let there be a letter. Please …*

"Cody! I was hoping we'd see you while we were in town today," Mary exclaimed as she hugged her youngest son.

Cody tipped his hat to Alana. "Have you been up to Dalles Bluff yet?" he inquired.

Alana smiled. "No, not yet. My guide hasn't been available to take me," she offered with sarcasm.

Cody laughed. "Well, I heard that things may be a bit slower next week for that guide of yours. How about I take you one week from tomorrow? I have been promised the entire day off, if no one goes and gets himself shot, that is. How does that sound?"

"I would be appreciative if you would escort me up the mountain. Next Tuesday would be perfect." Cody tipped his hat again, hugged his mama, and headed out the door.

Mary walked to the counter and asked for the mail. She was handed a bundle. Mary could not ignore Alana's curious stare, so she sat her bags down from the general store and began to sort through the mail.

"Well, Alana, I bet this will brighten your day." Alana snatched the letter and held it to her heart. "Go ahead … go find yourself a quiet place to read that letter of yours." Alana did not have to be told twice. She hurried out the door. Mary smiled as she watched Alana leave.

People were milling about everywhere as Alana made her way down the boardwalk. *Where could she go that was quiet?* The cemetery across from the church was absent of people. It seemed an odd place to be at the moment, but she was too excited to care. She hurried that direction.

She stopped under the nearest tree and closed her eyes in anticipation. Did Shay still love her? Was he coming back for her? She tore the letter open and took out the stationary.

Dear Alana,

By the time you receive this letter I will have already departed Sheridan and will be well on my way to Dalles with the sole purpose of claiming my girl. I trust you still want to come with me to Sheridan. If you have changed your mind—well, it is too late now, for I have already left and there is no way to inform me.

Alana giggled, clutching the letter in her fist. Her heart was beating rapidly as she focused on the words once again.

I love you, Alana. I love you with all my heart. I want you for my wife, forever and always. I know the proper way to ask a girl for her hand in marriage is to drop to one knee, and I plan to do that very thing upon my arrival, but I just want you to be fully prepared.

I also want to be a father to Jesse. I'm sure I'll make my share of mistakes when it comes to fathering, but I'll do my best by him. And for that matter, I'm sure I'll make plenty of mistakes when it comes to being a husband, but I feel confident that with you beside me, it'll be the most pleasurable profession I have yet learned or will ever learn.

I ache to see you ... to hold you ...

Alana's face reddened as she read his next words. She ached to be touched. He told about their house. He told about the town. And he described in more detail his brother's family. When Alana finally looked up, she saw Mary sitting in the wagon outside the cemetery. Alana made her way toward the wagon.

"I suspect you heard good news, if your face is any indication of what the letter was about."

Alana laughed. "You were right, Aunt Mary. We should have purchased that beautiful white material at the general store today." Now it was Mary's turn to smile.

o o o

The snow was beautiful. It glittered as the sun reflected off it. Alana rode next to Cody as they made their way up the mountainside. Cody had proven to be a very good tour guide. Because of his position as the assistant deputy, he knew every inch of the terrain covering the Oregon territory.

"April and May are the best months to come up here. The flowers are beginning to bloom. The snow has melted, causing small streams to glide down the mountains. If you are still here, I'll bring you back in May."

Alana smiled. "I received word last week that Shay is coming. He should be here any day."

Cody led her away from the small incline as they continued up the mountain. "You are excited he is coming, then? You haven't changed your mind?" he questioned.

"I was afraid he had changed his mind. I hadn't expected to be separated for so long."

Cody nodded. "You've been here since October, so that would be ... five months. It has been awhile. It seems a might odd that he'd stay away so long, especially when he's got someone like you waiting on him. If I were him, I'd be afraid you'd run off with someone else."

Alana smiled. "He knows I would do no such thing."

"Well then he's got himself a fine gal, and you can tell him I said so."

They traveled further up the mountain in silence. Periodically, water would drip onto her face or clothing from the trees up above. It was finally warm enough for the ice and snow to begin melting. It was also slippery in areas, but the horse seemed to know which path was best.

"Why do you enjoy being a deputy so much?" Alana asked.

"Are you sure you want to ask that question? I'll let you off the hook now ... before you get bombarded with—"

"I'm sure," she interrupted with a laugh.

"I guess it must have been born into me. From the time I could talk, I'm told that all I spoke about was guns and capturing the bad guy. I would play for hours, even by myself, pretending that I was the deputy hunting down a thief or killer in the dead of the night." Cody enjoyed Alana's smile.

"Go ahead and laugh. I know it's an entertaining tale. I even laugh at it now. As I grew older and I was too embarrassed to pretend anymore, I started reading true reports about experiences deputies had while tracking down a criminal. And now … now I get to write my own."

"It would be nice to know exactly what you were meant to do with your life right from the beginning. I've often wished I had some sort of purpose," Alana voiced.

"And just what is your part in Jesse's life? I call that some kind of purpose." Cody chided. "We are almost to the top. Just around this bend, you are going to see the most spectacular view you have ever seen."

They rounded the ridge. Cody smiled at Alana's intake of breath.

"It's beautiful." She could see everything from where she was standing. The pine trees covered the hillside and valley below. And the snow sparkled like diamonds from the tips of the trees. Way beyond she could see the outline of the town. It looked like a beautiful painting, certainly one of the most beautiful images she had ever seen.

They stayed and ate the lunch Mary had prepared for them. "I never see you in church," Alana voiced.

Cody shrugged his shoulders. "I guess I don't see much use in it. Some people take religion a bit too serious, it seems to me."

"But you believe in God?" she questioned.

He smiled at her concern. "I think that everyone would agree there is a God. Looking at...this right here in front of us," he waved his hand, signaling the beauty of it all. "It would be a hard case to convince me otherwise." They ate the rest of their meal in silence, each enjoying the scenery and sounds around them.

Finally, Cody brushed some crumbs from his pant leg and stood to his feet. "We should probably get going. It'll be dark before too long." He helped Alana pack up the remaining food, and they began the long descent down the mountain.

○○○

A knock sounded at the door. Mary hurried to answer it. She opened the door to find a young man standing on her doorstep. "May I help you?" Mary questioned.

"Is this the Bratten home?" the man asked. Before Mary could answer, Jesse came running from the kitchen, and upon seeing the visitor, ran with a scream of delight into his awaiting arms.

"You came! You promised you would."

Mary knew at once that the young man was Shay O'Connell. Alana's Shay.

Shay held Jesse out at arm's length. He could hardly believe how the child had grown. He hugged the boy again. "How's my horse. Did you take good care of her?" Shay asked.

Jesse grinned from ear to ear. "I sure did. I fed her every day. Mama helped some, and Uncle James taught me how to ride her."

Shay recognized the boy's new term for Alana. *Mama.* It sounded good.

"Do you want to go see your horse?" Jesse asked excitedly.

"I sure do. But where's Alana…I mean, your mama?" He looked around the room expecting her to appear any moment. Mary recognized the longing in his eyes.

"Mama went riding up the mountainside with

Cody. Let's go look at the horse." Jesse didn't intend to wait a moment longer. He grabbed Shay by the hand, and they set out the door toward the barn.

Shay's thoughts were running full force. Who was Cody? Where was Alana?

Jesse stopped suddenly and pointed off into the distance. "There's mama!" he exclaimed. Shay's gaze followed the small boy's finger. As his eyes adjusted, he soon saw the two riders. She was on horseback, and there was a young man beside her. Shay felt an instant pang of jealousy, but just as quickly, he put it aside. He stood next to Jesse, anxiously awaiting her arrival.

o o o

Alana stopped suddenly in mid-sentence. Cody noticed as her eyes intently scanned the surroundings in front of her. First she took note of the familiar horse tied to the fence post. Then she saw Jesse. And finally her eyes rested on the man standing beside him.

Alana reined the horse in and she paused to take it all in. She had known he was coming, yet knowing hadn't prepared her for the feelings that rose up within her when she saw him face to face. Excitement ran through her veins. Passion. She instantaneously leaped from the horse. Cody reached out to grab the reigns before the horse had a chance to bolt.

She picked up the end of her skirt and ran toward him. He hastened to meet her. Alana flung herself into his arms and buried her head into his neck. She hadn't realized how much emotion she had been holding inside, wondering if he might return for her. Suddenly, the dam broke, and she found herself sobbing on his shoulder.

Shay stroked her back, a little taken back. He hadn't

quite expected this. When her crying ceased, he held her back at arm's length. Gently, he brushed her left cheek with his lips. And then her right. Finally his mouth found hers. He had thought of this day for months. He kissed her with fervor. She yielded to his touch.

"Let's go see Heaven. Mama? Shay?" Alana realized they had an audience and was the first to pull away. Mary was standing on the porch with a satisfied grin on her face. Cody had dismounted and was standing silently holding the reins of both horses. Jesse stood directly behind Alana and Shay, waiting impatiently to show Shay the horse.

Alana blushed and Shay couldn't help but laugh at her expression. "I see you are still as bashful and timid as ever," he whispered against her hair. "I'm glad." Shay stepped around her and extended his hand out to the young man.

"Hello. I'm Shay O'Connell."

Cody extended his hand as well. "Cody Bratten."

Alana, Shay, and Cody set out after Jesse, who was already standing in the entrance of the barn, still impatient to show Heaven to Shay.

o o o

Later that evening, Shay was sitting on the porch swing with James sitting across from him. Alana had left moments before in order to put Jesse down for the night.

"So you've got your land all settled, I suppose?" James questioned.

"Yes. It's not far from my brother's place. In fact, both houses are visible to each other." Shay wondered how James felt about his desire to take Alana so far from them. She would be much closer than she had been before she had come west, but it was still a good distance. They certainly wouldn't be able to see each other often.

James sensed Shay's discomfort. "Thank you for allowing Alana to stay here with us. She is the only thing I have left of my sister. I was able to find out so much from her and hopefully she did from me as well. But she has missed you quite a bit, and I believe she's more than ready to follow you farther west."

Shay was relieved James held no grudge against him. "I know Sheridan is a long way off, but you, Mary, your sons, you're all welcome anytime for as long as you're able to stay."

James nodded his gratefulness. "We'll be sure to take you up on that offer. Were you pleased with the look of your horse?"

"Yes, I was. Thank you for allowing Heaven to stay here. And thank you for taking the time to teach Jesse to ride. It means a great deal to him, I can tell. It will make our trip home much easier."

James laughed. "I suppose it will. Even ten days out of the saddle will make you mighty sore when you get back on."

"Mr. Bratten?"

"Please call me James."

"James ... Alana doesn't have a father, and you're the closest relative Alana has right now. I would appreciate your blessing to ask for Alana's hand in marriage."

James smiled. "You wholeheartedly have it. I know you'll both be very happy together."

Alana walked out on the porch and sat down next to Shay. "He's finally asleep. You caused him quite a bit of excitement today." Shay intertwined his fingers with hers.

"Well, I've had a long day too. I think I'll head to bed myself. Good night." James got up and went inside.

Shay intently fixed his eyes on Alana. She blushed under his scrutiny, but moved closer to him. "I missed you, Alana, more then I ever thought I would. I never want to be parted from you again."

"I missed you too," Alana softly spoke.

Shay moved from the bench and dropped to one knee. He waited until Alana finally looked into his eyes before pushing forward. "Will you marry me, Alana?"

Alana smiled. "Nothing would make me happier." She watched as he slowly pushed the golden band onto her finger.

Shay grinned as he stood to his feet. He grabbed both her hands and pulled her to her feet. Then he slowly lifted her chin. Shay brushed away one of her tears with the back of his hand. And then he kissed her as he had never kissed her before.

o o o

Johnny was weary from traveling. He hadn't really paid attention to the fact that he was getting older, until he had begun this long trip west. Hours upon hours in the saddle were beginning to take its toll. Having never been much of a rider previously, the soreness and fatigue were inevitable.

Mr. Cohn seemed to be weathering the ordeal a whole lot better. *But he was young,* Johnny consoled himself.

Mr. Newman, an officer from Georgia, was also along on the journey. He would be needed in case

Johnny was questioned by any lawmen of his intentions to take Alana back with him. At times Johnny questioned what he was doing. He had already spent more than the reward would pay him for the girl.

But then he would remind himself that this had never been about money. He had no need for money. This was about revenge. He couldn't let go now. Something propelled him to continue. It was now more than just vindictiveness against he sister. He was controlled by this quest.

"Mr. Cohn...Mr. Newman, its time to get up," Johnny said loudly as he shuffled Mr. Cohn with his boot. Mr. Cohn groaned and turned to his other side. Johnny strode toward his horse and retrieved his canteen from the saddle. Cold water would wake even the deepest sleeper.

○ ○ ○

Shay made his way out to the barn. He had offered to help James round up the cows this morning. He turned right before he entered the barn and waved to Alana who stood watching him out the kitchen window. She smiled before turning away.

They had decided to marry before they departed. She wanted James to give her away. Mary had been cutting and sewing for the last three days, trying to finish the wedding gown she had started for Alana. And Jesse was thrilled that he would be carrying the rings to the minister. Shay moved toward the stall where Star resided and began to saddle her.

Back outdoors, Shay stood near James and his three sons. "Clay and Cole, you take the north side. Shay and Cody, take the west side. And I'll round them up from the east. We'll push the cattle into the corrals here on the south side." The men nodded, each heading in their own directions.

Shay followed behind Cody. "I'm not much of a cattleman yet. I'm sure I'll need some pointers."

"I haven't done it for a while myself. Father wasn't thinking when he paired us together."

"Alana told me you are a deputy. Seems like exciting work."

Cody raised his eyebrows. "Actually, I'm not a legalized deputy quite yet, although it all means the same to my family. I'm training with Mr. Miller, the deputy in town. He plans to retire sometime this year. By then I should have enough hours to be approved by the townspeople."

"So, is it as enlivening as everyone believes it to be? I mean chasing down the outlaw...keeping order in town and the like."

Cody smiled. "I enjoy it, but not everyone enjoys breaking up a fight or getting shot at." They both laughed.

"Have you ever been shot?" Shay asked on a more serious note.

"I've been shot at...twice. Luckily they were both too drunk to shoot straight."

Cody suddenly shifted the conversation. "How long have you known Alana?"

"I've known of her all my life. We both grew up in Independence. Her mother died during the time I was making plans to head west. When I heard she was interested in finding her uncle, I offered to assist her." Shay paused. "And then...I fell in love with her."

"She deserves the best," Cody stated. "You take good care of her."

Shay turned toward Cody. He tried to read his expression to see just exactly what his feelings were toward Alana. Fondness was unmistakable. Cody evidently had taken a special liking to Alana, enough to be concerned for her welfare.

"I plan to. You have a girl yet, Cody?"

"No. I'm gone too much to get involved with anyone."

"Is that why I didn't see you in church on Sunday?" Shay questioned.

Cody laughed. "You and Alana are two of a kind."

"Meaning?" Shay questioned.

"She's been concerned about my absence from church also. Instead of telling you why I don't go, why don't you tell me why you think I should?"

Shay laughed and then took a moment to think of a good answer. "The more time you spend with someone, the more you get to know him. And the more you get to know him, the more time you want to spend with him. The same pertains to Jesus. If you value a relationship with Him, then you'll value spending time with Him."

"I see where this is going. Going to church would be part of spending time with Him, right?"

Shay smiled. "Right. Some things require quite a bit of effort at first, but then eventually as they become habit...you can't imagine ever having not done it. Spending time with God is like that, a bit of an effort in the beginning, but well worth it in the end." The cows were in view now and the work would soon begin.

"That was a pretty good answer," Cody acknowledged. He found that he liked Shay. He was glad that

Alana was marrying a good man. "Would you like to ride out with me in the morning to check on an old man?"

"Sure. Is this part of your deputy work?"

"Yes. A few folks from town have purchased some whiskey from an old man who lives up in the mountains a ways. He makes the whiskey from scratch, but this last batch must have gone wrong because several of the customers have been to the doctor. The doctor thinks it may be mercury poisoning, perhaps from the water the old man is using."

"I look forward to it. Will I need to carry a gun?" Shay asked with raised eyebrows.

Cody laughed. "No…this old man is quite harmless."

◦ ◦ ◦

They had ridden for a couple hours, and Shay enjoyed the beautiful scenery. He was a bit partial to Sheridan, even though he had only called it home for a few months. "There must be times you are uneasy. Like today…are you nervous about confronting this old man?"

Cody guided his horse through the small stream. "Certainly there are times I feel a bit edgy, but not today. I wouldn't have asked you to come if I thought there was any danger."

Shay gave Cody a lopsided smile. "Then it must just be me, because I do feel somewhat uncertain."

"You can turn back," Cody offered. "You wouldn't get lost. It's a straight shot back to town."

Shay pondered his words before finally shaking his head. "No … I'm not uncertain enough to turn back."

"When I retire, I'd like to build a small cabin back in this valley." Cody surveyed the land around him.

Shay nodded. "It would be a pretty sight for sure. But then you'd have the whiskey man to contend with."

Cody laughed.

The small dilapidated shelter stood facing them as they rounded the next corner. A large, white dog made a beeline for them, growling and showing his sharp teeth.

Cody continued forward as if he hadn't noticed the dog. Shay followed warily behind. Cody slowly dismounted, taking in everything around him. Shay followed suit.

The place was a disaster. Tin cans littered the ground, as did parts and pieces of objects the man had taken apart to fix, only to leave disassembled.

"Mr. Johnson," Cody voiced. Besides the dog, who was no longer barking, there was no other living thing around. Cody moved toward the decrepit door. The bottom was missing a hinge allowing for a huge gap into the structure.

Shay noticed Cody's hand lingering over his gun. Did he feel the eerie presence as well? Shay now wished he had something on him to protect himself.

Cody stopped dead in his tracks. Something was not right. Suddenly, a bullet whizzed by his ear. Cody dove onto Shay, pushing them both as low to the ground as he could. Now he was thankful for the debris covering the yard. The scattered wagon was a better shield than nothing.

Cody realized he was still lying on Shay. "Stay down," he whispered, as he moved off to the side. Cody leaned in closer to hear what Shay was saying, but soon realized his new friend was offering up a prayer … for both of them.

"I guess you should have turned back," Cody acknowledged.

Shay couldn't resist a smile, even in the tense moment. "Why? You said the old man was quite harmless."

Cody smirked, but let the comment pass. "Mr. Johnson," he yelled. "You can come out with your hands held high … or I'll have to shoot you. And if you live … you'll wish you hadn't, because you'll spend the rest of your life in jail … surrounded by people. No more isolation for you." Another shot rang out. The man obviously didn't care.

Cody aimed his pistol for the right side of the house and took a shot. They heard a loud clatter within the shelter. "Dad blammit … you hit my whiskey bottle." Cody and Shay shared a brief smile.

"Get out here now, with your hands held high." Two more shots rang out.

Cody turned and let out another shot. A loud wail soon followed.

"My foot … my foot … you dang fool." Shay looked questionably at Cody. Had he really shot the old man in the foot?

"Now throw your gun out the window … and then slowly come out with your hands in the air. Or I'll shoot again." The gun landed a few feet away. The dilapidated door opened with a loud creak and an old man slowly crawled out the door, still moaning. Cody stood to his feet and cautiously made his way toward the man.

"Ya shot me in the foot, ya' blame fool." The man's thinning, silver hair was standing on end. And he smelled as if he had never taken a bath.

"It's your own fault, Mr. Johnson. I came in peace and you started shooting before I even got to the door. How many shots rang out, Shay, before I shot this man in the foot?"

Shay mentally calculated in his head. "Four shots."

"That's what I came up with too. Now lie still, Mr. Johnson. I'll find something clean to wrap your foot with. Cody moved toward the structure and went inside. It looked like it had been vandalized, not simply lived in. Finding something clean was impossible. Dirty pots and pans littered the countertop. Dirty dishes littered the floor. There was nothing clean in sight. He removed a torn curtain from the window and made his way back outside.

Shay already had the man's shoe and sock off. "The bullet is still inside. I could try to take it out, but it may be best to take him to town and let the doctor do it."

"I agree. He won't die from loss of blood, and there is nothing here that is sanitized enough to do the job without risking infection."

"Do you have a horse, Mr. Johnson?" Cody asked. The man shook his head. He had obviously enjoyed too much of his own whiskey because he was clearly drunk. "I guess you'll have to ride double with me then."

Cody and Shay gathered their horses. Shay helped the old man up behind Cody before mounting his own horse. They had traveled only a few feet when it became apparent that the man was not able to hold on tight enough without the threat of falling off the backside of the horse. Shay took a rope out of his pack and tied the man tightly to Cody.

"Sure am glad you are the deputy," Shay stated as he wrinkled his nose.

Cody laughed. "Now see, this is one of those moments when the job has its disadvantages.

"How did you know where he was located in the house?"

"I saw the direction the bullets were coming from. And the initial noise helped."

"But how did you know you wouldn't kill him?"

Cody smiled sheepishly. "I didn't know for sure I wouldn't kill him. But he was shooting random shots at us. I figured if someone was going to die, I would rather it be him than either one of us."

Shay remounted his horse with a smile on his face.

CHAPTER TEN

October 9, 1858

I am ill and have been for weeks. Dr. O'Connell has been monitoring my condition for the last two months. Today I read fear in his eyes—fear and sadness. I asked him to tell me the truth. He told me I am very sick indeed. Something inside is growing, depriving me of life, and I have only a few months to live. The money I have saved to go west has already been utilized for food. We are three months behind on our statement at the bank. I received a notice today, stating if no money is received by the end of October we will be forced to vacate the premises.

I fear for Alana. She knows no one here. She has no friends. She has no family. I have decided to tell her she has an uncle out west. I hope she will follow my guidance and begin the journey this spring to be with him. James will love her as if she were his own. He always had a special heart. But how will Alana find the money to travel west? I do not know, and for the first time ever, I pray that God will aid her.

God is more real to me in these last days. I should have taken Alana to church. I should have taught her from the Bible. I regret having not done so. She will find someone to show her the way; I must believe that.

° ° °

As their wedding day quickly approached, Alana began having nervous doubts about keeping her ethnicity from Shay. She tried to persuade herself that she could always tell him later, but deep down she knew why she wanted to wait. If she waited until after they were married, he couldn't change his mind.

"Not so far, Jesse. Stay where I can see you." Alana called out. Jesse was riding Heaven up ahead. Shay had mentioned a walk down the road, and they had both excitedly agreed.

"You have a lot on your mind," Shay stated. He looked into her brown eyes. "Are you doing all right? Not having second thoughts are you?"

"No … of course not." Alana turned her head away lest he see her frightened expression. Had James told him? She withdrew her hand from his.

"Why are you so despondent? Are you sure you want to get married? Are you sure you want to spend the rest of your life with me?" Shay's voice now held concern.

Alana slowed to a stop. "Shay, I love you. And I know you are the one I want to spend the rest of my life with. There is something that concerns me, though." There. It was out. She had said it. Now she had no choice but to tell him

"You're having second thoughts about moving?" Shay questioned.

"No. I want to move. I … I have some things from my past that I am still coming to terms with. I … "

"Alana Peterson. Your past means nothing to me. Nothing could change how I feel about you." Alana sighed. Jesse was riding toward them, ready to head back to the warm house. Another missed opportunity.

Alana sat quietly while Mary plaited her hair. In less than an hour she would no longer be Alana Peterson. She would be Alana O'Connell. She smiled as she realized Peterson would no longer be a part of her. She would leave that name behind ... and gladly. "There now, turn around and let me look at you." Alana turned toward her Aunt Mary. Mary nodded in approval. "Now lift your arms up ... a bit higher ... " Mary slipped the wedding dress over her head. "You look positively radiant," Mary admired. She turned Alana toward the mirror.

Alana smiled as she studied her reflection. Mary was an excellent seamstress. It was a simple gown, yet elegant. The sleeves of the gown were lace, displaying the beauty of Alana's tanned skin. Alana fingered the soft tendrils of hair dangling down both sides of her face. "The dress is beautiful. Thank you, Aunt Mary."

"It is the person who wears the dress that makes it so beautiful," Mary stated.

James walked into the room and whistled. "Mary, she's got to be the prettiest thing I've ever laid eyes on, next to you, of course." He stopped to kiss his wife on the cheek. "And to think that you made that beautiful dress," James complimented. Mary smiled at his praise.

"It's just barely after two, and Shay is beginning to worry," James turned to Alana. "Are you ready?"

Alana and Mary made their descent down the stairway. They had chosen to be married outside, and it was a beautiful day. As they stepped out the door, Alana did not miss Shay's penetrating gaze. She looped her arm with her Uncle James as she made her way toward him.

Alana lay still, listening to the heart-beat of her husband. Her husband! It still seemed incredible. She was now married to this man. Shay twisted one of her curls around his finger. Alana turned toward him and smiled.

"I thought you had fallen asleep," she whispered.

"I'm awake now." He rolled her over onto her back. Alana stared into his blue eyes.

"Have I ever told you how beautiful you are?"

"I believe you have … once or twice," Alana softly answered. "But I haven't heard it in the last hour." She blushed under his scrutiny.

"Well let me change that. You are a very beautiful woman. But it's not just your outward beauty, Alana. It's your inward beauty as well. Thank you for marrying me, Alana O'Connell. You'll never regret it."

Alana smiled. "Well, see that I don't."

Shay laughed. "Who would have known someone as quiet and shy as you would have such a haughty disposition. I bet there is a lot I still don't know about you."

Alana suddenly tensed. She closed her eyes, no longer able to look into his tender eyes. "Shay … there is something … "

Shay covered her mouth with his hand. He was in no mood for serious conversation. His mouth soon found hers.

They arrived at church early and many congratulations went around. Alana blushed at the Bratten boys' teasing. Shay smiled, taking it all in stride. Just as the preacher was walking to the pulpit, Cody appeared smiling a greeting their direction.

Afterward, they all met for lunch at James and Mary's. Cody found a moment to talk to Shay alone.

"I thought about what you said, Shay. And you're right. I've been too content with my life the way it is, and it's time I do something about it."

Shay laughed as he patted Cody on the back. "You won't regret it."

"So you're taking my cousin away tomorrow? We'll miss her a great deal—my father more than any of us." Cody glanced over at his father who was laughing at something Jesse had said.

"I know … and I hate to take her away, but sometimes life doesn't deal us simple decisions," Shay responded.

Cody held out his hand and Shay shook it. "Goodbye, Shay." Cody turned toward Alana and pulled her into a warm embrace. "Goodbye, Alana, my favorite cousin."

"Your only cousin," she added with a laugh.

Cody kissed Alana's cheek and then bent down to say goodbye to Jesse. "You be a good boy, Jesse. Treat your mama real good, and she'll spoil you forever, I can promise you that." Jesse laughed. Cody hugged his own mother before leaving the house.

o o o

Alex closed his eyes, savoring each bite. He hadn't tasted food so good in days...or actually, weeks. He eyed his boss Mr. Bratten. "What do you say we stay here tonight and have some fun? We haven't had a day to ourselves for weeks now."

Johnny glared at him, though the idea did sound

appealing, only because he himself was completely exhausted. He'd give anything for a real bed to sleep in. Johnny turned his gaze to Mr. Newman.

"I second Alex's suggestion," Mr. Newman stated. Johnny muttered his agreement and got up to find the hotel clerk. He couldn't get to a hotel room fast enough.

Later as Johnny lay enjoying the soft hotel bed, he let his thoughts drift to his brother. James. How had James fared out west? He'd soon find out, for Dalles was only a week's ride away. Johnny was never so relieved to finally be to the end of his destination.

Johnny knew James had married and had children of his own. Poor James, he would be devastated by the news of what Johnny planned to do to their sister's daughter. James always had too big a heart. And for that reason their father had loved him more, even though Johnny had been the one to stick around. He hadn't abandoned his parents like everyone else had.

James and Charise had been dearly loved by their parents, and no matter what Johnny did to make them love him more, it didn't change the fact that James or Charise could do it better. But they had deserted their family, leaving the entire inheritance to Johnny. He couldn't have asked for a better ending. But deep down he knew his parents had been displeased with the way he did business. But how could a banking business thrive if you consistently extended notes or forgave balances? It was the profit of the bank he cared about and nothing more.

His brother and sister had taken a part of their parents with them when they had deserted everyone. Johnny had hoped that his parents would finally turn to him for support, that they would finally accept him. But they had only pushed him further away.

° ° °

Shay tucked the blanket more securely around Jesse before turning to the fire. He reached for a couple pieces of wood, hoping there were enough embers left to get the fire going again. It had chilled considerably since they had retired for the night.

Shay watched the fire for a few minutes. The dry wood ignited rather quickly, and he held his hands over the fire, trying to warm them. He slowly added more wood. Finally content that the fire would continue burning, he rose and moved toward Alana.

Alana opened her eyes as he lay next to her on the ground, pulling the blanket up over them both. She snuggled up close to him, gathering heat from his body. He pulled her closer still, breathing in the scent of her.

"Having someone to share my bed with has most definitely made my nights warmer," Shay whispered against her hair. "We should have married before we left Independence. All those cold nights on the wagon train … " He shivered against her.

"You are the one who insisted we come as brother and sister," Alana teased.

"As if you tried to change my mind." He ran his fingers through her long hair, enjoying the softness of it.

"I was shy. But I would have married you then." Alana intertwined her hand with his. He had such strong hands. She felt safe next to him.

"Really? I'm not so sure. It took quite a bit of persistence on my part, if I remember right."

"Oh really, because I distinctly remember telling you I loved you first."

Shay rose up on one elbow. "That's right, you did." He fingered the outline of her mouth. "I'll never forget that night." He lowered his head and kissed her lightly, but as he brought his head back up, she pulled him back toward her.

° ° °

"If you hurry your movements, you'll only scare the horse. Be gentle … yep, just like that." Shay helped Jesse loosen the cinch on the saddle.

"Can I take the bridle off too?" Jesse whispered quietly.

Shay smiled. "Let's finish the saddle and then … yes, you may take the bridle off."

Shay looked over and found Alana watching them. "Ma'am, it is very impolite to stare," he said with good humor.

Alana laughed. "Then I'll do my best to control myself," she teased back. She turned back to the fire and began to prepare supper.

"We'll be there the day after tomorrow," Shay announced between mouthfuls. Alana was relieved. Sleeping out under the stars had been a new adventure for her, but she was more than ready to be back in a real bed. Jesse, on the other hand, was thrilled about sleeping outdoors. After the first night, he had stated with a huge smile, "I'm a real cowboy now!" Shay had laughed, and she had seen the pride in his eyes.

Alana took Shay's plate and scooped another large spoonful of stew on it.

"Thank you, ma'am," he said as he winked at her.

She sat back down next to him and smiled as he took another bite, closing his eyes in satisfaction. His blond hair was disarrayed from the wind. He had faded freckles on his nose, making him even more handsome in her eyes.

"Are you staring at me again?" he voiced, his eyes still closed.

o o o

They had just left the small town of Sheridan and were now only three miles from their new home. Shay was greatly anticipating Alana's reaction when she saw the house for the first time. Jesse, who sat in front of him on Heaven talked all the way. Was this the same withdrawn child who wouldn't even come near Shay in the beginning? Shay smiled when he thought about how their lives had all changed, and all for the better.

Shay pointed out his brother Cal's house and land. He debated stopping, but decided against it. They would have plenty of time together soon enough. They rounded the curve in the road, and Shay turned to see Alana's response.

Alana stopped and stared, completely astonished at the size of the house. It was huge compared to the small, dilapidated house she had grown up in. Alana turned to Shay, completely speechless.

"I told you before that I did carpentry work. And I was able to save a lot of money from my work. I've always wanted to build a house for myself."

"But this is incredible. I had no idea you could build something like this."

Jesse begged to be let off the horse before they even arrived, and he took off to investigate his new surroundings. Alana saw the wagon sitting by the barn. "I thought you said you sold the wagon we came in?" she questioned.

"I did. That's the Hubbards' wagon." Alana looked at Shay, confused. "I asked Mr. Leaver if we could keep it. I thought it might mean something to Jesse someday. Some of their things are still inside, and he might like to look through them when he is older."

Alana's eyes welled with tears. "I think you're right." Her look of appreciation said enough.

Shay led Alana into the house. She examined the kitchen stove and cupboards. He then took her through the parlor and living room. She dropped into the chair by the wood stove and closed her eyes. "I feel like I am in a dream." Shay laughed, enjoying her contentment.

He grabbed her hand and pulled her back up. "There's still more," he whispered against her hair. He led her up the staircase. They went through four bedrooms, the last being theirs.

"Just how many children are you expecting us to have?" Alana finally found the courage to ask.

"Many," he replied. She fingered one of the wooden side posts on their bed, before walking to the window and taking in the amazing view below.

"I believe I have married the most skilled and accomplished man alive," she declared with pride.

"And don't you ever forget it," Shay replied as he stood behind her.

◦ ◦ ◦

They had finally reached Dalles, Oregon. Johnny was never so glad to be anywhere in his entire life. He had inquired at the general store the whereabouts of his brother James. The three men decided to stay at the hotel in Dalles. Johnny would venture out to his brother's in the morning alone, and if he later needed his companions' assistance, he would send for them.

Johnny's night was restless. He couldn't help playing over in his mind the way he hoped things would go. He awoke early and ate breakfast before setting out in the direction the store owner had pointed. He had traveled a few miles before finally recognizing the description of the place. It was a nice house. Not big, nor fancy, but nice. He rode up to the house and dismounted. He didn't see anyone outdoors, so he made his way to the front door.

He knocked firmly and soon found himself face to face with a middle-aged woman. Though slightly overweight, she was rather attractive.

"May I help you?" she inquired.

"Is this James Bratten's residence?" he asked.

"It is. James is out feeding the cattle at the moment. But he'll be in for breakfast shortly. May I ask who is inquiring?"

Johnny stared determinedly at the woman. "I am James' brother, Johnny Bratten."

Mary invited Johnny inside and offered him a drink. She periodically glanced over at the man who claimed to be James brother. She didn't know much about him, but the small amount James had disclosed had not been favorable. Johnny sat drinking a hot cup of coffee. *Why was he here?* Mary didn't question him. In fact, she said nothing as she nervously awaited her husband's return.

She didn't have to wait long. James strode in the back door, stopping at the basin by the door to wash his hands. "Gretchin got out again. This is the third time this month. And no matter how hard Clay, Cole, or I search, we just can't see how she does it." He looked up and noticed his wife's concerned expression. It was then that he noticed the shadow. He walked the rest of the way into the kitchen and stood face to face with his brother. James' face went white as he quickly searched for the right words to say.

"Johnny," he stated evenly. "Why are you here?"

Johnny sized up his brother before speaking. "It is a very long story, brother. Shall I start at the beginning?"

James walked to the table and sat down. His hunger had suddenly dissipated. He waved to another empty seat at the table. "I don't really have much choice, now do I?" James replied.

Johnny took the seat across from him. "First of all, I'm looking for Alana. Alana Peterson. I'm under the presumption that she traveled this way and is now staying at this very residence. Am I correct?" Johnny drummed his fingers on the tabletop.

"What could you possibly want with Alana?" James hesitantly asked.

Johnny viciously smiled. "She's my niece too. Is it so terrible that I'd like to meet my own niece?"

James frowned. "You've never wanted anything to do with us before. Why now? What do you want with her?"

Johnny was done fooling around. "First, I want to know if she is here?" he glared at his brother.

James shook his head. "She's not here."

"Is she in Dalles? I know you know where she is. You never were a good liar."

James knew Johnny could see right through him. But what else could he do? He wouldn't just hand her over to his brother. Not without knowing his intentions. "I don't know…"

"You can't hide her from me forever. Someone in this town must know where she is. And I will find her. Mark my words, I'll find her." James knew Johnny was right. He could ask anybody in town, and they would know about Alana, her recent marriage, and departure to Sheridan.

"What do you want with her?" James pleaded with him.

Johnny laughed at his pathetic concern. He probably didn't even know who Alana's father was. It wasn't something she would share with just anyone. But Johnny would tell him. And he'd enjoy every second of it.

"Her mother…"

"Charise…Charise…you can't even say your sister's name?"

Johnny waved his hand in disgust. "Her mother married Jesse Blackwell. Do you remember him? Of course you do. He was the son of our gardener. Alana was born of their union. Jesse died, but our sister ran off to have his daughter. She thought she had everyone fooled, but she didn't.

"She married a no good drunk, thinking she could pass Alana off as his child, and for awhile it worked, she thought, but I knew the truth, and so did our father. But father didn't have the courage to do anything about it. Now he's dead. And I have set out to do what I have wanted to do for so long. I am going to find our sister's daughter and take her back to where she belongs. They have a warrant out for her arrest and delivery to a plantation in Georgia where her father was sold years ago."

James stared at his brother as if he were out of his

mind. "Why? Why are you so intent on ruining her life? What joy could there possibly be in that?"

Johnny screamed in fury. "Our sister ruined our family. She killed our mother … devastated our father. Our business almost went under because of her lurid behavior. She deserves every terrible thing imaginable."

"But this is Alana. She didn't do it. So be it that our sister caused you all this grief. But Alana—she is innocent in it all. Leave her alone. Let her be."

Johnny stood to his feet. "I can see you will be of no help to me. You never were. I will find her. Nothing you say will stop me." He strode to the door and let himself out.

Mary watched in agony as her husband slid to the floor in great anguish.

◦ ◦ ◦

Shay had decided to lease most of their property to Cal, who in exchange would have more pasture for the cows to graze. This would allow Shay more time to do construction work, but also try his hand at ranching. Already several businesses were asking Shay to build or remodel their stores.

Jesse and Peter had become good playmates for each other and ventured back and forth between the two houses during the day.

"Have you heard from Maggie and Tom?" Alana asked Shay one evening over supper.

Shay instantly left the table and soon returned with two envelopes and a sheepish smile. "I picked up the mail in town two days ago and forgot to give this to you." Shay handed her one of the envelopes.

"Who is the other envelope from?" Alana asked, still eyeing the other envelope in his hand.

"It's from you," Shay said with a smile.

Alana blushed. "You're not going to read it now … you were supposed to receive it before you came to get me." Alana reached for the envelope.

Shay laughed and held the envelope up higher. "Yes, I am going to read it."

"It's mine. I would like it back." Alana reached again, only to have Shay hold it up even higher. Alana began to turn away but reddened when she heard the sound of tearing paper. "No … read it outside somewhere … "

"Dear Shay, I miss you more than … " Shay left the kitchen, his voice still carrying into the kitchen from the other room.

Alana shook her head at his teasing. If she would just pretend it didn't bother her, he would probably cease teasing her, but some matters were more difficult to change than others. Alana stirred the pot of chili and checked the cornbread one last time before sitting down at the table. She quickly tore open the envelope holding the letter from her friend.

Dear Alana,

I miss you so much. Some days I fear I will never be content due to the absence of my dearest friend. I will never forget our days as we traveled on the wagon train headed west. When I look back, they remain my fondest memories.

Alana felt a presence behind her and turned to find Shay staring over her shoulder. "Did you enjoy my letter?" Alana asked.

Shay laughed. "I did … immensely. Would you mind

reading Maggie's letter aloud?" Shay asked as he took a seat next to her.

Alana nodded, and continued on.

There was much talk on the wagon train after you left us to stay with your uncle. For days, the fact that Shay went from being your brother to your betrothed was our most talked about topic!

Many rumors spread, which were entirely untrue of course. Poor Shay had to endure it all on his own. But he did very well under the circumstances. He never uttered another word about it, neither did he try to justify himself. And before long the talk died down.

Allan, of course, was the most hurt by the news! He most certainly had his eye set on you. Shay had a talk with him, and the day that Allan departed the wagon train I noticed a handshake between the two men, so all must have been forgiven.

"What did you say to him?" Alana questioned.

"Not on your life ... "

"It did concern me; therefore, I have a right to know," she pried.

"No, absolutely not," he stated. Alana raised her eye brows as she turned back to the letter.

I hope by now you have arrived in Sheridan. Shay, I'm sure, has been pining for you something awful. He felt the absence of his girl, just on the short trip to Sheridan. In case you don't know already, you have a man who loves you very much. Never forget that.

Alana looked up at Shay's arrogant smile. "I guess you better keep that letter as a reminder," he commented. Alana laughed and continued reading.

We made it to Pine Grove. Jonathan Thomas was born on December 26th. He is a beautiful baby boy. He has his daddy's dark hair and my blue eyes, just like you told me he would. He is everything I imagined him to be.

Pine Grove is a nice community. There is a tiny church here and a preacher that comes every other Sunday. The people of Pine Grove are nice and have kept Jonathan dressed in style with all the clothes they have sewn for him.

I have begun to feel the absence of my family since Jonathan's birth. I miss them very much. Tom has noticed my melancholy and has told me to invite you to visit. I am sure you are trying to settle into your new life, but I would love nothing more than a visit from my dearest friend. Please write.

I love you,
Maggie

Alana sat the letter aside. "Poor Maggie. She sounds like she needs a friend."

"Would you like to go?"

"Could we? Should we leave again so soon?"

"Now would be best. I haven't started remodeling anything in Sheridan yet. And Cal can take care of the cows. When you're packed and ready, we'll go."

"That reminds me," Alana voiced. "Did you remember to give the canister of money to Jane?"

Shay reached across the table and grabbed her hand. "I did. Jane went to town that day by herself. Jay stayed to fix the wagon's axle, as it had cracked the day before. When she returned, she had tears streaming down her cheeks, and she told me to tell you thank you. Her exact words were, 'She'll never know how much this means to me,' or something like that, anyway." Alana smiled, glad she had been able to help someone else in need. She stood to her feet and began to set the table for supper.

∘ ∘ ∘

Mary was distraught when she knocked on the door to the deputy's office. Mr. Miller answered the door.

"Hello, Mrs. Bratten. I suppose you are looking for Cody. He should be in right soon. I sent him on an errand over at the Johnson farm, but that was over three hours ago. Come in and have a seat."

Mary took the seat he offered, glad that he was busy with paperwork.

Ten minutes had passed before the door opened and Cody returned. "Hello, Mama," Cody said. He could see the fear etched in her eyes and instantly knew something was wrong. "What's wrong? Is Papa all right? Clay? Cole?"

Mary waved her hand indicating it was none of the above. Mr. Miller, sensing their need for a private discussion, excused himself and left the office. Cody sat down and took his mother's hands in his own. She told him of Johnny's arrival and what he planned to do to Alana.

"Why would he do such a thing?" Cody questioned. "Is he that mean-hearted?"

"According to your father, he is that and more."

"How is father taking it?" Cody voiced.

"Not well. He is barely speaking and just goes through the motions during the day. The last three nights, he hasn't even come to bed."

"I read something last night, Mama, right out of that Bible you bought me for Christmas last year. It said to cast your cares upon the Lord, and He will sustain you. It said He won't let the righteous fall. Shay and Alana need our prayers right now." Mary nodded at her son's encouraging words. "God is not going to let them fall. I have that feeling in here." Cody pointed to his heart.

"I'll see what I can do. Perhaps Mr. Miller will give me some time off. I'll be out to see Father this evening." Cody walked his mother to the door and helped her into the waiting wagon.

When Mr. Miller returned to the office, Cody approached him. "Mr. Miller, did you notice any newcomers this past week?"

"As a matter of fact I did. A young man stopped by here. His name was Alex. He said he was looking for an escaped slave. I told him we hadn't seen any escaped slaves around here."

"Did you see who he was traveling with? Did you notice when they left?"

"I saw three men leaving town the day before yesterday, an older man, and a middle-aged man, and then the young man who came in here. Why are you so interested?"

"I need some time off. It is important that I follow these men. I really can't say too much right now."

"Well, I'll expect a full report when you return. How long do you suppose you'll be gone?"

"I can't promise you anything, but for sure, a few weeks."

Mr. Miller brushed a hand through his thinning hair. "I managed for seventeen years alone, I suppose a couple more months won't kill me, but you hurry back. I'd like to retire while I still have a beating heart."

There was no time to notify Maggie of their soon arrival, so it came as a complete shock when Maggie opened the door and saw her cherished friend standing on her doorstep. Maggie screamed with delight and embraced her friend. The noise of a crying baby reached both their ears, and Maggie hurried from the room to get her son. When she returned, Alana reached for baby Jonathan, who looked so much like his mother.

"He's beautiful, Maggie," Alana exclaimed. Jonathan cried and reached out for his mother. "No, you have to let me hold you for awhile. I came all this way just to see you."

Alana followed Maggie into the kitchen and entertained Jonathan while Maggie began to prepare supper. Shay took Jesse out to the fields to find Tom.

Later, after supper, Alana and Maggie began to gather up the dirty dishes. "I haven't been myself since our arrival here," Maggie shared as they began to wash the supper dishes. Alana had noticed Maggie's lack of liveliness, for it had once been so much a part of her. Alana hated to see her unhappy.

"What changes have taken place, Maggie, since your arrival?"

"I missed you something awful. I knew that I would, but I wasn't totally prepared for how I'd feel with no female companionship. But I still had Tom and that helped. But when we got here, to Pine Grove, Tom was so busy. He's always dreamed of farming."

Already Alana was starting to understand Maggie's discontent. On the way west, she and Tom had so much time together. But now Maggie was a mother, and Tom had other things that required his attention.

"I barely see him anymore. He's out in the fields before I awake, and most nights I am already asleep when he comes in. I spend much of the day alone ... with Jonathan, of course, and that helps some, but there's only so much you can talk about with a baby."

Alana felt sorry for her friend, Maggie, the girl who had led her to the Lord. She had been so patient ... so caring.

"Have you spoken with Tom about how you are feeling?" Alana voiced with compassion.

"Yes, and he says things will slow down soon, but so far they haven't, and I don't see when they will, either. Every season requires so much of him, and we just don't have the funds yet to hire on help.

Alana sighed. "Maggie, I feel so unqualified to be giving you answers. You've always been the strong one. I know it seems like your husband has deserted you at the moment, but God is still here, willing to be your friend when you have no friend. Contrary to how we feel sometimes, He is there in the tough times. Repeating your words to me that night so long ago on the trail, my prayers will be with you every step of the way."

Maggie turned toward Alana with tears in her eyes. "Thank you, Alana. It is so easy to forget when you become overwhelmed."

"Don't ever feel bad, Maggie. We all have our peaks and valleys. Someday I'll be begging you for a visit."

"And I'll come, you can be sure of that. I knew you were special the first day I met you. God knew how much I'd need you."

Alana reached for Maggie's hand. "And I you."

°°°

"Maybe you could talk with Tom. If he really knew Maggie's pain, I'm sure he would be more compassionate. He might even be willing to slow down a bit and spend more time with his wife and son."

Shay raised his eyebrows. "Why is it that I always seem to be faced with the confrontational issues?"

Alana laughed as she lie down next to him in the bed. "You handle them so much better than I do."

"I'll talk to him," Shay stated with a yawn. "And just what is that smile for Mrs. O'Connell? If I didn't know any better, I'd say you're becoming somewhat spoiled, always getting your own way." He turned and began tickling her. Alana squirmed to get away, holding her breath so she would not scream out.

"Stop," she pleaded. "We'll wake Maggie and Tom." Shay reached to pull her close, but she stiffened her arms against him.

"I guess I'll have to tickle you until you succumb," he teased. Alana sighed in dismay and moved in closer.

"That's my girl," Shay whispered against her hair.

○ ○ ○

Johnny's patience was beginning to wear thin. He had just been at the O'Connell's house, but there had been no answer. He was so tired of false leads. He began to ride back toward town, when he saw a young woman hanging clothes on the line up the road. He rode toward her.

"Hello," he called. "I have just been at the home of Shay and Alana O'Connell, but there was no one there. Can you tell me when you expect them home?"

Annie walked toward him. "They went to Pine Grove

to visit a friend. They should be home any day now. Can I have your name? I'll let them know you stopped by.

"They'll meet up with me soon enough." Johnny turned his horse around and headed back to town.

Annie stared after him. There was something about that man she did not like. Why had he refused to give his name?

"Mama, Candice is awake," Peter called out the door. Annie turned toward the house, the rude man soon forgotten.

° ° °

"Thank you for coming, Alana. It meant everything to me." Maggie hugged Alana for the third time. Tom also was there to see them off.

Alana and Shay left with high hopes and a promise that Maggie and Tom would be coming to visit them near the end of summer. They wanted to bring some of their garden produce to sell at Sheridan's town social.

Jesse was anxious to go home. He missed Peter, because "at least he could walk and talk," he had exclaimed over supper the night before. Alana had admonished him for his comment, but Maggie had brushed it off with a laugh.

They rode for much of the day, but after such a late start, they agreed to settle down for the night and ride the rest of the way in the morning. Alana fell asleep, snuggled against Shay's arm.

Her brow was drenched in sweat and pain seared through her body. She screamed over and over again. A man was standing over her. He was telling her something, but she couldn't hear him. She tried to focus.

"Push," he told her. "Push."

Alana pushed with all her might. Finally the pain began to cease. She looked at the man who was holding the baby. Her baby. But the baby was black. Black as coal. The man's face had gone white. He stood staring at the infant with an angry expression on his face. He handed her the child and walked out the bedroom door.

Then Shay appeared. He was standing over her and the baby. She looked up into his eyes, which were filled with contempt and hate. She screamed.

"Alana? Alana? Wake up, Alana." Shay shook her gently. Finally her eyes opened and she felt his arms wrap around her. "What's wrong," he comforted. She shivered and he pulled her closer. "Alana, what's wrong?"

"I'm fine," she whispered against him.

"Are you sure?" he questioned

"Yes, I'm fine," she restated.

Shay nestled her as close as he could to his body and clasped his arms in front of her. She lay completely still until his deep breathing indicated he had fallen back asleep. Alana rested her hand on her belly. She was with child. She needed to tell Shay. She wanted to. But first she needed to share with him her ethnicity. He would understand. Wouldn't he?

CHAPTER ELEVEN

Shay took Alana's hand, and then Jesse's, before bowing his head in prayer. "Thank you for this food, Lord. Bless it to our bodies. Be with us today; guide us; protect us. We ask this in Jesus' name. Amen."

Alana began dishing up their plates. "What do you have planned today?" Shay asked Jesse from across the table.

Jesse hurriedly swallowed his bite of scrambled eggs. "Peter and I are going to go down by the river and fish, but first we got to find us some worms along the river bank."

Shay laughed. "You sound all grown up, young man. Who's going to watch you down at the river bank?" Shay asked with a smile.

"Mama … and maybe Annie … and if Annie comes then Candice will come, but she jabbers so much, she scares the fish away."

Alana and Shay shared a glance, humor displayed in each of their eyes. "If Candice and Annie come, we will walk farther down the river bank so we'll not disturb you," Alana announced.

A knock sounded at the door, and Jesse hurried from the table to answer it. Hearing an unfamiliar voice, Shay also stood to his feet, making his way to the front room. There were four men standing outside the house. Three were unfamiliar to him, but he recognized the sheriff from town.

"What can I help you with?" Shay inquired.

An awkward silence passed before an older gentleman stepped forward. "My name is Johnny...Johnny Bratten."

Shay smiled. "You're James' brother? I thought I saw some resemblance." Shay motioned for them to come into the house. "We're eating breakfast at the moment. Do you care to join us?"

"No, we ate in town," Johnny stated. "We have a matter to speak of with you. You are Shay O'Connell, correct?"

"Yes, I'm married to your niece...Alana." Shay didn't miss the man's raised eyes over his words. "Why don't we take a seat at the table? You can share the news you have, and I'll finish my breakfast." The four men followed him to the kitchen table.

Alana glanced up as they entered the kitchen. She quickly jumped up, serving them each a cup of coffee. "I see no reason to waste any more time." Johnny slid a piece of paper across the table towards Shay. Shay took it and carefully studied it. It spoke of a man named Jesse Blackwell who was wanted by a plantation in Georgia. How odd that Mr. Bratten would travel so far to bring him this information.

Shay glanced up at Johnny. "I don't see what this has to do with us. I've never known any man by the name of Jesse Blackwell." Alana shot up out of her chair, her face instantly losing all of its color.

Johnny smiled a very bitter smile. "You haven't told your husband?"

Shay turned toward Alana. "What haven't you told me, Alana?"

Tears flowed down her cheeks. "Jesse Blackwell ... is my ... father."

Shay's eyes widened in shock, and he studied his wife intently. "Your father was a slave?" Shay questioned. Alana nodded. "And you didn't think that detail was important enough to share?"

"I didn't know ... "

"Did you know before you married me?" Shay voiced. Alana could hear the mistrust in his voice.

Alana placed her hands over her face, but he could see the nod of her head. Finally she dropped her hands. "I wanted to tell you. I was afraid."

"Afraid! Some things are worth sharing, even if you're afraid. This would be one of them."

Alana ran from the room, no longer able to look into her husband's angry eyes. He hated her. He didn't want her anymore.

Shay turned toward the four men, now slightly embarrassed. "Surely you didn't travel two thousand miles to share Alana's ethnicity with us. Why are you here?" Shay's eyes had taken on a hard look. His demeanor was no longer friendly.

"Read the notice again, Mr. O'Connell, and you'll see why we're here." Johnny couldn't keep the smile from his face.

Shay once again picked up the paper. His breathing became labored with each word that he read.

Jesse Blackwell, purchased by the Georgian Plantation, has escaped. A reward is posted in the amount of five hundred dollars for his arrest and return to the Georgian

Plantation. This reward also stands ... also stands ... also stands ... for any descendants that may have been born.

Shay shoved the letter back toward Johnny. "Alana's always been free. Surely you don't mean to take her into slavery now?"

"I'm sorry, Shay, but the reward still stands, even though eighteen years have passed. I'm sorry to have to do this to you," the sheriff from Sheridan explained.

"And what if I won't let you take her!" Shay stated angrily as his chair scraped loudly against the hardwood floor. He stood to his feet. "She's my wife. Do you actually think I am going to sit idly by and let you escort my wife into slavery?"

The sheriff also stood to his feet. "Shay, you'll either let her leave peaceably, or someone is going to get hurt. I certainly don't want to put you in jail over the incident."

"Jail," Shay screamed. "My wife is being taken from me, and you think I might be concerned about a night in jail." The sheriff reached out, grabbing Shay's arm. He nodded for the other three men to leave the room.

o o o

Alana held Jesse's small body against her own. Jesse pushed back, concerned by the tears he saw on his mother's cheeks. "Mama, what's the matter?"

"Jesse, I love you so much. But I may have to leave ... for awhile ... "

"No, Mama. No. I will go with you ... "

"You can't come ... "

They both turned toward the three men approaching them. "Ma'am, I hereby arrest you according to the indictment made years ago. Jesse Blackwell was bought by the Georgian Plantation before his death in 1841. The indictment states that any descendants of Jesse Blackwell are therefore also owned by the Georgian Plantation. You shall hereby proceed to the Georgian Plantation, as well as any children that you may have born."

Alana's eyes instantly went to Jesse, still in her arms. "His mother died on the wagon train coming west. He's not my child."

"Leave the boy," Johnny declared from behind the officer. The officer looked at Johnny skeptically before turning away from his loathsome stare.

"Will you come willingly or must I be forced to bind you?" the officer asked.

Shay was not present, and Alana found she was relieved. She never again wanted to see the look of hurt, mingled with anger, because she had been a coward, unable to tell her husband the truth.

"I will go willingly." Had she glanced toward the kitchen window she would have seen Shay watching as they led her away. She would have noticed him fall to his knees in distress, not knowing what to do.

Jesse followed the men to their horses tied along the fence. "Mama, where are you going? Mama?" He began to panic as she continued forward. "Mama! Come back!" he sobbed. "Come back, Mama. Please, come back."

Alex, Johnny's attendant, stooped and picked the child up. "Your mother has to go now." He didn't know what he had expected, but certainly not this. She was married. She had a child. Alex would never forget the man kneeling in the kitchen window as they led his wife away.

"Mama, please come back," the boy continued

to wail even after Alex sat him back down. The small desperate voice resonated in their ears, long after they had left the house. "MAMA, PLEASE DON'T LEAVE ME!"

∘ ∘ ∘

Jesse ran back into the house. "Shay?" Jesse reached down, pressing his small hand against Shay's shoulder. "Shay! They've taken her. They've taken Mama."

"Alana," Shay whispered.

Jesse turned and ran from the house. He ran as fast as he could to his Uncle Cal's house. "Cal!" he screamed. "Cal!"

Cal came running from the barn. He fell to his knees in the grass beside Jesse who was crying inconsolably. Something was wrong. Terribly wrong. "Jesse, tell me what's happened?"

Jesse pointed down the road. "They've taken her. They've taken my mama. She's gone."

Annie soon appeared in the doorway of the house. "Annie," Cal shouted. "I'm going down to Shay's. Something is wrong. Will you take Jesse inside?"

When Cal arrived at Shay's, the door to the house was wide open. He walked in and saw his brother sitting at the kitchen table, his head buried in his arms. Cal knelt down beside him.

"Where's Alana?" Cal probed.

Shay shook his head, unable to speak.

"Jesse came to the house. He's upset. Has Alana left?"

Shay finally glanced up into his brother's eyes, and Cal was surprised to find not only sorrow but anger as well. "She lied to us," Shay finally said. "She knew her father was a slave, and she didn't tell me."

Cal knew his eyes betrayed his surprise. *Alana was black?* He had noticed her beautiful skin the first day he met her, but it had never crossed his mind that she could be colored. "So, she left?"

Shay shook his head. "They took her. She's a slave, Cal, an escaped fugitive. My wife is gone … " Shay stood to his feet and left the kitchen, not able to face the deep emotions he felt within.

∘ ∘ ∘

Four days passed. Four days of unanswered questions and a deep sorrow that penetrated each person in the O'Connell family. Jesse stayed with Cal and Annie. He had not seen Shay since Alana's departure.

"Where's your mama?" Peter asked, as he sat next to his cousin in the dirt.

Jesse's eyes moved to the road where his mama had ridden away only days before. "Cal said she had to leave. She is needed somewhere. But I need her too." Jesse fought past the tears rising to the surface. He swiped his cheek with the back of his hand. Hearing an approaching horse, Jesse hopefully glanced toward the road once again, trying to make out the figure approaching.

"Uncle Cody!" Jesse proclaimed. Annie hurried to the door, also hearing the approaching rider. Jesse, who had been playing in the yard with her son Peter, was already running toward the man. He obviously knew him. The man grabbed the boy and threw him in the air before hugging him tightly.

"They took my mama," Jesse stated.

"I know. But we'll get her back."

"You will?" Jesse voiced. His eyes beheld excitement for the first time in days. Jesse squeezed Cody's hand with his own as they made their way toward the house.

"Your father and I will bring her back." Cody promised the small boy.

Cody introduced himself to the lady at the door. Annie smiled and invited him in.

"Where's Shay?" he asked after he was seated at the kitchen table with a hot cup of coffee in his hand.

"He's at his place." Annie pointed further down the road. "We haven't seen him since she left four days ago."

Cody nodded. "And Jesse's been staying here?"

"Yes. Are you hungry? We have leftover ham from supper last night."

Cody downed the last of his coffee and stood to his feet. "Thanks, but I'll take you up on that later. I think I'll head down to Shay's and see what kind of plan we can come up with. It'd probably be best if Jesse stays here for the time being."

Jesse's smile disappeared with those words. "Don't you worry. I'll be back." Cody reassured Jesse as he patted the boy's head. Cody closed the door behind him and moved toward his horse. The short reprieve had done them both good.

"We're not goin' far," Cody assured the mare as they moved in the direction Annie had previously signaled. Cody admired the rolling hills. Shay had chosen a spectacular piece of land. Cody had intended on going to the house first, but upon hearing several loud noises coming from the fields, Cody instead moved in the direction of the sound.

Cody found Shay several moments later digging

fence post holes. He looked exhausted, like he hadn't slept in days, and he probably hadn't. Shay briefly looked up at the approaching rider, yet showed no surprise on his face at the unexpected arrival of Cody.

Cody had wondered what he would find when he arrived. He knew Shay would be devastated, afraid, and perhaps overwhelmed, but he hadn't expected to find the angry person who now stood in front of him.

"So, that's your plan? You're just going to let them take her? You're not even going to go after her?" Shay made no indication that he heard anything. "You promised me only a few short months ago that you would do your best by her. Is this your best?"

Shay threw down the shovel and punched Cody square in the jaw. Cody landed with a thud on the ground. "She lied to me. I trusted her and she ... lied ... "

Cody stood to his feet and brushed himself off. "Would it have changed anything?" He sucked in his lower lip at the taste of blood. "Would it have changed how you felt about her? The only thing it would have changed is how you lived. You would have been more cautious. You would have hid her from civilization just to be with her. Admit it." Shay turned away from him, but not before Cody saw the deep emotions pass through his eyes.

"We both know Alana, and the Alana we know is trustworthy and honorable. There is a reason she didn't tell you. Was she trying to protect you? Was she trying to protect Jesse? Could she have had any mistrust in you? There was a reason." Cody paused a moment to let his words penetrate.

"The way I see it, Shay, you have two choices. You

can give up and let her go, or you can trust God and go after her."

"Why would He let this happen? Why?" Shay stated in agony.

"There aren't always answers to life's injustices, but you can go after the woman you love, or you can stay here. What's it going to be?" Cody's shoulders slumped for the first time since beginning this journey. Shay had already given up. Cody turned and walked away.

Later, over supper at Cal and Annie's, Cody focused on Jesse, beginning to wonder what would become of the young lad. His childhood had been full of suffering; Cody hated to see Jesse suffer any more, but life wasn't always fair.

"Is Daddy going with you?" Jesse voiced at the table.

"I'm not sure, Jesse. He's … " Cody looked toward Cal for help.

Cal reached over and placed his large hand over Jesse's small one. "Your daddy is very sad … like you … " The front door opened, and they all glanced up with surprise when Shay walked into the house. His gaze moved over each individual at the table, his eyes still betrayed and hurt, but Cody read hope for the first time as well.

Jesse ran from the table and into Shay's waiting arms. Shay held the boy close. "I have to leave for a while. I'm going to get your mama."

Jesse pushed back and smiled up into Shay's face. "Can I come?"

"It's too far, and may be dangerous. I think it would be best if you stay here with Cal and Annie."

Jesse nodded. "All right, but you will bring Mama home?" he questioned.

"I will do my very best." Shay glanced over Jesse's shoulder and met Cody's gaze for the first time that day.

∘ ∘ ∘

Alana doubled over and lost the remains of her supper. She was exhausted and weak. She knew the reason why. She found Alex Cohn's eyes on her and closed her own. Was it pity she saw? She wiped her mouth on her dress and walked back to the fire. He handed her a cup of water. She drank it thirstily.

"Are you hungry?" Alex asked. She shook her head. "I'm riding into town in the morning to pick up some supplies. Can I get you anything while I am there?"

"A Bible," she uttered.

"A Bible?" he said as he lifted his eyebrows. "I was thinking you might need something more practical, shoes … a hair brush … anything of that nature?" She shook her head. Alex walked away. Why would she ask for something of such little value?

The next afternoon when Alex returned from town, he handed her the Bible. The preacher at the church had been glad to give it to him. Alana reached for it. She did not try to hide her smile. Alex eyed her curiously, not understanding why a book would mean so much to her.

"Thank you," she offered. Alana quickly grabbed some fabric and wrapped the Bible up tight.

"Well, I won't pretend to understand why you would ask for such a thing in the predicament you are now in, but you're welcome just the same." Alex turned to prepare the horses for departure. Alana followed him.

Alex knew she was afraid. He was afraid for her. For the last six months his entire life had revolved around

Mr. Bratten's quest for revenge. And now ... now he wished he had never come. He wished he had never become a part of the horrible scheme.

"You're safe with me. I promise you that." Alex didn't know why he voiced those words aloud. He turned so she would not see the heat creeping up his face.

Alana stood to the side, waiting for him to finish saddling the horse she would be riding. "I know," she whispered.

∘ ∘ ∘

"Why did you come?" Shay asked as they sat around the campfire.

"I felt like I was needed," Cody answered. He reached for the can of beans, hoping they were warm by now.

"I can hardly believe I am retracing the very same steps I just took." Shay reached for the plate of food Cody held out.

"I know it," Cody responded. They ate their food in silence. Their first intentions had been to catch up with Alana, but as they continued to talk about their plan, they realized that following behind was probably the best idea. They didn't want to risk someone getting shot even killed. Plus, Johnny had the warrant, and under law, he was in the right.

"Do you think we'll be able to buy Alana's freedom?" Shay questioned.

"I don't know, but it is the only thing I can think of at the moment."

Later, as Shay lay cloaked in the darkness staring up at the stars, he wondered if he'd ever hold his wife again. Just in the three short months they had been husband and wife, he had grown used to her being next to him. But she was not next to him tonight and probably wouldn't be for many weeks, possibly months.

Shay knew why she hadn't told him. She hadn't trusted him. She knew he loved her. But she had been uncertain if he'd still love her if he knew she was born of a black man. And she had every reason to doubt him. As a child, he had treated her horribly. Now that he thought of it, he wondered how she had ever learned to trust him in the first place.

Suddenly that night on the trail came back to him. They had been talking about the incident with the rock. She had wanted to know if he had thrown it. He hadn't, but he might as well have. It had been his idea. He told her that. He had been honest, and she had forgiven him of the incident.

Then the night before their wedding, when they had been walking on the road, she had tried to tell him. But he had said her past meant nothing to him. She had wanted him to know. Did it matter to him? Would he still love her? But he had failed...failed miserably. Why hadn't he noticed? Because at the time he hadn't wanted to face the reality that she might be. He wasn't near as strong as he thought he was.

Tears coursed down his cheeks and a sob escaped his lips. "Give me another chance," he whispered in the dark. "I don't want her last memory being that of me letting her go. Please, God, I need another chance."

∘ ∘ ∘

Alana chose not to think about Shay and Jesse. She couldn't. Mentally ... emotionally, it would be her breaking point. In the evening, when they were not riding, she read the Bible Alex had brought her. She often read until the fire light became too dim for her to make any sense of the words. Inside she felt strength, a strength that could only come from her Father. It was comforting to think that at least He would always be there.

"What is in that book? It's like you are entranced by the thing." Alana looked over at Alex who was on watch that evening. Mr. Miller and Mr. Bratten were already asleep.

"We eat food to sustain our physical bodies, don't we?"

Alex rubbed his belly. "Don't I know it? And there certainly hasn't been enough of it to go around these days." Alana laughed and it sounded strange to both of their ears. "It's nice to see you finally smile." He looked down then. "I'm sorry. I shouldn't have said that."

"No, it's all right," she said. A brief silence lingered between them. And then she continued with her illustration. "Just like food feeds our physical bodies, the Bible feeds us spiritually."

"Well, the least you could do is read the thing aloud." Alex stood to add some more wood to the dying fire.

"I'm reading in Jeremiah, chapter sixteen: 'O Lord, my strength and my fortress, my refuge in the day of affliction...'"

o o o

Johnny stared at the woman on the horse up ahead. She was carrying on a lively conversation with Mr. Cohn. So far, the only pleasure he had gotten out of the whole ordeal was watching the little boy wail as they rode out of sight.

Johnny had not figured on her being so beautiful. She had the bronze color to her skin, but so did many other people who worked hard in the sun all day. The only difference was her skin color was permanent. Her eyes were captivating. The shape of her eyes reminded him of his mother, Catherine, as much as he hated to admit it. How he detested his sister for allowing it to happen.

Even Alana's demeanor reminded him of his mother—soft spoken, yet strong willed. Ironic how two women who had never before met could be so much alike? Johnny found himself ready to be rid of the girl, and he couldn't wait to finally reach their destination. Once he turned her over to the plantation, he would never think of her again.

∘ ∘ ∘

Alana awoke suddenly. She lay cloaked in darkness and briefly wondered what had awakened her. Then she felt it again. Movement from within. Her hand went to her belly. Another movement fluttered across her hand. A smile stretched across her face. A part of Shay lived on inside of her. In the midst of all her turmoil, Alana had one ray of hope, one reason to continue living. Was this the way her mother had felt years earlier?

∘ ∘ ∘

Alex studied Alana from across the fire...the way she touched her stomach, as if she were pregnant! *She was with child?* Only a woman carrying her child would caress her stomach in such a way. Alex glanced away, unable to accept her joy over the event. This child would have no father. How could Alana smile, knowing that her baby would grow up on a plantation, knowing that her child would never experience freedom? Did Alana's husband know that his wife was with child? Did he know she was going to have his baby?

Alex turned his gaze to Mr. Bratten, who was sleeping soundly on the other side of him. How many lives had Johnny ruined just in the few short years Alex had worked for him? Alex knew he needed to get Alana away from him. He would not be a part of delivering her to a plantation to be worked like an animal, not in her present condition. He had to come up with a plan. In another month, it would be too late.

CHAPTER TWELVE

Beads of sweat began to form on the back of his neck. Someone was behind him. It was a sense that he had experienced several times before. Being a deputy often put him in intense situations. Cody shifted his gaze to where Shay lay sleeping. After a few more moments, the form behind him moved in closer. Within seconds he had the individual flat on his back, with his hands and feet pinned to the ground.

The commotion woke Shay, and he made his way toward Cody with his gun aimed at the figure lying on the ground.

Shay studied the individual and recognized the man at once. "Let him up," Shay stated. Cody hesitated, sending a questioning gaze in Shay's direction. "I know him. Let him up." Cody let the man go. The Indian stood to his feet.

"You scout?" the Indian questioned Cody.

"I'm a deputy," Cody responded.

"You move fast." The Indian turned to Shay and reached his hand out in greeting. "We meet again. You have horse. You like?"

Shay grabbed his hand in a firm handshake. "Yes, I like the horse. You trained him very well." The Indian looked toward Heaven with pride.

"Your name?" the Indian asked.

"Shay. Shay O'Connell. What is your name?"

"White Eagle. I follow all day. You not know?" White Eagle questioned. Shay looked to Cody who shook his head.

"No, we didn't hear or see a thing. I'm glad we are on friendly terms." They all laughed.

"Why ride east? You not like west?"

"It is a very long story," Shay answered.

"Come to camp. Close by. You tell story. Horses rest. They tired." Shay once again looked at Cody who nodded his approval.

∘ ∘ ∘

"For I know the plans I have for you, says the Lord. They are plans for good and not for your disaster, to give you a future and a hope. In those days when you pray, I will listen. If you look for me in earnest, you will find me when you seek me. I will be found by you, says the Lord. I will end your captivity and restore your fortunes. I will gather you out of the nations where I sent you and bring you home again to your own land." Alana closed the book and looked over at Alex. "This is my favorite scripture. It is found in Jeremiah chapter twenty-nine."

"And what are God's plans for you, Alana?" Alex shook his head. "I don't see Him saving you from this disaster."

Alana sat the Bible aside and snuggled down deeper into her warm blanket. She didn't know how to answer him.

"Alana, I'm sorry if I seem harsh. I guess I'm frustrated. I ... I don't want to see you get hurt."

Alana sighed. "I know. But contrary to what you may think, God does have a plan for me."

"Maybe he expects us to make our own plans. I'll help you make a run for it. It is the only way. The closer we get to Georgia, the more complicated it is going to be."

Alana shook her head. "If I run, I will be hunted and brought back. You know my uncle better than any of us. He won't ever give up. And if you help me escape, you will be a fugitive also."

"That doesn't matter to me, as long as you are free," Alex insisted.

"But I won't be free, Alex, don't you see. If I run, I'll never be free. Everyone I love will be in jeopardy because I chose to run."

Alana turned on her side and looked at Alex. "I admire you for wanting to help me. But I have lost my husband. And I have lost my son. I can't go back to them. I could never stand to see the pain in their eyes a second time as they led me away. And I'm afraid ... if I escaped, it would be ever so hard not to return to them because I ... I love them so much." She turned her head so he couldn't see her tears.

Alex reached across and grabbed her hand. "I'm sorry. I can think of nothing else but your freedom. I forget that your loss is much greater."

"It's all right. And I am appreciative for everything you've done." She squeezed his hand and released it.

"Where are your parents?" Alex asked, changing the subject.

"My mother passed away over a year ago. I never knew my real father." Clyde suddenly entered her thoughts, and she was surprised to feel no resentment toward him. God had changed her heart. Alana offered up a prayer for the man who had never once offered her anything of worth. *Send someone to show him the way.*

o o o

"My people glad to see you. They honor man who heal my son."

"You have given me the horse. I don't need to be honored," Shay stated.

"No ... we honor you with feast and dance." White Eagle turned to his people and spoke to them in their language. White Eagle then motioned for Shay and Cody to follow him. He led them into the same tepee Shay had been in the year previously.

"My son," White Eagle proudly proclaimed as he pointed to the boy sitting by the fire. The boy was sharpening knives. "Chequoa?" he gestured for the boy to come to him. The boy walked toward them with no limp whatsoever. One would never know the ordeal he had faced nearly a year ago.

"Chequoa my first son. You save from sickness. He chief someday." It was then that the reality of the situation struck Shay. White Eagle was the chief. Shay knew how important the first born son of a chief was. No wonder White Eagle was so intent on thanking him.

Chequoa reached out his hand in greeting. "I thank you for my life."

"You know English well," Shay complimented.

"My father says it is important to communicate with white man. He is right. It saved my life." White Eagle sent his son back to the fire.

"Tell me story. Why go east?" White Eagle questioned.

The feast and dance lasted several hours. When it finally came to an end, White Eagle held up his hands for silence. He turned to Shay.

"What you want for reward?" Anything? What?"

Shay shook his head. "No gift. You gave me a horse. She is a fine horse and more than enough."

"No, I give something else. What? You want weapon?"

Again Shay shook his head. "Nothing," he voiced.

White Eagle ignored him. "You want new wife?"

"No, I want my wife back. I am on my way to get her."

"Ah," White Eagle's mind was busy forming a plan. "We go fight ... get wife back."

Cody finally jumped in. "We plan on fighting with words ... not weapons."

White Eagle looked confused. "Weapons work better," he argued. Shay and Cody laughed. White Eagle frowned.

"Thank you, White Eagle, for your generosity. You have given me more than enough." Shay reached out his hand. "Farewell, good friend."

White Eagle raised a hand. "Wait," he stated and then walked away. He soon returned with another horse. "Present for wife. She need horse to ride west." Tears filled Shay's eyes at the man's generosity and encouraging words. Alana would indeed need a horse to ride west. He tied the black horse behind Heaven.

o o o

When they began passing workers in the fields, Alex

knew that they were getting close. He watched as a woman struggled to pick up her barrel of cotton and transport it to the bin. Alana would be one of them soon. Alex cringed at the thought.

They soon came to a large plantation house, and Johnny ordered them all to wait while he went inside. He later returned with the supervisor.

Charlie, the supervisor, studied the young woman in front of him. One would never know she was black, not unless told, anyway. "Alana, I will show you to your living quarters. Follow me."

Alex quickly dismounted and helped Alana from her horse. "Sir?" Alex inquired. The supervisor turned. "I'm looking for employment. Do you have any openings?"

"Wait here. I'll be back shortly." Charlie replied.

Alex nodded. He watched Alana until she was out of sight, desperately trying to control his emotions.

"What do you think you are doing?" Johnny angrily retorted. "You work for me."

"Not anymore. I am now giving you my resignation."

"You stupid fool. You make more money for me in a week, than you'll make at this place in a month. I can guarantee that."

"At least I'll be able to sleep at night." Alex would not look away. Johnny would not get the last word.

Johnny turned from the revulsion he saw in Alex's eyes. He brought his horse to a gallop and rode away.

o o o

Charlie pushed open the door to the small room. "You will share this room with four other women. That bed over there is empty." Charlie watched as she placed her small bundle on the empty bed. "You will begin working in the fields tomorrow. You may not leave the premises under any circumstances. You are not allowed near the main house. You cannot speak to Mr. Stanton, his wife, nor his children. Is this understood?" Alana nodded. Charlie turned and walked out the door.

Charlie moved back toward the main house. *Why had Johnny been so intent on bringing her in?* He knew there was a reason behind it all. Charlie had signed the petition stating he would not sell Alana. Johnny had paid him handsomely for signing it. More money than anyone would ever offer him for the girl. As he came upon the house, the young man who had previously asked him for work stood to his feet.

"Your name?" Charlie asked.

"Alex. Alex Cohn."

"Are you of any relation to the girl?" Charlie demanded.

"No, of course not. I helped capture and bring her in."

"I need another overseer. You will be required to ride out in the morning when the slaves go out to the fields. You will watch them. Make sure they stay on task. Make sure they are all accounted for and then ride back in when they return to their living quarters." Charlie noticed the young man's brief hesitation.

"I'll take it," Alex finally replied. He followed Charlie inside.

° ° °

"Anotha one. Thangs are cramped enough. They's thinks we's animals or somethin'." Alana looked away from their stares.

"Are yous sure yous black? Yor daddy must a been ta white owna, an they sent yous away I's suppose. Poor thang. Just enough black to make yous a slave."

"Josie, stop it," another girl said. "She's not always so mean. I'm Hannah," she introduced.

"I'm Alana." She now knew two of the women's names.

"That's my's bed," Josie announced.

"The man ... he said it was ... empty," Alana voiced with uncertainty.

"It's not," Josie stated angrily. "I's planning ta move there tis mornin' but I's dinna have time to move my's stuff. Now get yor stuff off my's bed." Alana moved to do so, but Hannah stepped in.

"Stop it, Josie. Stop it right now. You have no claims on that bed. You've slept on the top one for months now." Josie stomped her foot before flouncing outside and slamming the door.

"I can move my stuff," Alana voiced.

"No," Hannah said sharply. "You let her boss you around like that and she'll make your life miserable." Hannah turned and lay down on her own bed.

∘ ∘ ∘

"Someone is coming," Cody voiced. Shay also saw the dust accumulating from behind. Shay and Cody continued riding, but at a slower pace, allowing the rider to gain on them.

"That horse looks familiar." Cody stated as he turned back. "I'll be ... It's father!"

"James?" Shay said incredulously. It wasn't long until James joined them.

"Father ... what are you doing here?" Cody stated as he got off his horse and gave his father a hug.

"Mary told me to leave," he said with a grin. "She said I could stay and wonder what was happening, or I could come and help it happen. I thought I could be of some assistance. I grew up in Georgia. I know the best routes to take."

"I appreciate that, James," Shay expressed with gratitude.

"They took Alana then?" James questioned.

Shay nodded. "Yes ... a few weeks back. We've decided we'll approach the plantation and try to buy her freedom.

"That might work. Alana's not used to hard work. She means nothing to them. Surely they'll be reasonable," James replied.

"That's what we're praying," Shay stated hopefully.

"Well, let's not be wasting any more time on account of me," James stated with a smile. The three men once again began riding across the dusty terrain.

o o o

Alana picked up her full container of cotton and moved toward the loading wagon. Sweat drizzled down both sides of her face. Her throat had never felt so dry. She knew she needed water. Suddenly she tripped, and her basket flew from her arms, toppling over and spilling the cotton.

"Watch where's yous goin," Josie spat in her direction.

Alana stooped and began to pick up the fallen cotton.

"I saw what happened," Alex yelled as he made his

way toward them. "You tripped her. If you ever lay so much as a finger on her again, you'll be punished."

Josie bowed her head. "It will not happen again, sire."

Alex moved toward Alana. "Are you all right?" he asked. She nodded. He knelt beside her and began picking up the spilt cotton.

"Don't ... you'll bring attention to us," Alana voiced as she noticed the peculiar glances their direction.

Alex paused before standing to his feet and walking away. Alana turned back to the task at hand. A tear slipped down her cheek, and she quickly wiped it away. She didn't want to be weak. Moments later Alex returned with a dipper full of water. How had he known? Sometimes it scared her how well he could read her thoughts ... her emotions. Alana gazed into his saddened green eyes, hoping he read the thankfulness behind her own.

Alana reached out for the dipper and hurriedly drank the water. "Thank you," she whispered before reaching for the basket once again and moving toward the wagon.

○ ○ ○

"We should be there in three more days." James stated. "Possibly two if we continue at this pace."

Shay stretched and then yawned. "I've never been more tired in my entire life."

It's the anxiety that is so wearing," Cody added.

James eyed Shay from across the fire. He had a plan, but would Shay adhere to it?

"Shay ... I've been thinking. What if I went out to the plantation ... alone ... now wait, Shay," James held up his hand motioning for Shay to hear him out. "If you stayed in town and let me go, I think it would be best. Someone who is not so imminently impacted by the dilemma at hand would be able to come away with more information." James paused to the let his words sink in.

"Say, for example, I go as an esteemed older gentleman looking to purchase a slave. If I come across Alana, I'll put forth an offer for her." James hurried on when he noticed Shay begin to shake his head. "Shay, you are too caught up in the emotion of it all. That is understandable, but it could be to your detriment."

Shay looked away, hating the fact that James was correct. "You're right." Several moments of silence passed. Finally, Shay's eyes met James. "I'll give you one day. Just one day. And if your plan doesn't work, I'm going to the plantation. I've been away from her for long enough."

. . .

Alex studied Alana's movements. She was not using her right arm. He watched as she pushed the full basket of cotton over the wagon. Why was she using her left arm and not her right one? When she turned, he could see pain etched in her eyes. She had seemed fine last night when the work day had ended. What had he missed? He would find out tonight.

Later, after curfew, Alex stood outside Alana's bedroom window. He tapped on it once. Nothing. He tapped again. A shadow moved toward the window and the curtain parted. He could see it was her, but he knew she could not see him in the darkness. "Alana," he whispered. "It's me, Alex. Come outside." He moved to the door and waited for her. The door creaked open and Alana slipped out quietly.

"I know you're in pain. Is there anything I can do?" Alex gasped as she lowered the back of her nightgown. The initials, *GP* were initialed across her right shoulder blade. He reached out and traced the inflamed letters. She flinched at his touch.

"When did it happen?" Alex angrily stated.

"Last night … when you were in town."

Alex reached for her hand. "Come with me." Alana followed him to the barn where he grabbed some wire and picked the lock to the tack room. He rummaged around until he found what he was looking for.

"This is used to treat infection with horses." He opened the bottle and motioned for her to turn around. He felt her tense as he gently rubbed the ointment on her skin. He paused, trying to stop the shaking in his hand. He felt the fury building up inside of him. Nothing could be done now. Nothing. Wasn't it enough that she had to be here? Did she now have to be scarred for life? Where was her God, the God that she served so faithfully.

"It's all right, Alex. I'll be fine." He hadn't realized she had turned. He stood studying her. How could she be so strong? How could she be so forgiving?

Alex thrust the bottle toward her. "Take this and apply it to your back twice a day." He strode out of the barn, lest she notice the tear that had fallen on his cheek.

° ° °

Alana was returning to her room after supper when she overheard the confrontational voices close by. She knew it would be wise to bypass the area entirely, but she could not bring herself to do so. She stood hidden by the edge of the barn, watching the two people argue. The man she had seen several times from afar. He was the master's son. The woman next to him was a slave and as soon as she spoke, Alana recognized her voice.

"You cannot come near me anymore. It is unsafe."

"Unsafe for who?" Josie spat back at him. "Ya didna thank it unsafe a few weeks ago."

The man tried to go around her, but Josie reached out and grabbed his arm. "David ... ain't ya' gonna help me."

"To you I am Mr. Stanton. My position deserves respect." He walked away, while Josie slid to the ground, sobs shaking her entire body.

Alana slowly moved toward her, not knowing what to say ... what to do. "Josie? Are you all right?" Alana consoled.

"Go away," Josie cried. "Just go away."

"Maybe I can help," Alana offered.

"Ya cannot help me now. No one can."

"Josie, perhaps I can if you give me a chance." Alana reached out and touched the young woman's shoulder.

"I said *go away*," Josie screamed. Alana slowly backed away.

○○○

James rode toward the big plantation house. He had always hated slavery. And after having been away from it for all these years, the thought of owning another individual was even more oppressive. He soon rode into the courtyard. A man met him at the gate.

"May I help you?" the man asked.

"I hope so. I am here in Atlanta on business and am interested in purchasing a slave. I have heard such high regard for the workmanship and respect of the slaves you have here at the Georgian Plantation."

The man nodded. "You need to see Charlie. Follow me." The man knocked on the door to the side of the house. The door opened a few seconds later.

"Charlie, this man is interested in purchasing a slave."

Charlie nodded. "Come in and have a seat. Are you interested in a male or female slave? We have several we might part with—for a nice price, of course."

"I'm looking for a female. My wife has been feeling under the weather lately and needs help with cooking and cleaning and the like.

"I think I have just the girl. She is strong and well behaved. Would you like to go out to the fields? I'll let you take a look from a distance, and you can see what you think."

"Yes, I'd like to go take a look."

Charlie smiled. Only a few days ago, Mr. Stanton's young son David had come to see him, asking him for a favor. He had told him there was a young slave by the name of Josie. Josie Tally. He wanted her to be sold as soon as possible. Before leaving his office, David had thrown a large sum of money on his desk. "You'll receive the other half when it's done," David had said. This was Charlie's chance to get the other half.

James asked several questions as they rode out to the fields, wondering how he'd ever find Alana in the midst of so many people. Charlie finally stopped and pointed to a girl picking cotton only a few feet away from them. James feigned interest.

"What do you think?" Charlie asked.

"And you think she'd be reliable?" James stated, trying to buy more time to look around. "I do have some more business to attend to before I make any definite decisions … ." He stopped mid-sentence as he saw Alana for the first time. How could he have missed her?

"You were saying?" Charlie inquired.

James still found it hard to find his voice. Alana. His niece. James studied her. She looked fine. Healthy. Shay would want to know every detail.

"Do you see someone you'd like better?" Charlie asked.

"Actually … I was wondering about that girl there. What is her name?"

Charlie followed James' finger, but instantly tensed when he saw who James meant.

"The plantation cannot sell her."

"But why? I can pay more if that's the problem."

Charlie shook his head, firm with his decision. "She's under an old contract. Her ancestors have been here for generations."

"Not for any amount of money?" James persisted.

"No amount of money," Charlie insisted.

Charlie was lying. James knew that. Alana had only been there a few days. James looked away as Alana turned toward them. He did not want her to see him. Charlie turned also, and they rode back to the plantation house.

"Thank you, Charlie. I'll be in touch," James stated as they separated at the gate.

° ° °

"What do you mean, they won't sell her? What is she to

them?" Shay was furious with the news James had just given him.

"I tried everything. I asked for a dollar amount, and he wouldn't budge. The only thing I can think is that my brother is in on it somehow. It just doesn't add up."

Shay stopped pacing and sat back down at the table. "Tell me again. What did she look like? I want every detail. Was she sad? Hurt?"

James reached out and touched his shoulder. "She was fine. She looked good in spite of her circumstances. Perhaps a bit tired. The work is exhausting, I'm sure. But all in all she looked like she was holding up rather well."

Shay stood to his feet again. "I'm not sure I can stand it anymore. I need to do something. I can't just sit here. I'm sorry, but I'm going there tomorrow. If only to get a glimpse of her, I'm going." Shay strode to the door and walked out.

Cody looked to his father. "We're going to have to come up with another plan."

James ran a hand through his graying hair. "I know, but what? Buying her freedom was our best option. Nothing else will be nearly as promising."

CHAPTER THIRTEEN

Alex knocked on the door. He already knew the office was empty. He had just seen Charlie leave, but he wanted to make sure. He checked the handle. Sure enough, it was locked. He reached inside his shirt and took out the wire. He looked around. All was quiet. He quickly picked the lock, opened the door, and slipped inside.

Alex had been standing right next to them—Charlie and the gentleman looking to buy a slave. Alex had gone weak when the man had pointed directly to Alana and asked to buy her. But when Alex had turned to look at the man, he had seen the heartache and pain behind his eyes. And as the man had stared at Alana with compassion, Alex had finally grasped the situation. The gentleman knew Alana. There was no doubt in Alex's mind that he knew her. And he loved her. But who was he? And why wouldn't Charlie let him buy her?

He rummaged through a few drawers, not finding what he was looking for. Johnny had to be the reason Charlie would not sell Alana. A black box under the desk caught his attention, but of course it was locked too. Where would one hide a key? Alex turned and glanced at the picture on the wall. He walked over to it. Slowly he withdrew the picture and sat it on the floor. There was a small key on the nail. And the key fit the black box.

Alex lifted the lid and grabbed the stack of papers, anxiously flipping through them. Finally, he found what he was looking for.

In exchange for one thousand dollars, the Georgian Plantation agrees not to sell Alana Blackwell or any of her descendants by request of Johnny D. Bratten of Atlanta, Georgia.

Alex slammed the box shut and relocked it. He hung the key on the nail and replaced the picture. Taking one last look around to make sure everything was in order, he turned the lock on the door and swiftly pulled the door closed behind him.

○ ○ ○

Alana listened to the short gasps coming from above her bed. She stood up in the darkness. "Josie? Josie, what's wrong?" she asked.

"I need the midwife. Will ya' go an' get her?" Alana recognized the fear in Josie's voice and quickly left to find the midwife. The night was dark, but Alana hurried her steps in the direction of the midwife's room. Alana was thankful she knew where she was going. Had she not been carrying a baby, she never would have thought to ask Alex about it.

Coming to the door, Alana reached out her fist and knocked on the door. "I'm coming," a tired voice answered. The dark woman opened the door, a black bag firmly placed under her arm. "Who's having a baby at this hour?" the midwife questioned.

"Josie. Josie Tally," Alana answered.

"Josie? I had no idea she was expecting." They walked quickly toward Alana's room.

After examining her, the midwife turned to face the others in the room. "You should probably leave. It might be some time before ... this ends." Lena, Hannah, Sally and Alana turned to go.

"Alana ... I want Alana ta' stay," Josie pleaded. Alana looked to the midwife who nodded her consent. Alana went to Josie's side and took her hand.

"How long have you been bleeding?" the midwife asked.

"Since yesterday mornin'," Josie voiced.

"You should have come sooner. The baby ... you are losing your baby. You may have already."

Alana watched as Josie turned her head in shame. Had she known? Why would she purposefully not go to the midwife, unless of course, she didn't want the baby? The confrontation from the other night played through Alana's mind. The realization of the situation began to dawn on her.

"Do you know how far along you may be?" the midwife asked.

"I'm not sure ... three months." Josie let out another long gasp before finally relaxing.

"It's ... it's done," the midwife stated. Alana turned to Josie who lay expressionless, her eyes staring at the ceiling.

"No work for two days," the midwife instructed while she cleaned up the area. "The more rest you get, the sooner you will recover." The midwife finished and then left.

Josie turned to Alana with tears on her cheeks. "I wanted it ta' die. I wanted it, but I didna' know it would feel like this. I didna, know."

"God loves you, Josie."

"I dona' deserve His love."

"None of us deserves it, but it is there just the same."

Josie turned her head away, tears still streaming down her cheeks. "Tell the otha's they's can come back now," Josie finally said.

o o o

Alex stood on the sidewalk wondering where to look for the gentleman. He knew the man would be staying at some sort of lodging. But how could Alex ask around when he did not have a name to go by? Many men would fit the description.

A man passed by Alex on the boardwalk and Alex turned and studied him as the man stepped off the boardwalk and began to cross the street. A chill ran down Alex's spine when it finally dawned on him who the man was. He had seen the man as he fell to his knees. He remembered the man's face, full of agony. Alana's husband had come for her!

Alex felt joy for the first time in weeks. Alana's husband coming would mean the world to her. Alex had seen the rejection in her eyes. She had thought her husband wouldn't want her anymore, because she was black. But she had been wrong. He did love her.

Alex watched as the man went into the hotel. Alex crossed the street and entered the hotel, watching as the man went upstairs and into the third room at the top. Alex waited a moment and then went up the stairs. He hesitated before knocking. He had no idea what to expect. He would completely understand if the man met him at the door with a gun. He had taken his wife, after all. Before he could decide what to do, the door opened. It was a man he didn't recognize.

"Can I help you?" the man asked, staring at him with question.

"Yes... may I come in please?" Alex asked. The man studied him, leery of letting just anyone in. Who wouldn't be on guard after what they had just been through?

"I have some information about Alana." The man stepped aside and Alex walked in. He surveyed the room. Two men sat at a table. One was the gentleman who had been at the plantation. The other was Alana's husband. Shay recognized him immediately and flew across the table onto Alex.

"You took my wife..." Shay wrestled Alex to the floor, quickly pinning Alex beneath him.

Both James and Cody dragged Shay off Alex. "Perhaps we should hear what the man has to say before we finish him off." Cody stated with only a hint of a smile.

"How could I ever trust the likes of him?" Shay resisted.

"I didn't say we had to trust him... just hear what he has to say," Cody reminded.

Alex took the offered seat, rubbing his arm that had been crunched beneath Shay's elbow. "It didn't take me long to realize I had made a huge mistake. Mr. Bratten hadn't told me the entire story. I thought we were tracking down an escaped slave, not a married woman who had a child. I would change it all if I could. I planned a way for us to escape, but she wouldn't leave..."

"Why... why wouldn't she leave?" Shay questioned with doubt.

"She said that if she escaped, it still wouldn't mean she was free. She didn't want the people she loved to live in jeopardy. And she didn't want you to face her being taken away again. She felt it would be selfish.

"When we got to the plantation, I asked for a job and was given one as an overseer. I will do absolutely everything in my power to help you free her."

"Why? Why are you suddenly so willing to help? You took her from her family to live as a slave. How do I know you're not still working for Alana's uncle?"

"I guess you don't know ... for sure ... but ... I'll prove it ... Come out to the plantation and ask her yourself," Alex finally voiced.

"I can see her?" Shay shot to his feet, excitement immediately replacing his anger.

Alex nodded. "Come tomorrow ... in the evening. I'll wait by the gate, and I'll take you to her."

○ ○ ○

Shay's hands were shaking as he tightened the cinch on his saddle. He mounted his horse and rode out in the direction James had told him. Heaven sensed his urgency and traveled quickly. Shay noticed Alex by the gate.

"I want you to follow me. We'll go out to the fields. Alana must not see you until all the other workers have gone. When I ride off, that is your signal that it is safe to go to her. When I find Alana missing, I will notify the other overseers that I am returning for her, and I will come back to fetch her. You must stay in the fields until we are completely out of sight. Then ride out slowly. If you are questioned, tell them you were here to see me."

"I appreciate this ... "

Alex sighed. "It is the least I can do. Be prepared for

the impact your appearance may have on Alana. She has given up hope of seeing you again."

They rode toward the fields, and Shay couldn't help but stare at the slaves as they passed by each one in the fields. Their shirts were drenched in sweat. Their children played nearby, oblivious to their parents' hard work. He found himself searching for Alana. After some distance, Alex stopped.

Shay saw her before Alex even had time to point her out. It was as if his eyes drew right to her. He saw how she smiled at the woman who worked next to her. He watched as she picked up her basket and carried it to the cart. His eyes never left her.

The bell sounded five times, and the workers made their way to the carts with their baskets in hand. Then they began the walk back to their quarters. Alana started to go with them but Alex had already ridden toward her, and Shay watched as he bent and whispered something in her ear. Alana began to backtrack to where she had been working previously. It seemed an eternity before everyone was gone. Alex signaled for Shay to go ahead, and he rode out of sight.

Shay took a deep breath. "Stop shaking," he whispered to himself. He began to walk toward her. Alana's back was to him but as he drew closer she turned. "Alex?" Alana turned and her face went white. Shay watched as she fell to the ground.

"Alana. ... Alana, I'm here. I'm here." Alana opened her eyes. Was she dreaming?

"Alana?" She looked up into Shay's face. "Alana, I love you." He was on his knees in front of her.

She reached out and touched his face. "Why did you come?" she asked.

"You're my wife. I had to come."

"But what kind of life can you have here? Your wife is a slave."

Shay shifted on the ground in order to find a more comfortable position. Once seated, he pulled her onto his lap.

"I'll find a lawyer. We'll find some way to get you free." Hope filled Alana's eyes, but she wasn't completely convinced.

"Where's Jesse?" she voiced with concern.

"He stayed with Cal and Annie. I thought it would be best. He won't be happy until I bring you home. I won't be either."

Alana looked away. "I lied to you. I'm sorry."

Shay turned her face back toward him and looked into her eyes. "Alana, you tried to tell me. I wouldn't listen. But even if you had told me before our marriage, it wouldn't have changed anything. I would have married you anyway." He caressed her cheek and knew she was trying not to cry.

"I thought ... you didn't care anymore. I thought you—"

"I could never stop caring...never," Shay whispered against her hair.

They both stood to their feet as they heard the rider approaching. Shay turned toward Alana, and for the first time noticed her belly. His eyes rose to meet hers, full of question, full of wonder. She took his hand and placed it on her stomach.

"We're going to have a baby," she said. Shay took his other hand and placed it on her belly too. His baby? He was going to be a father? He dropped to his knees, placing his face against her. The baby moved against the pressure, and they both smiled. Then Shay and Alana turned as they heard a horse approaching.

Alex stopped short, hating to interrupt them, but knowing they had already had too much time together. "We need to go, Alana," he finally forced himself to say. He watched as Shay reached for her one last time.

Shay's mouth found Alana's and he kissed her fervently, wondering if this would be the last time he ever would. Finally he relinquished her, and Alana slowly made her way toward Alex.

◦ ◦ ◦

Shay lay in bed … alone … remembering every detail from just a few hours before. To see Alana again after months of separation … to hold her again … to feel her lips … and then the feeling that had risen within knowing that she carried his child.

"Why, Lord? Why?" A tear slipped unchecked down his cheek. Perhaps he would never know why, but it would not stop him from praying for Alana's release from slavery. He would never stop believing.

A feeling of anger rose up within Shay as he thought of Alana's calloused hands. He had felt the blisters and had pretended they were not there. Shay had experienced hurtful moments during his lifetime, but nothing like this. There was no feeling that compared to the devastation he now felt. The feeling of watching someone he loved more than anything else on earth be hurt, and feeling completely helpless to do anything about it. But God was not helpless! Shay knew he must remember that.

Shay smiled as he thought of Alana's round belly. How had he not noticed the moment he saw her? It had been so obvious, yet he had been so excited about seeing her, he must have ignored the small detail. He would be a father … and he was scared … more scared than ever. The possibility of never knowing his child rose to the surface, but he instantly threw the thought aside. He couldn't afford to think that way. He would speak to a lawyer tomorrow. Surely something could be done. Shay's body finally gave into his exhaustion and his eyes closed in sleep.

◇ ◇ ◇

"Are you Mr. Webb?" Shay asked.

"I am."

"I hope you can help me. Do you have time to talk?" Mr. Webb nodded and led Shay into his office.

Mr. Webb watched as Shay surveyed his walls, studying the articles. "I've won several cases here in Atlanta, and my practice has become quite large. I hired an associate attorney two years back and just recently a second. Even with three of us, we stay quite busy."

Shay shared with him the story of Alana. Mr. Webb listened intently, but his frown deepened as Shay spoke.

Finally after a few moments of silence, Mr. Webb began to speak. "Mr. O'Connell, I don't make a habit of dealing with slavery issues. It is such a controversial subject. In fact, one of the cases I lost several years ago dealt with a man in slavery, and I vowed to never again represent a case of that nature. People never forget the cases you lose, and I struggled for quite a while to overcome it. Don't get me wrong, I feel for you and your wife. It is most definitely an unfortunate circumstance. But I'm afraid I can't help you. I'm sorry." Mr. Webb stood to his feet, and Shay knew that their conversation was over.

Shay walked to the door and let himself out. He stood for a moment on the boardwalk, a bit shaken by Mr. Webb's refusal to take Alana's case. The door opened behind Shay, and he turned to see if perhaps Mr. Webb had changed his mind. It wasn't Mr. Webb, but rather a young man not much older than Shay.

"I overheard your conversation with Mr. Webb. I'm the new attorney he just hired, and I'd like to take your case.

Shay eyed the young man curiously. "Have you ever tried a case before?" Shay asked.

"Not my own," he stated honestly. "But I have sat in on several, and I'll do a good job. You will not be disappointed."

Shay stood studying the young man. "I'm sorry … I'm just … a bit taken back. I really need to win this case … "

"And what makes you think I can't win this case, besides my inexperience," the young lawyer said with a smile.

Shay finally smiled. He was already growing quite fond of the man.

"Listen … I don't want to disappoint you, but you won't find another lawyer willing to take a case dealing with slavery issues, at least not in this area."

"So why are you interested in taking it?" Shay couldn't help asking.

"I've never been known to hide behind the coattails of the influential. Also, I don't usually eavesdrop, but I overheard the story you shared with Mr. Webb. I'd like to help."

"It would be nice to know the name of my new lawyer," Shay stated, holding out his hand.

The man smiled. "Mr. Sawyer—Brady Sawyer."

"My name is Shay O'Connell. Do you have time to come by the hotel? I'd like you to meet some other people here with me. Then you could fill us in on what you have planned for this case."

"Sure. Lead the way," Brady stated.

They walked to the hotel, and when Shay opened the door to the hotel room, he could see the shocked expressions of both James and Cody.

Whether Brady could hold up in court would remain to be seen, but he knew the legal system well and shared with them his goal for Alana.

"So, Alana is pregnant? I will present that before the court in hopes that they will hear us as quickly as possible. We certainly don't want Alana to have the baby at the plantation. I would desperately like to see her freed before that time."

"And do you think that's possible," James responded with question. "That is only a few short weeks away."

"It is entirely possible, Mr. Bratten."

"You can't just go into the courtroom demanding that they hand her over. You've got to have a plan," James persisted.

Brady wasn't unnerved in the least. "I do have a plan in mind," Brady offered with a smile. "I need a couple days to research some information. There have been cases that, after they've been won, are used to bring the same ruling in another case, even though there hasn't been a set decree prescribed."

"I'm not sure I understand," Cody admitted.

"Say, for example there was a man who died of a

sickness. His family believes that the medicine the doctor prescribed had added to his sickness, instead of helping him, and so they take the doctor to court. The jury agrees with the family and the doctor who gave them the medicine now owes them a lot of money.

"Then, say, several more months pass. Now a woman dies of a similar sickness. After reading about the man who died previously, the husband realizes his wife had been taking the same medication. He now takes the doctor who prescribed the medicine for his wife to court, using the ruling he read about as his persuasion. He also wins."

Cody nodded, now understanding. "So, what you are saying is that we need to find a ruling or verdict that is similar to Alana's situation and use it as our persuasion in court to bring about her freedom."

"Exactly. If another trial of the same sort has been tried, and they have a ruling to prove it, the judge will often stay with the same verdict. I have rarely seen it otherwise."

"You had me somewhat scared when you entered this room," James stated to Brady. "But I do think he knows what he's doing," James directed across the table to Shay. They all laughed.

o o o

Josie lay reading the Bible Alana had left with her.

At dawn he appeared again in the temple courts, where all the people gathered around him, and he sat down to teach them. The teachers of the law and the Pharisees brought in a woman caught in adultery. They made her stand before the group and

*said to Jesus, "Teacher, this woman was caught in
the act of adultery. In the Law, Moses commanded
us to stone such a woman. Now what do you say?"*

*They were using this question as a trap, in order to
have a basis for accusing him. But Jesus bent down
and started to write on the ground with his finger.
When they kept on questioning him, he straightened up and said to them "If any one of you is
without sin, let him be the first to throw a stone
at her." Again he stooped down and wrote on the
ground.*

*At this, those who heard began to go away one at
a time, the older ones first, until only Jesus was
left with the woman still standing there. Jesus
straightened up and asked her, "Woman, where are
they? Has no one condemned you?" "No one, sir,"
she said. "Then neither do I condemn you," Jesus
declared. "Go now and leave your life of sin."*

John 8:2–11 NIV

Josie closed the book. Jesus had accepted the woman
in the Bible. He had loved her regardless of her sin. Josie
could not change her past, but she did have the ability
to change her tomorrows. "Lord … I believe," she whispered in the empty room.

A loud knock sounded on the door and Charlie
entered. "Pack up your belongings. A man from Savannah has purchased you. You'll be leaving shortly." Josie
nodded. She knew this was coming, and it was for the
best. She needed a place where no one would know her
past … her failings.

"Sir … " Charlie turned toward her. "Could ya'
please write a note in this here Bible?" Charlie walked

toward her and hesitantly took the pen. Josie spoke the words she wished him to write as she moved to pack her belongings.

　　　　　　　　　　○ ○ ○

Shay and Cody sat combing through books, newspapers, and any other written materials that were relevant.

"The library will be closing in an hour." Both men glanced up at the librarian, nodded, and turned back to the articles they were reading.

Black Slave Goes Free. The title instantly grabbed Cody's attention. As he read, beads of sweat began to form upon his forehead. He screeched his chair back, causing Shay to look up in surprise. "I found it," Cody announced.

Shay dropped the article he was reading and followed Cody toward the door. The librarian followed them.

"You aren't allowed to take documents of that sort out of the library."

"Can you please make an exception this once? Upon my life, I promise that I will return this document as soon as we are finished with it." The woman hesitated for a moment and then shooed them out the door.

　　　　　　　　　　○ ○ ○

Brady looked over at Shay and Cody with a pleased smile on his face. "This might work. It just might work." Brady paced the room in deep thought.

"I'll need all of your help. Who is willing to travel?" They all raised their hands. Brady laughed. "All right. I need to go to Charleston, where this trial took place. I will need to know exactly what took place in this trial so we can match Alana's trial accordingly.

"The next thing I'll need is a document showing the lineage of Alana's father, Jesse Blackwell. It should have come here with Alana. It is supposed to follow the owner of the slave. Alex, can we depend on you to weasel into Charlie's office again?" Alex smiled and nodded.

Brady turned to James. "Do you remember anything about Jesse's father or mother?"

James nodded. "My father purchased them both when Jesse's mother was pregnant with him. She died during childbirth. Jesse's father raised him alone."

"Do you remember anything about their ancestry?" Brady questioned.

"Jesse's mother was Spanish and wasn't dark like his father."

"If the lineage papers are in Charlie's office, it will benefit us greatly, but it would be of further help if I could explain to the jury where these people came from and who they were married to." Brady continued to pace the room. "If the jury sees them as people with lives instead of merely as slaves, Alana's dilemma will have a greater effect on them." Brady turned toward James. "Do you think you can go to the estate where you were raised? Could there be any information that your father once had on Jesse's parents tucked away in his files somewhere?"

"I know just the place to look. I'll do it," James replied.

"I'd like to ride along with my father," Cody requested.

Brady nodded. "You'll get more done together. It would be nice if someone could come with me ... "

"Anything's better than sitting here waiting," Shay interrupted, standing to his feet.

CHAPTER FOURTEEN

When Alana returned from the fields, she was startled to find Josie gone. Darkness soon fell and Alana became concerned. As the other women got ready for bed, Alana set out to see if she could find her. She stopped and asked a few women whom Josie had spent time with before, but they had not seen her. Alana made her way toward the barn in search if Alex. As she came closer, she could see the figure of a man. She realized it wasn't Alex as she came upon him and turned abruptly, but not before the man saw her.

"Where are you going?" he asked. He walked closer. "Why are you out so late?" She recognized him from the night he had been arguing with Josie.

"I'm looking for Josie Tally," Alana voiced timidly. "She wasn't in our room when I returned from the fields this evening." She saw his eyes skim her entire body. She instantly felt uneasy.

"The whereabouts of Josie are none of your business," he stated as he took a step closer. A horse whinnied from behind them. Alana breathed a sigh of relief when she saw who it was.

"Alana!" Alex said in a sharp tone of voice. "You know better than to be out of your quarters at this hour." Alex quickly tied his horse to the post and walked to her. "If I ever find you out again after curfew, Charlie will be notified." He grabbed her arm a bit roughly and began to escort her back to her room. After walking several feet, Alex glanced behind him before quickly pulling Alana behind an old outbuilding.

"Alana, you scared me to death. David Stanton is not a safe man to be around. Especially alone. I've heard rumors about his treatment of the slave girls, particularly the ... more ... attractive ones. Don't ever come out here again after dark, unless you're with me." Alana trembled under his touch.

Alex tipped her chin up. "Don't cry. I'm sorry I spoke to you like I did, but I didn't want Mr. Stanton to think I was rescuing you." He gently squeezed her arm, and they began walking again toward her room.

"I was afraid for Josie," Alana finally voiced. "I have not seen her all evening."

Alex sighed. He might have known Alana was only looking out for someone else's wellbeing. "I'm sorry, Alana, but Josie was sold this morning. She has gone to a plantation in Savannah. I had the opportunity to speak with her new owner. He seemed like a very kind man. Hopefully that will give you some consolation." They reached Alana's room, and she bid Alex goodnight.

○ ○ ○

James was amazed at the new buildings and farms that had sprung up from what he had once known as bare land. Cody listened intently as his father spoke of the life he had lived as a child. James pointed out the homes he recognized and talked fondly about the families who used to live there.

When they came to the outskirts of town, James saw the big estate situated way back from the road. How many times had he traveled this road? Tears came to his eyes as he thought of his childhood. His parents had done what they thought was best with their children. They didn't know they were pushing their children away by their strict rules and demanding expectations.

James felt bad for the way his mother's life had ended. He had learned of her death from his brother, Johnny. It had been the only letter he had ever received from home. He remembered the painful words, even to this day. *Our mother is dead. She lost her mind and will to live due to the loss of three children, one who drowned, and two who deserted her.* Had he truly played a part in his mother's death? James supposed he would never truly know.

James wished his father were still alive. He wished he could tell him he was sorry. He wished he could tell him that he loved him. James dismounted his horse and stared in silence at his childhood home. Cody stood silent, allowing his father to dwell on memories from the past. Finally James turned to his son.

"Well, what should we do? Waltz in like we own the place, or be devious and sneak in?"

Cody laughed. "I'm sure we won't get far if we waltz in, so let's leave our horses tied back behind those trees. We'll walk in a little further and stake out the property." James agreed and they led their horses out of sight.

After several minutes of no activity, James stated he would go in. "I know where father kept the legal documents. If you see anyone coming, make a signal of some kind." Cody chirped three times like a bird. James smiled and moved quickly toward the front door. The door was not locked and he slipped inside the house.

Everything was as he remembered it. The same rug

still lay in the center hall. The stand was still by the door with a vase of flowers on it. James made his way down the hall. He could hear no one. He passed one door and then another. At the third door, he opened it and went inside, gently closing it behind him.

The study looked the same as well. He walked over to the cabinet where all the important documents were kept, including any papers pertaining to the slaves. He began to sort through them. He eventually came to those of Judas and Phineas Blackwell. James withdrew the papers and sat down in the chair at the desk as he began to scan the words, making sure the papers contained what they had come for.

James glanced around the office slightly unnerved. His father had never allowed any of the children in his study. He felt like a badly behaved child about to get reprimanded for doing something wrong.

James turned back to the papers. They did include important information—from where Judas and Phineas had been born, to whom they had been born, whom they had been sold to, even when they had married. The papers would be very useful.

James stood and sifted one more time through the cabinet, making sure he hadn't missed anything. He hadn't. As he moved toward the door, he heard footsteps sounding in the hall. Why hadn't Cody warned him? The door pushed open and in walked an old man. He was stooped from hard labor. James gasped in recognition. It was Judas Blackwell. Alana's grandfather was still alive? It had never crossed his mind before.

"Masta' James! You's scared me half ta' death. What are ya' doin' here?" James was amazed that Judas recognized him. It had been many years since he had left for the west.

"It's a very long story, Judas. And as strange as it may seem, this story pertains to you as well."

"Me?" Judas questioned. "I would surely like ta' hear it then. Go's ahead." James shared with Judas how Alana had been born of Jesse and Charise. He told of how Alana's mother had died over a year ago, and Alana had come west to find him. James also explained how Johnny had come and taken her to the Georgian Plantation, where she was now a slave.

James paused as he saw tears begin to well up in the old man's eyes. "I'm sorry. This is too much for you," James stated with concern.

Judas waved his hand. "No … please … go on. I's just overjoyed at haven' a granddaughter. I's thought my family was gone." James finished the story and waited while Judas composed himself.

"Where's ya' takin' those?" Judas said pointing to the papers in James' hand.

"I need this information in an effort to convince the court to set Alana free. I am going to take them to a lawyer."

"I would like ta' come. I would like ta' see my granddaughter before I leave this life."

James looked at him surprised. "But my brother, won't he notify the authorities if you leave the premises without permission?"

"Yor fatha' and I become close afta' yor motha die. Befoe he die, he write out a deed grantin' me my freedom to come and go as I please. Though I's a slave ta' this here property, I's allowed ta' leave as I feel the need."

James realized his father had changed quite a bit

later in life. James wished he would have had the chance to see his father before he passed away.

"We need to leave now. Do you have a horse you can ride?"

Judas nodded.

∘ ∘ ∘

Brady and Shay had returned and were relieved to see Alex had already found the document of Alana's lineage and had left it waiting in the hotel room.

Meanwhile, Brady poured over the information he had. He wanted to know it well, down to the tiniest detail. He asked Shay questions about Alana. Some Shay knew. Some he didn't. Brady also posed questions to Alex, who in turn asked Alana and then brought the information back to Brady.

One evening, past the time Brady should have retired, he sat reading over more documents. The door to his office creaked opened, and Brady looked up to find Mr. Webb standing across from him.

"Mr. Sawyer, I don't want you working on this case. It will bring bad publicity to our office when you lose this case. And mark my words, you will lose this case."

"How are you so certain I'll lose, Mr. Webb? Because I feel like I have a fighting chance."

Mr. Webb laughed. "That's why I hired you, because you were a stick of dynamite waiting to be lit. You remind me of myself when I was young and innocent to the legal world." Mr. Webb moved forward and pressed both hands on the desk. "Drop the case, Brady. I mean it."

Brady stood to his feet. "And what if I don't, Mr. Webb?"

"Then I am going to have to ask you to resign from your position here. I will not jeopardize my career because of some foolish young lawyer who doesn't have any sense."

Brady grabbed an empty crate and set it on his desk. "I'll be gone by morning."

Mr. Webb stared at him with a puzzled expression. "You are going to risk your practice over the freedom of a slave girl, a girl you have never even met. Brady ... I thought you were smarter than that." Brady said nothing. Nothing he could say would make Mr. Webb understand. Mr. Webb finally turned and exited the door.

∘ ∘ ∘

Alana opened her Bible and there inside the cover was a note from Josie.

Alana,

I've been sold to another plantation. Please don't worry about me. You will be happy to know I believe like you do now. I will try to live for Him. I can never thank you enough for not giving up on me, even when you had every reason to. You are a true friend,

Josie Tally

Alana's hand moved to her belly. The baby moved frequently and was quickly running out of space. She smiled. She was now in her seventh month, and Shay would be shocked if he could see her now.

∘ ∘ ∘

Shay and Brady's conversation came to an abrupt end when they heard commotion outside the hotel room.

The doorknob turned and in walked James, Cody, and an older black man.

James walked toward Shay with a smile on his face. "Shay, this is Judas Blackwell, your wife's grandfather." Shay turned to the elderly man. He was considerably darker in color than Alana, but they shared the same cheek bones and chin.

Shay stretched forth his hand. "Mr. Blackwell, it is an honor to meet you," he stated. Judas eyed him with growing respect and then offered his own hand in greeting.

A confident smile spread over Brady's face. "Mr. Blackwell, what would you think about testifying in court?"

Judas eyed the lawyer cautiously. "I's suppose it would depend on why's I's in court."

"I need a personal witness to verify the facts I will be presenting in court in hopes that they will grant Alana her freedom."

Judas smiled. "Well then, I's be obliged ta' help... obliged."

"Are you staying here at the hotel?" Brady asked.

"I's have no room here … "

"Stay in my room, Mr. Blackwell," Shay stated. "I have a feeling you can fill in the missing links to Alana's past."

"I's will, if ya' will call me Judas." Shay smiled and patted the older gentleman on the back.

Later that night, after they had retired, Shay listened to Judas' story about Jesse. When Jesse had been killed years before, Judas had been devastated. He had desired so much more for Jesse's life. At first he had been angry that his son had run off, and with the master's daughter, no less. Judas had not seen it coming. He knew that Jesse and the girl spent quite a bit of time together, but had he known how deep their relationship had really become, he would have put a stop to it immediately.

It would seem that Mr. Bratten, his master, had been paying more attention than he, because it was soon made known that Jesse had been sold to a different plantation. Judas had been upset and had planned to speak with the master about it, but Jesse had eloped with the girl before he had the chance. And then they had returned with the body of his dead son...

"But I's now have a granddaughter. What a blessin', a sure blessin'."

o o o

Brady pushed open the door to his home and stopped short, taking in the overturned chairs and torn papers littering his floor. Brady set his briefcase on the floor and moved into the kitchen. It had been ransacked too. The only clean area was the kitchen table and on the table laid a white piece of paper with hurriedly scribbled handwriting. Brady placed both hands on the table, squinting in order to make anything of the scribbled letters. A chill ran down his spine as the words began to make sense.

You're going down a path that will get you hurt. If I were you, I'd rethink the case you're about to represent. It could be your last.

Brady picked up an overturned chair and sat down in it. Placing his head into his hands, he took two deep breaths. For the first time since taking this case, Brady realized he wasn't only fighting for Shay's wife's freedom. This was a battle against slavery, against the white and black race. And most of the population in Atlanta would be against him.

Brady grabbed the piece of paper and scrunched it in his fist before tossing it into the waste basket. He couldn't let it get to him. He had come too far to back down now. "Protect us, Father," Brady whispered into the silent room.

○ ○ ○

Shay was sitting at the hotel café reading the paper when a shadow fell over the page. "Father!" he exclaimed as he glanced up. "What are you doing here? How did you know I was here?"

Luke helped himself to the chair next to his son. "Your mother left. She went back to Boston."

"When?" Shay asked.

"Not long after you did. I was out delivering the Abbotts' baby. When I returned the next day, I found a note on our dresser saying she had never been happy in Independence and was returning home."

The pain Shay felt inside was only sympathy for his father. He would not miss his mother. He had never known her. "I'm sorry, Father."

"Well, that's not why I'm here. I sent a telegram to Cal, stating that I wanted to come visit my boys. He sent one back saying that you were here in Atlanta. You can imagine my surprise. At any rate, I decided perhaps you could use my moral support."

"What about your practice?" Shay questioned.

"After you left, the Evans' boy returned from his training out east. He had high hopes of starting his own practice, so I talked him into working with me for a while and eventually taking over mine. I've doctored long enough." Luke smiled at his son's shocked expression. "I can see by your expression you're surprised."

Shay nodded. "I am surprised. I never thought I'd see the day you'd give up doctoring. It meant a lot to you."

"More than it should have...I realize that now. I've missed out on my family, and I started thinking to myself, *should I live in regret for the rest of my life or make amends for the future?*"

Shay stared at his father in awe. He had changed. No doubt about that. His father reached across the table and patted his hand. Shay stared at the hand covering his own. When had his father ever touched him?

"How are you, son? I was sorry to hear about what happened. I told the Raymonds, and they have been praying. They sure took a liking to that girl." Shay knew they had grown quite fond of her before they had headed west.

His father cleared his throat. "There are some things I'd like to get off my chest. First, I'd like to apologize for not being a father to you or Cal when you were growing up. My home was an unhappy place, and I chose to find solace in my work. Will you forgive me?"

Shay stared across the table at his father. He knew the shock was transparent on his face. He was sitting there with his father carrying on a conversation. When had that ever happened in his life? "Yes...of course ... I forgive you."

"When Lydia left, I was devastated. Why? I am not sure. It wasn't as if we ever had a happy marriage. Mr. Raymond came over every night...to see how I was doing. I began spending time with the Raymonds, and I suppose you could say they rubbed off." Shay's smile widened. Was his father saying what he thought he was saying?

"As much as I disliked the idea of you leaving for the west, I could see the change in you. And it opened my eyes. You proved to me that there was something more this life had to offer. I believe like you. Every care … every burden I once had is now gone."

Now Shay reached across the table and grasped his father's hand. "I'm glad, Father. Remind me to hug the Raymonds if I ever see them again." They shared a laugh.

"How's Alana holding up?" his father asked with concern.

"She's doing well under the circumstances."

"You know, I delivered her when she was born. I've always watched her from afar. As soon as I saw her, I knew that she'd have a rough go of it. But she was a strong one. She obviously still is."

"So you knew? You knew that she was black, didn't you?" Shay wondered how much more surreal the entire situation could be. His father had known his future wife was black, yet her husband had no idea.

"She had a very dark complexion when she made her appearance that cold March morning. I was shocked to say the least, and her mother could read my expression. She begged me not to say a word. And I never breathed a word, not even when there was question among our community. Alana's skin lightened bit by bit every time I would see her, and by the time she started school, one wouldn't have known a thing. If only the rumors had died down. She still had to endure the teasing and taunting by the town's people. But she was brave, and I was proud of her."

A brief silence passed over the table. Luke smiled.

"Who would have ever guessed my own son would escort her west, fall in love, and marry her?" Luke laughed, and Shay smiled at his humor.

What was even more surprising to Shay was how enjoyable his father was to be around. "Thanks for coming, Father. It means a lot."

CHAPTER FIFTEEN

Charlie reread the notice. A trial? What was going on? Who was up to this? He glanced again at the paper in his hand. *Alana Blackwell must appear in court....* Why would she be needed in court? He rode out to the fields and finally saw her amongst the workers.

"Alana... come here for a moment." Alana moved toward him and Alex came as well.

"I have a notice here that says you are to appear in court in just a few days. Do you know why?"

Alana stared at him as if she knew nothing. "I... haven't done anything wrong—" Alex interrupted her.

"Charlie, if I may," Alex responded. "I learned only a few days ago that her husband is in town. He is trying to fight for her freedom."

"Well, of all the nonsense in the world. He doesn't stand a chance. Surely he realizes that." Charlie walked away mumbling to himself.

Alana smiled at Alex before walking back to her empty basket. Shay was still fighting for her freedom. He still loved her.

Several minutes later a slight ache entered her midsection, but quickly passed. The midwife had warned her that brief pains could be expected as her body readied itself for the birth of her baby. Throughout the rest of the afternoon, the aches continued, deepening in length and discomfort. Alana tried to ignore the pain as much as possible, but by curfew she knew something was not right.

Alana readied herself for bed, but sleep would not come. She prayed for peace, but it evaded her. Then a pain hit her, this time with such force that her breathing became labored and she cried out. It was too soon. *God, oh God, please not now.* But the pains continued to come. Shay! She needed her husband. But he wasn't there. He couldn't come. "NO!" she screamed out.

Lena appeared at her side. "Alana, what is it?"

Alana curled into a ball. "ALEX!" she cried. Lena ran from the room. It seemed like an eternity, but finally Alex was beside her. He slid to his knees next to the bed, cupping her face in his hands, alarmed by the pain he saw in her eyes.

"Alana ... what can I do? Is it the baby?" She clutched his hand in her own. She nodded and then screamed again as another pain tore through her body.

"Fetch the midwife," Alex ordered Lena. This couldn't be happening. Not now. Not when they were so close.

"It's too ... too early," Alana gasped between pains.

"Maybe you are wrong on the date, Alana. Maybe ... " the midwife rushed in before he had a chance to finish. Alex stepped back from the bed.

"How far along are you?" the midwife questioned.

"Sev ... seven months."

"Well ... it's coming now, that's plain to see. I hope you are wrong for the baby's sake." Alex paced back and forth in the room. Never had he heard such anguish. He could barely stand it, but he couldn't bring himself to leave." He pace and prayed.

"Push, girl, push now," the midwife scolded. "We're never going get this baby out if you don't push." The midwife turned to Alex. "Help her focus, will you?"

Alex hurried to Alana's side. "Alana...look at me." Her eyes beheld a glazed look. Was it shock? "ALANA...LOOK AT ME," he panicked. Her eyes turned toward him, finally focusing on him. "You're going to be fine, Alana. Now I need you to work with me. You can do it. When I say push, you push with all your might." Another contraction hit, and Alex waited for the midwife's signal.

"Push," Alex stated. Alana's entire body tensed as she bore down with all her might.

"The head is out," the midwife relayed. "One more time should do it."

Alex cupped Alana's face in his hands. "Did you hear that? One more time. Only one more time. All right. This is it." Alana screamed out and then fell back depleted. Alex watched as the midwife carried the baby away and began working with the small bundle.

"The baby..." Alana whispered.

Alex rubbed her cold hand between his own. "Everything is fine," he consoled.

The midwife suddenly looked up. Alex did not like the expression he read on her face. "I'm sorry. It was too early. She's...she's gone."

Alana began to sob. "Not my baby!" She tried to crawl from the bed. Alex pushed her back.

"You're too weak..." his voice broke. He wanted to be strong for her, but he could not.

"Here, let me tend to the mother. You go...go and

dispose of the baby." Alex shuddered. He couldn't. He wouldn't. He meant to walk by the table, but could not without glancing at the infant. He stopped. She was beautiful. So fully human. Beautiful black hair. A perfect nose and perfect lips. And then he saw it. Or did he imagine it? A small rising of the chest. He moved closer. Yes! He saw it again.

An idea suddenly began forming in his head. He wrapped the blanket around the infant before quickly walking out the door with the small bundle wrapped in his arms.

o o o

Shay sat up in bed. A light tap sounded at his door again. Groggily, he made his way to the door and opened it. "Alex?" Alex moved past Shay into the room and quickly kicked the door shut. Shay's eyes went to the bundle he had in his arms. Alex ever so gently pulled back part of the blanket. The first thing Shay saw was the black hair.

"What... who?" Shay gasped as the rest of the blanket fell away and he saw the tiny infant. "Is he all right?"

"She..." Alex stated. "She was born a little over an hour ago. The midwife pronounced her dead, but when I went to carry the baby out, I realized she was breathing. You said your father is a doctor?" Shay nodded. "You should probably get him." Shay hurried from the room and soon returned with his disheveled father. Luke immediately took the baby into his arms.

"Tell me what happened. Every detail," Luke requested as he carried the baby to the bed and laid her upon it. As Alex recounted the recent events, Luke checked the infant thoroughly. Alex spoke in a hurry, as everything vividly flashed through his mind. He would not forget this evening's happenings for a very long time.

"So the midwife proclaimed her deceased?" Luke questioned for reassurance. Alex nodded. "Her breathing is not labored. Her lungs seem fully developed. That is an answer to prayer." Luke gently swaddled the baby in the blanket and put her in Shay's outstretched arms.

"Why did you not leave the baby with Alana when you discovered she was still breathing?" James asked as he paced the room. He had just come in moments before.

"I ... if she is thought dead, then ... the baby can be free ... no matter what happens, for they do not know she exists." Light registered in all their eyes.

"Good thinking," James stated.

"Even if Alana is given her freedom, it is much better for the newborn to be here than with her, for she only has two maternity days before she must return to work," Alex voiced.

"What do other mothers do with their babies?" Shay questioned as he stared at the beautiful infant that lay in his arms. He could not take his eyes off her.

"Most of the women bind the baby to their bellies, but it is uncomfortable for both the mother and infant. Some leave them with the old women who can no longer carry on with hard labor. Either way, it is not a healthy environment for an infant as little as she."

"You did the right thing," Luke assured Alex.

The door opened and Judas emerged with a leather pouch. He walked over to Shay and rubbed the small end gently on the baby's mouth. The baby caught on quickly and all five men chuckled at the loud sucking noise the small infant made.

"What is it?" Shay asked.

Judas smiled. "Goat's milk. My wife.... died in childbirth ... I spent many nights feeding my son Jesse. I spoke with the maid, and she knew of a goat nearby, and the shopkeeper next door donated the leather pouch."

"She has very strong suction for one so small," Cody stated as he admired her from behind Shay. "And she is very noisy for one so small."

"I must go ... I must get back to Alana," Alex voiced.

"You'll tell her ... won't you ... that I love her and the daughter she has given to me," Shay voiced with tears in his eyes.

"I will," Alex answered before he turned and walked out the door.

Shay stared after him, wishing it were he going to his wife's side and not Alex. Shay glanced down at his daughter once again, amazed at the deep desire that took hold of him to protect her from harm.

o o o

Alana lay still in her bed. Out of habit, she reached to her stomach. It was empty. Lifeless. Her baby...dead. How could this happen? Where was God? Did He care? *And lo, I am with you always, even to the end of time.* "But I don't feel you," Alana whispered in the dark room. *Call upon Me and I will be with you in times of trouble.* "I need you, Lord. I can't bear this sorrow." *You have made Me your Lord and because of that, no evil shall befall you, nor shall any plague come near your dwelling.* "But Lord, I feel alone." *I have given my angels charge over you. In their hands they shall bear you up.* "Oh Lord, deliver me from this heartache." *I will deliver you, and I will honor you. With long life will I satisfy you.* Alana finally fell into a peaceful sleep.

Alana was still sleeping when Alex returned. He let her sleep, knowing that she needed her rest. He picked up her hand. It was calloused from the hard work she had been enduring. Yet she never complained. An hour passed before her eyelids fluttered open. He leaned over and whispered in her ear. Her eyes became large with wonderment. Tears of joy and gratitude flowed down her cheeks.

"You need more sleep. Get rested up. You have a hearing in three days." Alana nodded and closed her eyes.

∘ ∘ ∘

"What does she look like?" Alana asked when Alex brought her breakfast the next morning.

"She's beautiful," Alex said with a smile. "Black hair, like yours. And she has high cheek bones like you too. But she has her father's nose and chin."

Alana smiled. "I like his nose ... and his chin."

"Shay won't let anyone else hold her, but his father Luke, and that is only if he is checking her over for medical reasons. He's mighty proud." Alex enjoyed the way his words made Alana's eyes dance. "And that daughter of yours, why she eats like a pig. You would never believe that one as tiny as she could eat so much ... and make so much noise doing it." Alex tried to mimic the infant's noises and had Alana laughing.

Alana clutched her stomach. "That hurts," she admitted. "No more funny stories ... at least for a couple days."

Alana reached out and touched his arm. "Thank

you, Alex. I've needed you. You've given up so much to be here with me."

Alex brushed her words aside. "Ah, well, I'm honored to be here. You know ... this is the first time I've ever done anything for someone else. It feels good." Alex looked away from Alana's thoughtful gaze.

CHAPTER SIXTEEN

Brady and Shay made their way across the street to the court house. Shay glanced back at the hotel, and Brady knew he was worried about leaving his daughter.

"She'll be fine, Shay. I know Marty very well. She's raised eight children and has sixteen grandchildren. Marty is more experienced with infants than you or I will ever be." Brady and Shay shared a laugh. The laugh was cut short when they noticed the picketers lined along the walkway of the courthouse. Several held signs denouncing the cause Brady was about to argue for. He surveyed the crowd, wondering if one of them had written the note. He hadn't told Shay about the threat. He was under enough stress without adding anything more.

They entered the courtroom, and Brady's eyes quickly scanned the room. He motioned for Shay to take a seat beside him. Brady followed Shay's gaze to a beautiful woman sitting on the other side of the room. Brady stared at the girl he was about to represent. The realization of what he was doing finally took hold of him. He would be speaking on her behalf. Her freedom rested on his shoulders alone. Anxiety began to grip him. What if he failed? He stood to his feet and exited through the back door, thankful there was no one around.

"In Your Word, Father, You say that You make the simple wise. You also say that You give understanding to the simple. I come before You now, admitting I am a simple man. I need Your understanding. I need Your wisdom. Speak through me today. Let the questions I ask come from You, not my own understanding. Amen."

Brady noticed Shay watching him when he re-entered the court room. He gave him a reassuring smile. Brady loved these people. He had spent hours upon hours with them. He had followed every procedure he had learned during his training, except for one, not allowing himself to become emotionally involved with the people he was representing. He had done away with that theory as soon as he had heard Shay's story.

Brady realized it was a slim chance. He wasn't oblivious to the stringent laws set for the slaves. But he also knew that this case was different. Brady's gaze settled on Alana once again. If she had ever doubted Shay's love, she never would again.

Brady was surprised at the number of people showing up for the trial. Several people from his church were there in support. But there were also several people there he didn't recognize, yet their angry glances his direction made Brady quite aware they were not in agreement with his decision to represent the O'Connells. He also noticed Mr. Webb sitting in the first row. Mr. Webb smiled at Brady, and Brady nodded his direction. It increased Brady's confidence, seeing Mr. Webb there. Perhaps Mr. Webb believed in him more than he thought he did.

A hush fell over the courtroom as Johnny Bratten walked through the door. Johnny was a very influential man in Atlanta's society. Even the people that did not know him knew of him. Behind Johnny was his lawyer, Lawrence Casey.

◦ ◦ ◦

Lawrence Casey was not a man to be toyed with. He was well experienced and very popular within their district. He prepared a good defense and was short and to the point. He didn't believe in being soft-hearted. It got you nowhere. People were looking for someone to take control of the situation. They bowed to power. Domination was the only tool he used, and it had served him well over the past twenty years.

Lawrence looked over at Brady Sawyer. He had spoken with Mr. Webb, and he knew this was Brady's first trial. He knew that Brady's inexperience would be an open door to overpower him before the trial even began. It was then that Lawrence noticed Mr. Webb. He was sitting directly behind Brady. Lawrence was unnerved by it, but he didn't let it show. It was unacceptable to show any sign of weakness.

Mr. Webb hadn't hid his admiration for Brady during their discussion. But Lawrence realized why Mr. Webb had to let the boy go. Mr. Webb was smart enough to realize that Brady's loss today could affect his entire practice. But that didn't mean he didn't like the boy. "Brady has the backbone of an ox," Mr. Webb had stated. And he had stated it with pride.

Lawrence focused his eyes on the girl he would be fighting to keep in slavery. He felt a sting of pity, and it took him by surprise. He hadn't had that feeling since he first started his legal practice. He quickly pushed the feeling aside. It hadn't helped him then, and most assuredly it wouldn't help him now.

The judge entered the courtroom and took his seat at the front. "I'll let the defense begin."

Lawrence immediately stood to his feet. "Your honor, I think it would save us all a great deal of time and money if we dismiss this case without further delay. We all know that the issue of slavery has not and will not change. The outcome of this trial is decided before it has even begun. I propose that we all go home." With that said, Lawrence sat back down.

The judge looked at Brady. "What is your proposition, Mr. Sawyer?"

Brady never dropped his gaze. "Your honor, on behalf of a man who has traveled well over four thousand miles, I ask that you hear this case today. We are not basing our case on unworthy appeals. We have done much work on our part, and I believe what we have to say today should be heard by you, your honor, and by these people." The judge sat in silence pondering his decision.

Lawrence stood back up. "Your honor, this is ludicrous. This young lawyer has nothing to say that we haven't already heard."

The judge frowned and turned his gaze toward Brady. "Let's go forth with the trial. The boy at least deserves an opportunity to acquire some experience." Brady smiled, while Lawrence glowered from across the room.

"Mr. Sawyer, state your purpose for this trial and then call your first witness."

Brady turned toward the crowd. "I come before you today in representation of Alana Charise Blackwell O'Connell. She was taken into slavery a few months ago. We desire nothing less than her freedom to return home with her husband. My first witness I call forth is Alana O'Connell."

Alana made her way to the stand. She laid her hand on the Bible and promised to tell the truth and nothing but the truth. Then she sat in the witness seat.

"Alana, when were you born?"

"March fourth, eighteen forty-two."

"So that makes you how old?"

"Seventeen," she replied nervously.

"When did you find out you were of Black descent?"

"A year and a half ago. My mother died and she left me her journal. I read in the journal that my father, Jesse Blackwell, was black."

Lawrence stood to his feet. "This is absurd," he stated. "We already know she's black. Does it make her any less black that she didn't know she was until later?"

The judge pounded his gravel. "Mr. Casey, I will ask for your opinion when I want it. Sit down. You may precede, Mr. Sawyer."

"Alana, did you know your father was a slave?"

"Yes. My mother's journal said he had been sold to a plantation in Georgia."

"But then your father died, before he ever got to Georgia. Is that right?" Brady inquired.

"Yes, that's correct."

"Did you realize that because your father was a slave that you were a slave also?"

Alana shook her head. "No … it did not cross my mind at the time."

"When did it cross your mind?" Brady knew that these would be some of the first questions Mr. Casey would ask her in his cross examination. He wanted to bring them out in the open where she could answer them without Mr. Casey putting words in her mouth.

"When I arrived at my Uncle James' house out west, I told him about my father. He told me it could bring trouble on me if I told anyone. I realized then that something was wrong."

"Did you know you were wanted by the Georgian Plantation?"

"No, I did not."

"Can you point out your husband to the jury, Alana?"

Alana stood and pointed to Shay.

"How long have you been married?"

"We married on March twenty-seventh."

"So, you've been married for eight months, is that correct?"

"Yes, that's correct."

"Thank you, Alana. That concludes my examination. Mr. Casey may cross examine her if he wishes." Brady took his seat.

Mr. Casey stood. He hadn't given the young Sawyer boy enough credit. He had asked every question Lawrence had written down on his writing pad. If there was anything a judge hated worse, it was repetition.

"Were you teased as a child? Made fun of?" He noticed her stiffen.

"Yes, I was teased."

"Why were you teased, Mrs. O'Connell?"

"Because I was darker than the other children."

"But you just said you didn't know that you were black until only recently."

"I didn't know for sure ... but it was rumored that I was."

"I see," Mr. Lawrence said crisply. "So, you didn't know for sure, but you thought you might be."

Alana didn't answer.

"No further questions, your honor," Mr. Casey sat down with a sneer.

Brady took a deep breath. Mr. Casey had just made Alana look like a fabricator. He was more experienced—that was evident. Brady called Shay to the stand.

"Tell me about your relationship with Alana before you married."

"We grew up in the same town. We went to school together. We didn't spend much time together, but when her mother passed away, I offered to assist her in going west."

"Did you know that your wife was of black descent, Mr. O'Connell?"

"No. As a child I wondered ... it was rumored around town that she was. But as an adult, I never gave it any thought."

"Do you think your wife should be free?"

"Yes. She grew up out of slavery. She has always lived free until now. I love her. She's my wife."

Brady sat down and Mr. Casey stood up.

"Did your wife tell you she was of black descent before she married you, Mr. O'Connell?"

Shay paused. "No, she did not."

"Would you have married her if you had known?" Mr. Casey persisted.

"Yes. It would not have changed my love for her."

"Were you angry with your wife when you first found out she was black?"

"Yes ... I was. But I soon realized it didn't matter. The only reason she hadn't told me is, she was afraid."

Lawrence laughed. "Maybe she didn't tell you because she thought if she married a white man, people would no longer wonder. Have you ever thought of that, Mr. O'Connell?"

"No," Shay openly stated. "She married me because she loves me." Lawrence dismissed the witness.

"James Bratten, please take the stand," Brady stated.

"Tell me what you know of Alana?"

"She's my niece. She is the daughter of my sister."

"How did you feel when she told you about her father?" Brady inquired.

"I was shocked. Then I was afraid for her well-being."

"Were you surprised when Johnny showed up at your place?"

"My brother is a harsh man, and I knew he was angry with our sister. It doesn't shock me that he is disturbed that his family line now has black blood running through its veins. He's always been a proud man."

"What did Johnny say to you that day?"

"He told me he was looking for Alana. He said that even though he couldn't hurt our sister Charise anymore, for she had died, he planned to take his revenge out on her daughter. I tried to talk him out of it, but he was determined to find her and take her into slavery."

"Thank you, Mr. Bratten."

Lawrence surprised James with his first question. "Do you think it was very smart of your sister to marry a slave, Mr. Bratten?" Dead silence followed. "Do you?" Lawrence demanded.

"No ... it wasn't smart. Nothing good could come of it. But she did and we can't change the past."

"Should your father have sold Jesse Blackwell to the Georgian Plantation?"

"Yes … he was a slave."

"But Alana, his daughter, she doesn't belong there?"

"No," James replied. "It wasn't her fault her mother married a slave."

"Come now, Mr. Bratten, are you not being partial because she is your niece, your flesh and blood?"

"If that is so, then why does my own brother, also Alana's uncle, want so desperately for her to live in slavery?" Brady smiled at James' answer. Mr. Casey signaled to the judge that he was done.

"Your next witness, Mr. Sawyer," the judge announced.

"I call as a witness…Judas Blackwell, your honor." Brady watched as Alana's face changed from one of hesitancy, to uncertainty, and then full realization. Judas made his way to the witness stand. He was older and slower in his movements. As he came by Alana, he stopped and stared at her. He reached out gently and patted her hand. A tear ran down his cheek. Alana also began to cry. Judas went forward and laid his hand on the Bible.

"Mr. Blackwell, how are you related to Alana?"

"Alana's fatha', Jesse Blackwell, was my son. Alana is my granddaughta'."

"How long have you known that you have a granddaughter, Mr. Blackwell?"

"Not long a'tal. James, he come to the ole Bratten homestead a few days back, and that was when I found out about Alana." Judas watched as Johnny's face paled.

It was the first that Johnny knew that James had been there.

"Why didn't you know you had a granddaughter?"

"My son, Jesse, ran off with the Bratten girl, but I didna know she was with child. Ya' see, my son died only a few days afta' they ran off tagetha.'"

"What kind of emotions are you feeling right now, Mr. Blackwell, at the sight of your granddaughter?"

Judas turned toward his granddaughter. "Well, she's a beautiful one ta' be sure. I see her fatha' in her. I's real happy to know I still have family. A part of my son still lives on."

Lawrence stood to his feet. "Your honor, is this going anywhere, because if it is not, I'd like to call a witness."

The judge looked at Brady. "Ask him what you need to ask him and let him go."

Brady nodded. "Mr. Blackwell, I asked you up here today because I have some information to ask you about your bloodline, as well as the bloodline of your wife. Do you mind answering a few questions for me"?

"I's be glad to help anyways I can. I kept good track of our ancestry, and I do have a good memory."

Brady smiled. "First, I'd like to know about your own father. Tell me about his ethnicity."

"He's black … and I's know he had some German, too, I's just not sure how much."

"And your mother? Do you remember what percentage she was black?"

Judas paused before speaking, calculating in his head. "My mama, she was part white. She was an illegitimate child of the former masta' of the plantation we was at." Some people in the room gasped in disgust.

"So, Mr. Blackwell, for the record, you're about sixty percent black, is that correct?"

"Yes, I suppose that's right. The other forty percent is a mixture of white and German, though that don't make any difference to my owner," Judas added with a chuckle.

"What about your wife? If I am correct, her name was Phineas, right?"

Judas nodded. "Her fatha' was a Frenchman. Her mother met him in France."

"So her father was not black at all?"

"No … he wasn't."

"And Phineas' mother? Tell me about her."

"Her mother was also French. She was black, and then I's guess forty percent French."

"So, Phineas was at the most thirty percent black?"

"Yes, sir, that sounds correct."

"Your son, Jesse Blackwell, was then not more than forty-five percent black, considering the ancestry of you and your wife, is that right?"

"Jesse had several different bloodlines flowing through him: German, French, white, black."

Brady turned to the judge. "Your honor, I have in my possession the percentages of the bloodlines regarding the Blackwell family. Everything Judas has just described is documented and is in my custody."

Lawrence also stood to his feet. "We've all heard that Alana Blackwell O'Connell is of black descent. Does it really matter how much of it runs in her veins? Come now, your honor, let's get beyond this."

The judge glared at Mr. Casey. Brady could tell he disliked Lawrence's haughty attitude. Finally, the judge turned to Brady. "I do hope all of this has an explanation behind it."

"Your honor, if I may have only a few more minutes, I will share with those present my reason for bringing this information out in the open." The judge motioned for him to continue.

"I would like to call Johnny Bratten to the stand." Johnny stood up surprised, but quickly made his way to the witness seat. "I have only one brief question for you, Mr. Bratten. I was curious about the ethnicity of your family. Does it have any black bloodlines running through it? I mean before the birth of Alana Blackwell."

Johnny looked aghast that Brady would even propose such a thing. "Absolutely not," Johnny declared. "Our family has had generation after generation of well-bred and highly esteemed white people birthed from it. That is until my sister made her preposterous error."

"So, to set the record straight, your sister, Charise, was in fact fully white?"

"Certainly. I defy anyone who would say otherwise."

"Thank you, Mr. Bratten. That will be all." Brady turned to the judge. "Your honor, will you please grant me the request of sharing a short, yet very significant story with you and the people present here now."

The judge looked skeptical, yet curious. "I do hope your short story will wrap up this question we have about the bloodlines."

"It will, your honor," Brady replied.

"Then proceed," the judge stated.

CHAPTER SEVENTEEN

Her name was Savannah. Savannah Rose Percelli. She was a slave of Sanford Cotton Plantation in Charleston, Georgia. Her mother and father had been slaves before her, just as their mothers and fathers had been before them.

The master's son had grown up with her. They had been playmates. And then as they both became of age, they fell in love. They exchanged vows underneath the oak tree they used to climb together.

The master soon realized it was not the passing interest he had once thought it to be. He promised his son that if he agreed to attend law school for the next three years, he would in exchange recognize Savannah as his son's wife and even allow them to exchange true vows in church. The son agreed to his father's pledge and soon left for training. Once gone, the son's father sold Savannah to another plantation.

But it was too late. Savannah was with child. A son was born. She named him Rosline Timothy Percelli. Timothy after his father, for she still loved him.

The master's son finished school and returned. He searched the plantation for Savannah, but she was no where to be found. His father refused to say anything. And he made known that anyone who relayed anything of Savannah's whereabouts would be severely punished.

Six years passed in which the son never married,

though often pressured in order to produce an heir to the family name. The master then died, leaving his plantation to his son. It was then that someone came forth with the whereabouts of Savannah, for they knew the love the son still harbored for the girl.

Timothy went and found her. Savannah had not married either. He brought her and their son back to the Sanford Cotton Plantation. But he was not satisfied having her as his slave. He married her, much to the dismay of the townspeople and his own mother, who was still living. Savannah lived in the main house as his wife. Their son attended school as any normal white child would do. The town was outraged and they brought the issue to trial.

The man was desperate to save his wife, and after many sleepless nights, he finally thought of something. It was his only resolve. He brought his wife before the court and brought up the issue of her ancestry. As it went, Savannah was only a small percentage black, her most prominent bloodlines being that of Spanish, German, and white.

The court saw the love that existed between the man and his wife, and they recognized the son, an almost exact replica of his father. It was decided in court that day that Savannah and her son were free individuals. The man was free to take his wife and son home.

There was silence in the courtroom as Brady ended the story. He paused to let the story sink in.

"If you would please take note that Alana's bloodline concerning that of her black ancestry is only a very small percentage. Alana differs from Savannah in that she has lived in freedom since her birth. And now she has married a free man whom she wants to share her life with.

"I ask you today, not to consider the fact that her father was a slave, but I ask instead that you consider today a girl who loves a man...her own husband...and would like nothing more than to return home with him." Brady sat down. Several agonizing seconds passed by.

Finally, the judge spoke. "Do you have any documentation of the trial you just spoke of?"

Brady gathered the documents and took them to the front. The judge turned to Lawrence. "Any last words before we meet to decide the outcome."

Lawrence sat for a moment before finally shaking his head. The judge stood to his feet and exited the courtroom.

Mr. Webb walked over to Brady, who was already busy shaking hands with a line of well-wishers. What a plot Brady had just delivered. Mr. Webb had definitely underestimated the boy. He glanced over at Mr. Casey who had yet to leave his seat. He was glad he wasn't in Lawrence's shoes today. He would hate to be Brady's opponent any day for that matter. The boy had a definite knack for persuasion in the legal field. Mr. Webb waited patiently until finally Brady turned and shook his hand.

"Good work, Brady. I couldn't be more proud."

"Well, I learned from the best," Brady complimented. Mr. Webb chuckled as he walked away.

Several more minutes passed before the judge returned. He walked to the podium. "We have met. We have seen the documents. We agree that the defendant, Alana Charise O'Connell, is deserving of a free life. She shall return home with her husband. They shall be free to have children and raise those children in freedom ... "

Shay was already out of his seat and on his way to claim his wife. The noise in the room was almost intolerable. No one noticed as Johnny Bratten and his lawyer, Mr. Casey, made their way out of the court room.

Shay picked Alana up and swung her around in a circle. Finally he put her down and pulled her against him. Tears ran down both their faces as he kissed her cheeks, then her nose until finally his mouth found hers. She was his now.

Brady tapped Shay on the shoulder. "Take Alana and leave through the back door. Take her to the hotel and don't leave your room until this chaos has died down."

"What about you?" Shay voiced with concern.

"I'll be fine. If I leave through the front, it will take their attention off of you."

Shay grabbed Alana's hand and slowly moved through the crowd and out the back door.

° ° °

Shay lay silently in bed, his head propped up by one arm. Alana was sleeping soundly next to him. He could no longer resist the urge to touch her. He reached across the sheet and caressed the top of her hand. Had it only been eight hours since the court decision—since the proclamation of Alana's freedom? Their child stirred in the cradle next to the bed, and Shay reached for her. *Savannah Charise O'Connell,* in honor of the woman who had effectuated his own wife's freedom.

Savannah took right to Alana, as if her mother hadn't been missing for three days. Shay laid the baby between them. She nestled in close to her mother and began to nurse. The rustle of the sheets interrupted Alana's sleep briefly, but her eyes only fluttered open, before closing again. Shay once again reached across the bed and stroked her hand. It was worn and calloused from the hard work she had endured.

Shay thanked God for the hundredth time that day for his wife's freedom. He now had a second chance to prove to her the sincerity of his love. He would not let her down again. Shay intertwined his fingers with Alana's, their arms encircling Savannah. He drifted off into peaceful sleep.

A couple hours later they both awoke to the baby's cry. Alana quickly soothed Savannah with her voice. Savannah instantly hushed at the sound. Alana smiled and looked up at Shay.

"She is the most beautiful baby in the whole world," Shay stated with emotion.

Alana smiled. "You say that because she's yours."

Shay's hand caressed his wife's cheek. "No…I say that because she's yours."

Shay reached his hand toward Alana's bare shoulder, hesitating briefly before he traced the two letters engraved in her beautiful skin. *GP.* They would forever be a symbol to him of *God's Provision.*

○ ○ ○

Alex lay in bed. All was silent around him. Too silent. Why did he feel so troubled? He got up and went to the window. He could see nothing out of place. There was no evidence anywhere that suggested unease. Why then did he feel the way he did? Alex sighed and lay back down. He continued to toss and turn. He had slept better when Alana had been in captivity. Now she was free…and he was happy she was free. But why wasn't he at peace?

For several long months his life had revolved around her. His every thought and deed had been to protect her and provide for her. And when Shay had come to fight for her freedom, he had helped with that as well. Maybe it was just the sudden change of events now that Alana was free. His emotions had been so caught up with her and the trial ... and now that it was all over, well, naturally he would feel ... different.

He wasn't sure what he should do now. He couldn't stay at the plantation. Shay had suggested he go west with them and try his hand at farming. Shay and Alana would be leaving ... leaving ... Alana would be leaving. And Alex finally accepted the fact that he would never see her again.

Sorrow crept upon him with no warning. He gasped at the final acknowledgement of it. He had buried himself so deeply in his work and his plot to free her that he had managed to keep it from his thoughts. But now... now he could no longer fight it. A tear rolled down his cheek and fell to his pillow.

"God," he whispered. "After all I've experienced these past few months, I have no doubt that You are who Alana says You are. Be with me now. Please, God, be with me."

○ ○ ○

James, Cody, and Luke stayed in Atlanta until Alana and Savannah were strong enough to travel.

Judas visited them frequently, enjoying the time he had with his granddaughter and great-granddaughter before they would head west. He knew he would most likely never see them again. But their faces would be forever etched in his memory.

Although Mr. Webb offered Brady his previous position with better pay than before, Brady declined, stating he was ready to venture forth on his own. Brady offered Alex a job, which he accepted. With all the publicity from Brady's recent trial, he had several cases already lined up.

Relationships and friendships had been formed, never to be broken, and distance was the only obstacle that stood between them. Saying goodbye was difficult. Alex stood off to the side, holding Savannah, who had already gained three pounds since her birth four weeks earlier. Luke had proudly stated that morning that Savannah now weighed in at a whopping six pounds. Alana joined Alex by the trees and smiled at the way her daughter gazed up into the eyes of the man who had saved her life.

"She loves you. Look at the way she looks at you."

Alex looked over at Alana and smiled. "Savannah's the first baby I've ever held ... and I must admit ... it feels real nice."

"Alex ... I could never repay you for your help these last few months. Thank you ... for fighting for my freedom ... for caring ... " A tear traced down Alana's cheek, and she could no longer speak.

Alex reached over and grabbed her hand. "I should be thanking you ... you showed me the true meaning of life ... If it weren't for you, I'd still be aimlessly pursuing dead dreams that would never amount to anything."

Alex kissed Savannah's forehead and handed her over to her mother. "Goodbye, Alana." Alex moved toward Shay and shook his hand before mounting his horse and riding out of sight. Alana turned toward Shay, grateful God had blessed her with such a man.

"Are you ready for another long journey?" Shay questioned.

"As long as you are coming with me…" Alana voiced with a smile.

"I'll be right beside you," Shay declared.

Epilogue

Jesse stood waiting by the fence post. They would be here any day now, his mama, his pa, and his new baby sister. Would the baby change anything? Would they still want him? Love him? Uncle Cal assured him they would, but it still plagued his mind. He knew it would until he saw his mama again.

"Je...ss...ee," he heard his little cousin call from the doorway of the house. Candice was a year old. And she had just started walking. "Jee...sss...ee," she called again. *Jesse* had been her first word, and she had a special place in his five year old heart. He went to her and grabbed her hand, helping her walk back to the fence post.

"My mama and pa are coming soon. Then I won't be able to stay here anymore. I'll have to go home." Candice frowned. "But I'll be back to visit every day. I promise. And—"

Jesse noticed the dust accumulating up the road. Someone was coming. Was it them? He waited. And then he saw her. His mama. Her horse came to a stop and she jumped down and began to run toward him. Jesse dropped his cousin's hand and took off toward his mama, forgetting he had any fears at all. Alana scooped him up in her arms. Jesse smiled and gently reached out to touch the tears on her face.

"You're free, mama. You're really free."

"Yes," Alana said as she caressed his soft cheek. "God has granted me freedom."

Jeremiah 29:11–14

For I know the plans I have for you, says the Lord. They are plans for good and not for your disaster, to give you a future and a hope. In those days when you pray, I will listen. If you look for me in earnest, you will find me when you seek me. I will be found by you, says the Lord. I will end your captivity and restore your fortunes. I will gather you out of the nations where I sent you and bring you home again to your own land. (New Living)

listen|imagine|view|experience

AUDIO BOOK DOWNLOAD INCLUDED WITH THIS BOOK!

In your hands you hold a complete digital entertainment package. Besides purchasing the paper version of this book, this book includes a free download of the audio version of this book. Simply use the code listed below when visiting our website. Once downloaded to your computer, you can listen to the book through your computer's speakers, burn it to an audio CD or save the file to your portable music device (such as Apple's popular iPod) and listen on the go!

How to get your free audio book digital download:

1. Visit www.tatepublishing.com and click on the e|LIVE logo on the home page.
2. Enter the following coupon code:
   6960-41dd-757e-c6e0-58f2-9212-a3f4-8e0e
3. Download the audio book from your e|LIVE digital locker and begin enjoying your new digital entertainment package today!